**Outstanding praise for Kasey Michaels and Maggie Kelly!**

MAGGIE NEEDS AN ALIBI

"Deliciously funny . . . Michaels handles it all with aplomb, gaily satirizing the current state of publishing, slowly building the romantic tension between Maggie and her frustratingly real hero, and providing plenty of laughs for the reader."—*Publishers Weekly*

"Readers will relish Michaels's clever and highly amusing mystery."
—*Booklist*

"The innovative Kasey Michaels comes up with a bewitching story that will have you laughing out loud. The plot is fresh, Maggie appealing, Detective Wendell charming, and Saint Just—well, meet him and decide!"—*Romantic Times*

"A great read . . . funny and well-written."—*Mystery News*

MAGGIE BY THE BOOK

"Colorful characters and humorous dialogue populate this wonderful sequel to *Maggie Needs an Alibi* and leave the reader waiting for more."—*Booklist*

"Romance and cozy fans will welcome this cross-genre sequel to Michaels's *Maggie Needs an Alibi*, with its original premise, sympathetic if reluctant heroine, and lively supporting cast."
—*Publishers Weekly*

"Once again, we're thrown into mayhem and enjoy every moment. Kasey Michaels's unique voice has developed another song—a true joy. Oh, what fun! More please."—*Rendezvous*

MAGGIE WITHOUT A CLUE

"Michaels delivers more fantasy and fun in her third witty, well-plotted cozy . . . a surprising conclusion will leave readers wanting more."
—*Publishers Weekly*

"Pure magic—if you love a good mystery, lots of laughter and a touch of romance, Maggie's your girl. As always, Kasey Michaels tickles the funny bone and touches the heart. If you haven't met Maggie yet, what are you waiting for?!"
—Mariah Stewart, *New York Times* best-selling author

"*Maggie Without a Clue* is magnificent . . . Ms. Michaels's delicious wit is generously spread throughout the book. I love this series and these characters. The Maggie books don't come fast enough to suit me."
—*Affaire de Coeur*

**Books by Kasey Michaels**

CAN'T TAKE MY EYES OFF OF YOU

TOO GOOD TO BE TRUE

LOVE TO LOVE YOU BABY

BE MY BABY TONIGHT

THIS MUST BE LOVE

THIS CAN'T BE LOVE

MAGGIE NEEDS AN ALIBI

MAGGIE BY THE BOOK

MAGGIE WITHOUT A CLUE

HIGH HEELS AND HOMICIDE

Published by Kensington Publishing Corporation

# High Heels and Homicide



KASEY MICHAELS

KENSINGTON BOOKS
http://www.kensingtonbooks.com

KENSINGTON BOOKS are published by

Kensington Publishing Corp.
850 Third Avenue
New York, NY 10022



All Kensington titles, imprints and distributed lines are available at special quantity discounts for bulk purchases for sales promotion, premiums, fund-raising, and educational or institutional use.

Special book excerpts or customized printings can also be created to fit specific needs. For details, write or phone the office of the Kensington Special Sales Manager: Kensington Publishing Corp., 850 Third Avenue, New York, NY 10022. Attn: Special Sales Department. Phone: 1-800-221-2647.

Kensington and the K logo Reg. U.S. Pat. & TM Off.

ISBN 0-7582-0880-4

First Kensington Trade Paperback Printing: December 2005
10 9 8 7 6 5 4 3 2 1

Printed in the United States of America

*There's nothing to writing. All you do*
*is sit down at a typewriter and open a vein.*
—Walter "Red" Smith, 1982

*I can truthfully say I will never*
*make a bad film.*
—Eddie Murphy, 1987

# Cast of Characters

**Maggie Kelly.** Writing as Cleo Dooley, the creator of Alexandre Blake, Viscount Saint Just, from the best-selling Saint Just Mysteries series. Both of them. Literally.

**Alex Blakely** aka **Viscount Saint Just.** The figment of Maggie's creative imagination, her perfect hero, inexplicably come to life some months earlier in her Manhattan apartment. It's a problem . . .

**Sterling Balder.** The obligatory loyal sidekick to Maggie's once-only fictional sleuth, now also living large in Manhattan, and a dear soul who would be too confused to ever answer to an alias.

**Bernice Toland-James.** Maggie's editor, recently sober, although she is not convinced sobriety is her natural condition.

**Tabitha Leighton.** Maggie's agent, married to the Bed-Hopping Champion of the Western World.

**Arnaud Peppin.** The director of *The Case of the Disappearing Earl*, the Cleo Dooley novel to be filmed for a television movie on location in England.

**Sir Rudolph Medwine.** The owner of the country manor house at which the movie will be filmed. Knighted for his creation of the Medwine Marauder fishing reel, Rudy thinks having a movie filmed at his newly purchased house would be smashing great fun.

**Byrd Stockwell.** Rudy's nephew, who thinks chasing American actresses of loose morals would be smashing great fun.

**Troy Barlow.** The perfect choice to play Saint Just, if the Viscount had been into bleach-streaked hair and surfboards.

**Nikki Campion.** The female lead, best known for being Nikki Campion, as well as the spokesperson for Boffo Transmissions ("When shifting gears, think Boffo!").

**Evan Pottinger.** A method actor cast in the role of the dastardly villain of the piece.

**Perry Posko.** An actor for whom playing the sweet, naive, often-bumbling Sterling Balder will be no stretch.

**Dennis Lloyd.** An English thespian hoping to make the roll of Clarence, the Saint Just valet, into an Emmy-winning performance.

**Sam Undercuffler.** The screenwriter who adapted Maggie's book for the small screen.

**Joanne Pertuccelli.** The regulation corporate bitch, employed by the production company to keep the filming on time and under budget.

**Marylou Keppel.** Script girl, stand-in, and gofer, hoping to add to her list of "Actors I Have Boinked."

# Prologue

*Dear Journal,*

*Once more I take up my pen to record the happenings of my life and of those around me. I must admit that I have been quite remiss in my entries these past six weeks or more, but I have been much occupied with assembling our apartment after the shambles it had become thanks to those horrible gentlemen I told you about not so long ago.*

*But everything is all right and tight now, and properly done up according to feng shui guidelines. (Mrs. Tabby Leighton has corrected me, and it is not feng* shoo-ee, *as I had thought, but feng* schway*—isn't that interesting? Saint Just says it isn't.)*

*My only problem now is that Mrs. McBedie, whom Saint Just has engaged to look after us, will persist in facing the three-legged money frog in entirely the incorrect direction whenever she dusts the "Wealth" corner of our main saloon (what Maggie calls a living room, which I think rather eerie, as who wants to lounge about in a* living *room?).*

*Unfortunately, we don't have much time to enjoy our new apartment, which now legally belongs to Saint Just, who is quite happily solvent now that he is half of the photographic modeling pair of himself and our own Mary Louise, posing for magazine and even billboard advertisements for Fragrances by Pierre. It is, I must admit, rather disconcerting to see Saint Just twenty-five feet tall in Times Square.*

*And we have just baskets and baskets of lovely toiletries now, courtesy of Mr. Pierre, but Saint Just persists in favoring Brut. Maggie finds this amusing.*

*Saint Just has been toiling night and day at this new venture, which, he told me rather proudly, entails considerably more work than he had supposed when he agreed to pose. Mary Louise has been able to forgo other employment (and more nefarious document-counterfeiting dealings), and is now a student only, completing her last year at what she calls NYU.*

*It's lovely to see so much progress since our arrival on this plane of existence just a few short, exciting months ago.*

*Saint Just still oversees the Streetcorner Orators and Players (or however he says it—I keep forgetting the order), with Mary Louise's cousin and houseboys in charge. The enterprise has grown to include forty-seven street corners. Just imagine. Saint Just now calls himself an entrepreneur, which also makes Maggie laugh. I like it when she laughs.*

*Because even all this to-ing and fro-ing by Saint Just does not explain the Decided Coolness I have observed between him and our Maggie, friend and creator of both Saint Just and me. I only hope that she is not so put out with us that she decides to stop writing about us, because I am not sure if we can continue to exist outside our books once Maggie has turned us off inside her head.*

*That's the problem with being imaginary characters come to life: this tenuous existence. Saint Just says he is working to ensure that we evolve, grow, and become more of our own persons, thereby enabling us to create our own identities, completely separate from Maggie, so perhaps this is why she seems to be sulking. I think Maggie likes to be Needed.*

*She has completed her new book in record time, a full three months early, which is explained by the fact that she has been all but living in front of her computer seven days a week. Regardless, she is now officially on vacation for the next month, before needing to begin her research for another Saint Just adventure, but has yet to put on an All Done party, as has been her custom in the past. Then again, considering what occurred after the last All Done party, I suppose she has her reasons and all of that.*

*But back to what is happening now, dear Journal, not what is already past. After all, I believe this journaling business is supposed to be a chronicle, not a history, yes?*

*Bernie has returned from her drying-out place, and seeing her editor and very good friend again has put the roses back in Maggie's cheeks, just a little bit, although I'm still concerned for her. She so badly wanted a cigarette the other night that she asked me to "light" the pretzel she'd been munching, poor thing.*

*But, as Saint Just reminded me, the weeks have passed by and the day is rapidly approaching when we must all travel to a place called Ocean City, in a state called New Jersey (quite unlike our own English Jersey, I fear), to partake of Thanksgiving dinner with Maggie's parents.*

*I know very little about Mr. and Mrs. Kelly, save that Maggie studiously avoids them whenever possible. In addition, the fact that Maggie has explained Saint Just and me to all in New York as the distant English relations she patterned her Saint Just books on in the first place could prove a tad sticky, as her parents are unaware of our existence.*

*Saint Just volunteered to have us remain here, safely out of sight in Manhattan, but Maggie looked at him with such* daggers *that he quickly rescinded that offer. Besides, we leave for England directly after the parental visit, invited guests of the film company that will be turning the very first Saint Just Mystery into a movie made just to fit television screens. I wonder who will portray me. I hope he isn't pudgy and balding. Then again, I am pudgy and balding.*

*My Henry will be well taken care of by Mrs. McBedie, who has quite a fondness for mice, thank goodness, although she will insist upon thinking of him as a hamster, a species she considers a more domesticated animal. I am happy to report, also, that I discovered the most lovely new home for Henry, with lots and lots of tunnels for him to run through, and a wheel for him to run on, and a . . . but I digress. It's a failing.*

*Bernie will meet us there—in England, dear Journal—along with Tabby, who says an agent's place is at her author's side. Saint Just calls that a tax-deductible hum meant to give Tabby a vacation overseas, but he smiles almost indulgently when he says it. Saint Just, you see, is greatly enamoured of something called loopholes in the American tax codes.*

*Socks, my very good friend who has taught me all about the Duties of a Doorman, will remain here in Manhattan, to celebrate this uniquely American holiday with his mother, and to toil nightly in the off-off-Broadway play he auditioned for after his paperback-romance cover-model debut proved less than auspicious. I shall miss him, and I have told him he is free to borrow my motorized scooter any time he wishes.*

*Lieutenant Steve Wendell, also sadly, will not be a part*

*of our entourage, and I will admit to you, dear Journal, if not to Saint Just, the trepidation I feel at his absence.*

*For, as you already know, dear Journal, we often seem to have need of a representative of the constabulary.*

*Respectfully,*

*Sterling Balder*

# Chapter One

Maggie Kelly sat at the desk in the corner of the large living room of her Manhattan condo. Sort of sat. She actually was rather *supported* by her desk, her headset phone jammed down over her uncombed hair, her forehead pressed to the desktop, her arms hanging on either side of the chair. She looked rather like one of those collapsible dolls, one whose button had been pushed.

She spoke into the headset. "Okay, okay. Once more, with feeling. *M*, as in *moronic*. *A*, as in *asinine*. *R*, as in . . . as in—*ridiculous*! Margaret. It's *Margaret*. My name is Margaret Kelly, not Missy. How difficult can this be? You'd think my name was Schwarzenegger. What? No! *Not* Missy Schwarzenegger! Margaret Kelly! Oh, God—what? *No!* Don't put me on hold. I've already been on hold three times, and I already know all the words to "It's a Small World." Don't put me on—oh, hell . . ."

"Talking to your knees, my dear? There are some, myself not included, of course, who might consider that a tad eccentric. But, then, I know you."

Maggie pushed herself upright to glare at Alexandre Blake, the Viscount Saint Just of her best-selling historical mystery series and currently known as Alex Blakely, her supposed distant relative and model for her fictional creation. He lived across the hall now, but had never seemed to be able to understand the concept of knocking first before barging in on her.

She liked having him around, now that she'd gotten her mind around the fact that, heck, he *was* here. But there were times when she wished he was more of an in and out—no, that might sound a little too sexual—a less-*constant* presence in her life. Okay, that was better. Not great, but better.

"Why are you always barging in here when I'm at my worst?" she asked him, looking down, to see that she'd buttoned her pajama top incorrectly. Nothing new there . . . including the faded pajama top that had been her favorite since college, or maybe high school. Junior year. She wore it now over ancient sweatpants, the knees and seat of the pajama bottoms having worn through a few years ago.

"Feeling snarly this morning, my dear?" Alex asked, one well-sculpted eyebrow raised Clint Eastwood style. (She'd thought she'd re-created Jim Carrey's expressive eyebrows, but in the flesh, they were definitely Clint's.) The young Clint of the spaghetti westerns. Young and yummy Clint. And she ought to know, because hidden deep in one of the desk drawers was her physical description of the Viscount Saint Just.

There was a lot of the young Clint Eastwood in the Viscount Saint Just—the lean face, the slashes in the cheeks, the long, sleekly muscular frame—along with snippets of younger versions of Sean Connery (voice in those Bond films), Paul Newman (bluer-than-blue eyes), Peter O'Toole (nose), and Val Kilmer (mouth—oh, dear God, yes—Kilmer's mouth in *Tombstone*: "I'm your huckleberry.").

Maggie had set out to create the Perfect Regency Era Hero, and she really did do good work, if she did say so herself.

Except for the arrogant part. The self-assured part, and maybe the brilliant-cutting-wit part. She might have gone a little heavy on those, at least she thought so once her fictional Perfect Hero had morphed into a living twenty-first-century man with all his early-nineteenth-century superior male sensibilities intact.

There were moments lately when she wondered if she could mentally incorporate a few more bits of Hugh Grant into the character of Saint Just, who already had a sexy shock of black hair, and then sit back and watch Alex to see if he'd change. Maybe a little something around the eyes—a small air of vulnerability, maybe?

It was a provocative thought, especially as she'd watched Grant in *Love Actually* late one Saturday night. Just she and her two cats and her burnt microwave popcorn with extra butter. She led such an exciting social life.

But that was beside the point, as was her on-again, off-again romantic interest in the gorgeous, perfect hero standing in front of her, which was currently very, very *off*.

"I have a good reason to be snarly," Maggie said, adjusting the headset, the better to muffle the sound of some twit telling her that she could save time by contacting the company on the Internet. "Tried that," she mumbled.

Alex made a small, circling motion with his right index finger. "Forgive the question, but is there someone on the other end of that?"

"There have been a *lot* of someones on the other end of the phone in the past . . ." she began, glancing down at her watch, to see that it was noon, ". . . the past forty-five minutes. And if I could talk to someone who has English as their first language, I would probably spend the first five minutes just sobbing my thanks into the phone. They call this a *help* line?" She turned in her chair, began shuffling through the mess on her desk. "Where's my *I Love Lou Dobbs* button?"

She felt Alex's hands on her shoulders as he slowly spun her around to face him. "Maggie. Concentrate. Tell me what you're doing . . . attempting to do."

She swallowed. Nodded. Swallowed again. Pretended not to notice that someone inside the earpiece was now asking her, musically, if she knew the way to San Jose. "Okay. I'm on the phone with the airline. I get flyer miles every time I charge something with my credit card, and I want to cash them in for our flight. It might have been easier if I'd asked one of the agents for a kidney."

"You didn't do that, did you, Maggie? That's crass."

She rolled her eyes. "No, I didn't do that, and I know it's crass, as well as a cheap joke. But I'm going nuts here, Alex. I don't understand what they're saying, they don't understand what I'm saying—and I swear to God, *nobody* understands all the rules. Look," she said, grabbing a card from her desk. "See this? This is a coupon for a free companion ticket. I buy one, you fly free. I buy two, two fly free. I understand this. This is fairly basic, right?"

Alex took the offered ticket. "Quite a few asterisks leading to several separate bits of barely readable print, aren't there? I do see the small *K* down at the corner. You've circled it."

"Right. It's a *K*. But guess what? I need a *U*. *An U*. Whatever. You can *have* a *K*, but you can only *use* a *U*."

Alex deposited the ticket on the coffee table. "I think I'm done understanding, thank you," he said, wiping his hands together.

"Oh, no. No, no, no, you're just getting *started*. I can use the *K* if I use a *U* with it. The second person I talked to told me that. I'm eligible for a *K*, but not for a *U*, and I can't use a *K* without a *U*—but they sent me a *K* anyway, because I qualified for that one. If I spend another bazillion bucks, I can get a *U* to go with the *K*, but by then the *K* will have expired. Machiavellian in its brilliance, isn't it?"

"American ingenuity at the corporate level. The *K* did get you to pick up the phone, didn't it?"

"Don't interrupt. I don't actually need the *K*, or the *U*. The third gal I talked to told me I have enough flyer miles to go from here to Hawaii and back, and take half a football team with me. Except that there are only about six seats a plane that are available for free miles, so you have to book in advance. We're talking *way* in advance here, maybe a decade. So I've got about a million free miles I can't use, sucker offers with the wrong letter on them, and the ditz who just put me on hold knows how to pronounce Schwarzenegger, but doesn't know how to spell Margaret. That's it, Alex. We're not going."

"You're only saying that because you're looking for an excuse not to fly at all. Because you're afraid of flight."

"Damn straight I am. This whole thing is driving me nuts. Do we fly out of Kennedy for one price or go to Newark for a better price? Or, since we can't leave until after Thanksgiving anyway, do we fly out of Philly? But which is the right choice? Do I go for convenience? Or price? And then, just when I think, okay, out of Philly, the idiot on the phone who told me about the flight says, No, that one's booked, so I start thinking, Okay, maybe God wants me to fly out of Kennedy, maybe he *knows something* about the Philly flight. Then again, he could *know something* about the Kennedy flight. But then again, maybe God's just pulling my chain. I could be making a life-or-death decision here, and God's trying to be funny."

Alex sighed. "Maggie, hang up."

"Hang up? Are you kidding? I spent twenty minutes online trying to figure out when the hell I'd tried online before and made up a user name and password, because I sure couldn't remember them. Then, once I'd gotten a new password, the damn site wouldn't recognize my credit card number anyway, so I had to call, wait, talk, be put on hold, talk, be put on hold, talk, be put—I am *not* hanging up until and unless this woman figures out how to spell Margaret!"

"Since *you* already know how to spell *stubborn*. Very well," Alex said, walking over to the credenza and pouring himself a glass of wine, as he had the Regency Era disdain for water. "Then you wouldn't be interested in knowing that thanks to my speaking last week with a representative of the production company, who happened to phone while you were out and I was here, doing nothing in the least nefarious, and after putting forth my personal recommendations on the matter, three airline tickets were delivered just minutes ago to my apartment. I, by the grace or possible cruel joke of God, decided on Philadelphia, by the way, with our return to Kennedy. We depart for Heathrow the Sunday after Thanksgiving, traveling in something called first class. And you Americans vow you aren't class conscious."

Maggie just sat there, stared at him. "You . . . it's all . . . so I'm driving myself nuts for . . . damn it, Alex, why do you keep doing this to me?"

The man had the nerve to look innocent and the panache to carry it off. "Doing what, my dear?"

"Oh, don't get cute. You know darn well. Stepping in. Taking charge. Never getting ruffled. Always getting what you want. Making me feel like an idiot because I always do things the hard way. And you got *three* free tickets out of them? I mean, okay, me I can understand. I'm the author. They could certainly spring for a ticket for me. But you and Sterling? How did you finagle that one?"

"*Finagle*? I'm not familiar with the term, but I'm confident the Viscount Saint Just does *not* finagle. But, as I am your personal assistant and liaison with the press and Sterling is your spiritual advisor, it was, of course, only logical that we should accompany you."

"And you're expecting me to swallow this? Oh, wait. The person who called? Female, right?"

"Why, yes. Miss Browning. She had a lovely laugh. Very like the soft tinkling of delicate silver bells tickled by the breeze of a clear spring day."

"As I'm sure you told her." Maggie made some sort of low, chuckling sound. "They don't even *see* you, and they go all gooey and do whatever you want them to do, just the way I planned you. Man, I'm good. But that's manipulative, Alex, do you know that? It's not nice."

He shrugged, put down the empty wineglass. "In point of fact, it's a woman who doubtless spent the remainder of her day spreading her joy to everyone. It is also, my dear girl, three free first-class plane tickets to England. I believe we are all to be considered winners in the exchange."

"Okay," she said, giving up. "I'm the last one to be arguing over saving money. Unless you're actually going to start paying your own way around here, Perfume Man."

Then she gave herself a swift mental kick because that blow had been below the belt. She knew better, she knew his vulnerabilities, because she'd created him. The Viscount Saint Just placed a lot of his pride on being self-sufficient, in *all* ways.

"Oh, God, I'm sorry, Alex," she said quickly. "You've paid back every cent I advanced you when you first . . . first showed up. And you're paying off the mortgage on your condo. You're an honorable, upstanding—oh boy, I'll grovel later. She's back on the line."

"Maggie, what are you—?"

Maggie held up a finger, motioning for him to be quiet. "Yes, yes, that's right. Missy Schwarzenegger. Two *g*'s? Oh, right. Two *g*'s. Boy, you're good. Uh-huh. Uh-huh, yes.

That's four round-trip tickets, first class, from Kennedy to Heathrow. And I'd like to add a leg from Heathrow to Oslo, back to Heathrow, and then to Kennedy. Oh, and I'll need two kosher meals and one diabetic meal. Uh-huh. And will there be room for the Way-Bac Machine? Uh-huh, Way-Bac Machine. That's *W–a–y–* capital *B-a-c*. No *k*. God knows we don't want anything with a *k* in it, right? Uh-huh. It's . . . it's kind of a . . . well, it's a necessity for one of the passengers. Uh-huh, my boy Sherman. You'll check? Yes, yes, of course I can hold."

Feeling better than she had in, oh, at least an hour and twenty minutes, Maggie took off the headset and laid it on the desk. "That ought to keep her busy for a good ten minutes."

"You are an evil woman, Maggie Kelly," Alex told her when she grinned at him.

"Uh-huh. Yes. I know," she said in the same too-sweet voice she'd just used on the phone, then slapped her hands on her thighs and stood up. "Then again, I suddenly feel *so* much better."

"How gratifying for you. Who is Sherman? And what's a Way-Bac Machine?"

"Hang in a sec, I need a Popsicle."

Alex was still standing, waiting for her when she came back from the kitchen, the thin, single-stick diet chocolate Popsicle in her mouth. She spoke around it. "I don't know how I'm going to exist without these while we're in England."

"Really?" he said as she slowly pulled the thing out of her mouth.

"Hey, addictions are addictions, and I'm addicted to these things. Hardly any calories, and they satisfy my chocolate cravings, as well as give me something to do with my hands, my mouth, now that I don't smoke anymore. I don't know, I guess I'm into oral gratification."

"Many of us are," Alex said quietly, and Maggie tried very hard not to look at him.

She aimed herself toward one of the couches, collapsing into the soft cushions before taking a big bite of the Popsicle, the better to disguise its form, she imagined. "Back to the Way-Bac. Didn't you ever watch any of those tapes I bought for Sterling? *The Rocky and Bullwinkle Show*? It's an American classic. One of the recurring skits is 'Improbable History,' with Professor Hector Peabody and his boy, Sherman. The professor is a dog, see, and he has a boy, and Peabody teaches Sherman about history using the Way-Bac Machine to time travel and—" She stopped, looking at Alex's impassive face. "I'm not getting through, am I?"

Alex shook his head. "Perhaps another time? If I applied myself?"

"No, never mind. You either get this kind of stuff or you don't. And you'd get it, I know you would, if you watched the tapes."

"I'll put that on my to-do list. In the meantime, are you happy with the travel arrangements? I could have made the departure date Saturday, but that would mean only two days with your parents, and I wouldn't want it to appear that you were in a rush to be away."

"Yeah, we don't want to appear in a rush," Maggie said, then sucked on the Popsicle once more, wondering how she was going to get through three entire days playing Happy Families. Since the thought was depressing, she changed the subject. "So, Mr. Transportation Arranger, how long will we be in jolly old England?"

"I'm not quite sure," Alex said, seating himself on the facing couch. "It's something called an open-ended ticket, I believe. We'll be arriving just after the featured players in the cast and the director, and departing just as the shooting begins, if I understood correctly."

"Because they don't want the writer getting in the way.

This trip is just flipping me a fish, hoping I'll be dazzled and keep my mouth shut," Maggie said, nodding. "Long ago I was told that if you sell your book to the movies, take the money and run—never look back. They change everything, and not for the better, either."

She took one last, large bite, knowing she'd never eaten a Popsicle so quickly, and hoped she wouldn't get an ice cream headache. She just knew she didn't want to watch Alex watching her as she licked and sucked on the thing. Not for another second. "I still can't believe we're going."

"And if the filming hadn't been so abruptly moved from California to England, we wouldn't be, not with your fear of an earthquake the moment the plane landed. I do agree that everything seems so suddenly rushed, but I look forward to returning to England."

Maggie closed one eye and lowered her head as she looked at him. "You've never *been* to England, Alex. I've never been there, so you can't have been there. Until you and Sterling somehow made a break for it out of my imagination, you've never *been* anywhere."

"Have you tried to pop us back in, Maggie?" Alex asked, his expression suddenly serious. "Lord knows, these past weeks have been difficult between us."

Mentally, Maggie was in her bedroom, her head under her pillow. "I . . . I'm really not ready to discuss that, Alex."

"And when would you be ready? I had no choice, Maggie. It was a matter of honor. I am obligated, as a gentleman, to protect my own."

She hopped to her feet. "There you go again. Your own? Since when am I yours? Who asked you to protect me? You . . . what you did . . . you—oh, forget it."

"The man had a choice."

"The *man* didn't know he was up against a freaking Scarlet Pimpernel! And do you know what's the worst?

You're not sorry. You don't see that you did anything wrong. A man is *dead*, Alex."

"A man who would have ordered you and Sterling and me dead, then gone out to supper with his cohorts. I know. The past is the past, and the incident over and done. Shall we just agree to disagree on this one?"

"We're not debating politics here, Alex. I want . . . I want you to understand that I made you, and that means I'm at least partially responsible for what you do, even if you are doing this *evolving* stuff you keep talking about."

Alex stood up as well, fished his quizzing glass out of his slacks pocket, and slipped the black grosgrain ribbon over his head. "So, I am not responsible for you, but you are responsible for me?"

"Yes . . . no! Oh, hell, I don't know." She touched his arm. "I just know I don't want to go on like this. Being so damn polite to each other, dancing around each other, but not really being friends anymore."

"We were never friends, Maggie," Alex said, his voice low, intimate. "We were very nearly lovers. What is it the Comte De Bussy-Rabutin said? Oh yes. 'Love comes from blindness, friendship from knowledge.' Perhaps it would be better if we were to become friends first."

Maggie wet her lips, tried to ignore that her heart had skipped a beat. "Start over, you mean? I don't know . . . I guess we could try. I mean, you're here. You're definitely here. I don't know if you'll disappear one day, you and Sterling, but for now? You are here . . ."

"And I've missed you horribly," Alex said, moving fractionally closer. He lifted a hand to stroke her cheek. "I've missed your smiles, I've missed your laughter, I've missed our occasional forays into that something more we'd begun to explore in each other."

He was doing it again. Oh, he was good. And, boy, she

was easy. "Alex . . . please, you said we'd start over. This isn't exactly starting over. This is more starting in the middle, and much as I—oh, hell!"

Behind her, she could hear the loud *buzz-buzz-buzz* from the earpiece of her headset.

She recognized a lucky escape when she saw one, and took it, hurrying over to hit the Talk button on the phone, cutting off the off-the-hook warning.

"I guess I'm not connected anymore," she said, trying to smile.

Alex smiled, too, and his smile hurt her. "No, we're not, are we? Well, if you'll excuse me, Maggie, I believe I should find my way to the bank, along with some other errands. I want to discuss something called traveling checks, for our trip. You understand."

"Traveler's checks, Alex, not traveling checks, although, literally, that is what they are," Maggie said automatically, reaching for the headset again, for the phone had begun to ring. "Takeout pizza for dinner?"

"I'm sure Sterling would enjoy that. I'll have him arrange an order for six o'clock. We could dine in our apartment, in front of the television machine, while I'm being educated in the matter of the Way-Bac Machine."

"Perfect," Maggie said, grabbing the headset, then turned her back on him as she hit the Talk button. "Hello? Oh, hi, Steve. Meet you for a late lunch? Ummm . . . I'm not sure. Where?"

She turned back, to see that Alex was still standing there. She grabbed the mouthpiece, squeezed her hand around it. "It's Steve," she said, smiling as brightly as she could.

"My regards to the good *left*-tenant," Alex said, and bowed himself out of the apartment before Bernice Toland-James could ask a third time: "Maggie? Is that you?"

"I'm sorry, Bernie." Maggie collapsed into her desk chair. "I don't know why I did that."

"Did what? Oh, never mind. Look, I want to come over, okay? I've read the manuscript."

"And?"

"And I'll bring lunch."

Uh-oh. Instant panic, insecurity about talent being the curse of every writer. Had her talent disappeared? Had she ever really had any talent? Maybe she'd been faking it for years, and now it had finally caught up with her. "Bernie? What did you think of the book? You have a problem with the book? What's wrong with the book? Nothing's wrong with my book, Bernie. Is it?"

"Give me an hour. I'll be there in an hour."

As she listened to the dial tone, Maggie considered, then discarded, the idea of collapsing headfirst onto her desk once more. "This day just keeps getting better and better . . ."

# Chapter Two

Saint Just returned to his own apartment, caught between amusement at Maggie's rather adorable fierceness when dealing with the vagaries of the uncaring world and a small sadness that the breech between them still sat like a huge elephant in the middle of her living room, with neither of them daring to do more than periodically mention its existence.

She could, it seemed, create a hero . . . she just couldn't understand one.

"Sterling?" he called out, snatching up his sword cane from its resting place in—how coincidental?—a plaster stand in the shape of an elephant. "Have you changed your mind about accompanying me to the bank?"

Sterling Balder, wiping his hands on the "Kiss the Cook" apron tied around his pudgy waist, emerged from the kitchen, his cheeks floury white. "I've nearly got it, Saint Just," he said, shoving his spectacles higher on his nose. "I think this next batch will be the charm."

"More scones, Sterling? I thought we'd discussed this. We have enough paperweights as it is."

Sterling's lower lip came out in a pout. "That's not nice, Saint Just. Mrs. McBedie insists on serving those English muffins, as she calls them, but I just know scones would be much more the thing, if I could only master them. You should have more faith in me, and all of that. Besides, Henry likes my scones. He's living in one of them, as a matter of fact, having eaten his way in."

Saint Just winced. He'd told himself to forget about the tension between Maggie and himself, but obviously he'd allowed it to color his mood. "My deepest apologies, Sterling, I've become a beast. I'll be happy to sample one of this new batch with my tea the very moment I return."

"Could you possibly stop at Mario's on your way back? It being Mrs. McBedie's day off, I thought we could have cold sliced meat for dinner."

"Maggie has already requested pizza, if that's all right?" Saint Just asked, heading for the door once more. "And you have enough on your plate with the scones." Saint Just knew that he'd have more than enough on his own plate—more stone-hard scones. "I'm also convinced this batch will be the charm."

"Thank you, Saint Just. You're a good man."

Saint Just considered Sterling's praise as he employed the tip of his sword cane to depress the call button for the elevator. Sterling was a good man, a good soul. He wasn't quite that certain about himself.

Once out on the street, Saint Just donned his new black, wide-brimmed hat—the one Maggie called his Riverboat Gambler hat—and tucked his cane under his arm, not in the least believing either accessory an affectation, or at all out of place with his midnight-blue silk knit pullover and tan slacks. And, because he was Saint Just, it all worked.

His confident, long-legged stride took him the few blocks to his bank, the one he had chosen after much online research; a choice Sterling had seconded because new account holders were rewarded with a chrome-and-black toaster oven.

He stepped into the building, his hat in his hand, and easily made his way to his favorite teller, Mrs. Halliday, as there was only one other customer in the bank at the moment. Two, if he counted a second gentleman at one of the tables, scribbling on a deposit slip.

"Good afternoon, my dear," he said. "Aren't you looking well today. And how is your son? Still with the footballers?"

"Yes . . . er, thank you," Mrs. Halliday said, not looking at him. "How may I help you today, sir?"

Saint Just frowned, lowered his voice. "Is something amiss, Mrs. Halliday?"

She smiled then, a rather plain woman whose smile could make her quite attractive. Except this smile was more of a rictus and eminently unflattering. "A very fine day, yes, it is."

The hairs on the back of Saint Just's neck began to prickle as he felt someone looking hard at his back. He reached into his pocket, slowly extracted his money clip. "I was hoping you could exchange this for smaller bills," he said, pulling out a one-hundred-dollar bill and slipping it across the countertop.

With fumblings fingers, Mrs. Halliday opened the drawer and pulled out five twenties, quickly counted them out. Not at all usual; Mrs. Halliday always gave him three twenties, three tens, and two fives, just as he preferred. "Have a nice day, sir," she said, folding her hands on the counter without picking up the larger bill.

"I'll make a point of it, madam. Good day," Saint Just said, then turned, seemingly oblivious of the man at the desk, the second man at the first teller's cage.

His cane in his hand, no longer tucked under his arm, he replaced his hat, setting it at a slight tilt, and strolled leisurely toward the door, then out into the street.

Where he stopped, stepped in front of the thick wall beside the glass doors, flipped open his cell phone, and pushed two buttons. Lieutenant Wendell's number was one Saint Just had in the phone's memory.

Three rings, and the Lieutenant answered.

"Wendell, my good man, Alex Blakely here. Would it be at all possible for you to stop by my bank?" He gave him the address. "You are nearby, correct? Or is Maggie meeting you somewhere?"

"Maggie? I haven't talked to Maggie in a week. She doesn't return my calls. I know she's got a deadline and everything, but I was beginning to—why should I meet you at your bank? What's up?"

"Possibly nothing, possibly quite a bit. You haven't answered me. Are you close by?" As for the other—how very interesting. But he'd have to consider Maggie's fib another time; Mrs. Halliday had very clearly put her dependence upon him.

"No, I'm way the hell up in—Blakely, what in hell did you do now? Are you playing hero again? No, don't tell me. Oh, cripes—tell me."

"So indecisive, my friend. Is it any wonder Maggie can't find it in herself to perceive you as a serious beau?" Saint Just stepped forward, held up his hand to a woman approaching the door to the bank, shook his head. "As you're unavailable, perhaps you'd allow for a substitute? Any of your number will do. Lights and sirens are always so welcome. But I really must go now."

He folded the phone, slipping it back into his pocket as he smiled at the woman. "I'm dreadfully sorry to inconvenience you, madam, but it would appear the bank is being robbed at the moment. Perhaps you could visit our branch on Broadway? It's also a full-service facility. Thank you, and please call again," he said, bowing, giving a slight tip of his hat as the woman all but ran down the street.

Saint Just then smiled at passersby, tipping his hat another time or two, before taking a final, quick peek through the gold-toned window, and moving to just beside the door, to stand at the ready.

The door opened, his cane came out and up at knee level, and the first man through the door found himself sprawled facedown on the sidewalk, what breath was left in him effectively expelled when his partner tripped and landed on top of him.

It was all rather lovely . . . quite a bit like slow-motion dominoes.

"Oh, how clumsy of me," Saint Just said as a loud alarm began to ring inside the bank, and people on the sidewalk variously stopped, stared, shrieked, or moved along with an intensity of purpose that all but shouted, "Not my table, not my problem."

With the tip of his cane pressed against one jugular, the heel of his classically stylish shoe firmly planted in one back, Saint Just then posed rather like a hunter with his first kill. An excited couple, speaking rapid Japanese, kept their mini videocam rolling, so that Saint Just, always polite, bowed to them.

He was, however, distracted by the sound that seemed to go *poof* inside the open black plastic bag one of the men had dropped—signaling the explosion of the dye pack an adventurous teller had placed inside it.

He was definitely distracted by the small, dusty cloud that served to turn one leg of his new slacks a garish purple.

"Oh dear, an unexpected punishment for performing a good deed. Ah, and look at you. That's going to leave a mark, isn't it, poor fellow?" Saint Just asked the robber closest to the open bag, but the man, his face and hair now purple, only coughed, blinking furiously.

More excited Japanese, with the woman hitting her companion's shoulder to get his attention, and Saint Just realized that the tourist was now eager to capture for posterity the arrival of a few of New York's Finest.

That was fine with Saint Just. He had been wondering what he was going to do when the robbers recovered their breath and realized they outnumbered him two to one. Brandishing his sword cane on a city street at midday certainly wasn't the action of a prudent man. He'd happily turn over the miscreants to the police, and be on his way.

At least, that was his intention. As it turned out, the uniformed policemen had other ideas for his immediate future, which, unfortunately, had a lot to do with slamming him up against the wall, telling him to "spread 'em," and then slapping him in handcuffs.

There was often no justice in this world.

But, Saint Just realized as he heard his name being called by none other than Holly Spivak, she of the traveling Fox News van, in America there is always the media.

Maggie opened the door and stood back as Bernice Toland-James swept into the apartment: tall, slim, her mane of inspired bushy long red hair flying like a flag in her self-created breeze. Designer clad, chemically peeled, silicone enhanced, suctioned and tweaked, lifted and toned, Bernie was that most dangerous of females: powerful in business, perimenopausal, and newly sober.

She was also Maggie's editor and very best friend.

"Here you go. Liverwurst is yours, salami's mine," Bernie said, flinging out her arm, so that the paper bag she held nearly clipped Maggie on the nose. "Got any cigarettes? I forgot mine at the office, damn it."

Maggie took the bag and put it down on the coffee table, beside the two glasses of lemonade she'd poured the moment the doorman buzzed Bernie's arrival. Socks would have just let her come up, but this new guy was by-the-book. Which was good, because Bernie's arrival could be startling enough, without her showing up unannounced.

"You know I quit, Bernie, and I'm carrying the extra ten pounds to prove it. What do you think kills more—cigarettes or obesity? Never mind. But I've got a spare nicotine inhaler around somewhere, if you want it."

"Yeah, right," Bernie said, kicking off her shoes before sitting on one of the couches, pulling her long legs up under her. "That's like a scotch on the rocks minus the scotch. No thanks. Besides, you look stupid with that thing in your mouth, no offense."

"None taken," Maggie said, collapsing onto the facing couch. "I love being told I look stupid. What's wrong with the manuscript?"

Bernie dug in the bag, pulled out the sandwiches. "Here you go. Let's eat."

"Let's eat and talk," Maggie said, taking the foil-wrapped sandwich, then grabbing a snack-size bag of potato chips, leaving the tortilla chips for Bernie. She ripped open the bag, carefully positioned five potato chips directly on her liverwurst, then replaced the top piece of seeded rye bread and squished the sandwich between her hands. Gourmet all the way. "What's wrong with the manuscript?"

Bernie held up a sienna-tipped finger as she nodded her head and chewed, finally swallowed. "You're a great writer, Maggie. The best. The Saint Just Mysteries are top drawer. I always knew you could write. Never a problem there. Really. Sales? Sales are terrific. You're carrying us on your back, Mags, so I can say as both your editor and your publisher, Toland Books is damn grateful."

"But? Come on, Bernie. We both know there's a big *but* coming."

Bernie took a sip of lemonade, winced. "But . . . how do I say this nicely? Okay, I've got it. But this book stinks on ice. One hundred thousand words that demonstrate why editors drink. Sorry, honey."

"It . . . it . . . oh, it does not!"

"Not the writing. The writing's great. Really. But who wants to read *The Case of the Lamenting Lordship*?"

"*The Case of the* Lonely *Lordship*," Maggie corrected. She'd never really been nuts over the title, which probably should have told her something. She hated working without a title. "It's a little dark, I admit it."

Bernie pushed her hair back, used its length to tie it in a knot. "Saint Just spends two thirds of the book contemplating his navel and the last third going around making amends for being a bad, bad man, like he's doing some kind of wacko Regency twelve-step program. I had to prop my eyelids up with toothpicks to read it for more than ten minutes at a time. Where's the joy? Where's the humor? Where's the murder in this murder mystery, for crying out loud? And we're not even going to talk about the sex, because there wasn't any."

Maggie looked down at her sandwich, her appetite gone. "He killed a man, Bernie. He had to come to terms with what he'd done."

"Oh, yeah, right. He killed a man. Big deal. The guy was no good anyway. Saint Just's a hero—*our* hero. If I wanted someone wringing his hands and beating his breast for four hundred pages, I'd buy—hell, I wouldn't buy that cheap, lazy, manipulative pap. I hate that drivel. Everybody cry? Spare me."

"Saint Just can't have a crisis of conscience?"

Bernie ripped open the bag of tortilla chips, spilling them out on her lap. "Again, spare me. It's the Saint Just mysteries, Mags, not the confessions of a tarnished hero. Heroes don't have crises of conscience. They bed the ladies and solve murders, both brilliantly, then go for drinks at

Boodles or White's or somewhere. End of story, watch for the next Saint Just Mystery, available soon."

"I . . . I think his character needs to . . . to grow a little." Maggie winced, then said the hated word. "Evolve."

"Oh, no. Not that. Please, not that. Are you planning on writing for the critics now, Maggie, instead of your loyal readers? You want a list of all the good popular fiction writers who bought into that crap about not writing *real* books? I know where I can't look to find that list—the *New York Times*, that's where. Your readers want Saint Just. Edgy, confident, brilliant, a bit of a bastard, but with heart. They don't want Hugh Grant."

Maggie tried to swallow, choked, and reached for her glass. "So . . . so you want a rewrite?"

"Honey, I want a bonfire, a big one. Except for Sterling's subplot. Poor guy, that's the first time in a half-dozen books he finally got laid. I wouldn't want to lose that—but giving Sterling that nice, tame little love scene *instead of* Saint Just, not *in addition to* Saint Just's rolls in the hay? Nope, that's a cop-out. It doesn't work. It's cheating."

Maggie wasn't going to cry. She refused to cry. She was a professional, damn it, and she was not going to—"I put everything I had into that book, Bernie. It all just poured out of me. I know it sounds dumb, but that was . . . that was a book of the heart for me, something I just had to do."

The editor put down her sandwich. "Aw, honey, I know that. What I want to know now is *why*? Are you going through some blue period or something? What did I miss while I was drying out at the happy farm?"

Maggie was on thin ice now, and she knew it. "Well . . . you know. Buddy's murder and everything. You being accused. And then Sterling? I was so worried about Sterling . . . and then Saint Just—I mean *Alex* . . ."

"Oh, brother." Bernie looked toward the sideboard and the bottles she'd insisted Maggie not hide just because her best friend was a boozer, recently retired. "I guess it was bound to happen. I mean, Alex is a god, we both know that, and you did base Saint Just on him. But one is fiction, Mags, and one is Alex. I know you don't like that Alex is always . . . well, always in the thick of things whenever there's trouble. But now you're mixing them up, kiddo, the real and the fictional. You can't control Alex, so now you're trying to give twenty-first-century morals and all that crap to a guy from eighteen-sixteen. You've got to keep them separated in your mind, Maggie."

"That . . . that's sometimes difficult," Maggie said, wishing for a cigarette with all her being. Should she tell Bernie the truth? Could she? Bernie was her best friend . . . but Bernie was sober now, and what Maggie told her today, the woman would remember tomorrow. Forever. Forever might be a long time to go around regretting opening her big mouth.

Bernie nodded. "I guess it is. But just because you could never see Alex killing anyone doesn't mean Saint Just has to morph into frigging Alan Alda. And don't say *who*, because I'm not that old."

"My God." Maggie looked at her liverwurst sandwich again, beginning to think it looked pretty good. Like she'd had a liverwurst-and-potato-chip-on-rye epiphany. "You're right, Bernie. Saint Just *is* Saint Just. The whole time I was writing, I felt like I was trying to shove a square peg into a round hole. It was . . . I guess it was just something I had to do. As . . . as a writer, hokey as that sounds."

"Okay, that's fair. But, now that you've done it, do us both a favor and don't do it again. Books of the heart are almost always just for the writer, not for public consumption. God knows I've read and rejected enough of them.

Just forget about the book for a while. Go do your penance in New Jersey with your folks, go to England, leave your laptop here in New York. Find a nice Englishman to flirt with or something."

"Yeah, that's what I need, all right. Another Englishman," Maggie said, wincing. And yet, she felt better. She really did. Maybe the book had been an exorcism of sorts, and now it was out of her system. Saint Just was Saint Just. Hadn't Alex told her that? "I yams what I yams," she said, and grinned.

"What?"

"Popeye, Bernie. I yams what I yams. Doesn't anybody watch the old cartoons anymore?"

"No, some of us have a life," Bernie said, and Maggie threw her sandwich wrapper at her friend, just as the door opened and Sterling raced into the room.

"Turn it on, turn it on! Miss Spivak is talking to Saint Just."

"No! Oh, cripes, now what? I let him out of my sight for two minutes and—" Maggie nearly toppled off the couch, reaching for the remote control, then hit the Power button. Moments later, she saw Saint Just on the screen, Holly Spivak beside him, the Fox News van behind them.

" . . . truly, Miss Spivak," Alex was saying, "the kudos all go to Mrs. Halliday, who so cleverly warned me that something nefarious was afoot. I, for my small part in the affair, merely reacted."

Holly Spivak pulled the mike back to her own face. "And there we have it, Kevin—Mr. Blakely's modest explanation of what can only be called an act of heroism caught somewhere between Zorro and the Keystone Kops, as two of New York's Finest nearly arrested our hero, mistaking him for one of the bad guys, when he had actually just single-handedly foiled a daring daylight bank robbery.

Thanks to Mr. and Mrs. Yasimoto, again, here's all the action, caught on tape by Mr. Yasimoto, who happened to be videotaping his wife as she posed in front of the bank."

Videotape. Of course. You couldn't walk more than five steps in any direction in Manhattan without bumping into some tourist with a videocam.

Maggie forgot to breathe as the tape rolled and she saw a woman who had to be Mrs. Yasimoto, smiling and pointing to the art deco facade of the bank. Suddenly the woman screamed, and the picture blurred, then refocused, to show Alex—with a rousing, theatrical flourish—placing the tip of his cane against the neck of one of two men sprawled on the pavement.

Maggie closed her eyes. "Ah, jeez, doesn't he ever give it a rest?"

"Look, Maggie, look!" Sterling shouted. "The constables! They're arresting Saint Just."

Okay, it was time to open her eyes again . . . and there was Alex, being pushed against the wall and frisked. And his pant leg was purple. Why was his pant leg purple? And did she really want an answer to that question?

"You know," Bernie said, munching on a tortilla chip, "at times like this, Mags, I can see why you sometimes get confused between Alex and Saint Just. He does make a pretty good hero."

"Yeah," Maggie said, and decided to take another bite of her sandwich. It was safer than talking to Bernie.

Saint Just was Saint Just. Sometimes, if you just sort of squinted, life was simple. Okay, she had to learn to live with it. She *could* live with it. Really. She could. Hoo-boy . . .

# Chapter Three

"You have everything? I could run back upstairs and get the kitchen sink? Maybe the drapes?"

Saint Just ignored the sarcasm and tapped his quizzing glass against his lips as he counted the multitude of luggage on the sidewalk. The viscount did not travel without all the amenities. After all, he had his reputation as a gentleman of fashion to consider. "I believe so. Thank you, Socks."

"Hey, I'm the doorman. I do this stuff," Argyle Jackson said, grinning. Then he held out his hand. "And you're the tenant. You tip me. It's a quaint American custom."

"Of course, how remiss of me," Saint Just said, removing a twenty from his money clip and passing it to Socks. "Now all we need are Maggie and our transport. You did say ten o'clock, didn't you, Socks?"

"Relax, Alex, I got it. And here it comes, one bad-ass SUV."

"And here's Maggie," Sterling said, pointing down the street. "Oh, dear, I don't think she and Doctor Bob had a productive session. She's scowling, Saint Just."

"Maggie, my dear," Saint Just said, manfully withholding a smile as she came to a stomping halt in front of him. "How go the wars?"

"I don't want to talk about it."

"You informed Doctor Bob that, now that you're no longer smoking, you have no further need of his services? That was the plan as you presented it to me so optimistically this morning, was it not?"

"I said I don't want to talk about it," Maggie told him through gritted teeth. Then she sort of slumped in place. "We talked about this trip."

"About your mother, you mean? So. How much longer will you be seeing the good doctor?"

"Christmas. I know I'm going to get roped into going home for Christmas, too. After that. I'm a big girl now. I don't need a shrink to hold my hand just because I'm going to see my—oh, hell, I should have asked the man if he has an unlimited-visit lifetime plan. You know, like dance lessons and gym memberships. Once you pay out the bucks for one of those things, you never go again. It could be my way out."

"I cannot tell you how anxious I am to make your mother's acquaintance, Maggie. Sterling is of the opinion she must breathe real fire."

"Venom. She secretes real venom, and it gets more lethal every year. I mean, she was never a happy woman, but lately? I don't want to think about it. This the rental?" she asked, pointing to the huge black SUV. "Do I need a trucker's license to drive this thing?"

"I could—"

"In your dreams, Alex. As far as I know, you're licensed to drive only high-perch phaetons in Hyde Park. In the eighteen hundreds. Oh, here comes Steve. He said he might be able to see us off."

Saint Just looked down the street to see Steve Wendell making his way toward them with his slow, lazy shuffle of a walk, his too-long sandy-colored hair hanging in his eyes, his clothes, although well tailored, looking as if he'd slept in them. "Ah, yes, here's our impeccably groomed Beau Brummell now. To bid us a fond farewell? How very touching. But about the good *left*-tenant, my dear. I believe you had planned a luncheon with him, and yet when I had reason to speak with him the other day, he mentioned that he hadn't spoken with you for—"

"Bite me."

"I look forward to it, yes." Oh, he was a bad man. A bad, bad man. And enjoying himself immensely, as he had begun to feel a thaw in Maggie's attitude toward him these past few days. And now she'd allowed herself to be angry with him. Much more usual, and much more pleasing than her previous disappointment, disillusionment. His Maggie was a damned obstinate woman . . . and he adored her for it.

"Maggie," Steve Wendell said, bending to kiss her. A polite kiss. Circumspect. Really, the man was a total loss when it came to romance. Not that Saint Just was displeased by the man's ineptitude. "Alex, Sterling. I guess you two are looking forward to getting back to jolly old England?"

Saint Just removed his quizzing glass, stuck it in his pocket. "Don't look so sad, *Left*-tenant. We are not passing out of your life forever. It is a visit only."

Sterling, who had been helping Socks load luggage into the SUV, said, "I'm so looking forward to flight. Another new adventure."

Saint Just counted to three before Wendell picked up on Sterling's verbal slip and asked, "New? But you flew over here, right?"

Maggie quickly stepped in front of Sterling. "Boat. They came by boat." She spread her arms. "*Big* boat."

"Oh, I don't think so, Maggie," Sterling, always truthful, if not always astute, said, poking his head out from behind her. "I don't think I like boats. Socks took me on a boat tour around Manhattan, and I was quite queasy by the time we were done."

"But, then, how did you—?"

"I believe that's obvious. We walked," Saint Just slipped in quickly. "Steve, dear friend, would you be so kind as to move away from the car door, so that Sterling may settle himself. You do wish to settle yourself, don't you, Sterling?"

"Um . . . I might want to go upstairs one last time. Maggie tells me that with all the increased traffic that is prevalent around American holidays, and all of that, it could be several hours before we reach her parents' home, and I . . ."

"Yes, thank you, Sterling. I believe we understand," Saint Just said. Socks told him he could use the restroom in the lobby, and Sterling ran back into the building. "How lovely," Saint Just went on, "now you two can prolong your farewells. Will you kiss her again, Wendell? It's very affecting to observe."

"Alex, knock it off," Maggie said in a near-growl, then took hold of Wendell's arm at the elbow and steered him a good twenty paces down the sidewalk.

"You're really cruising for a bruising, you know that?" Socks said, shaking his head. "That guy carries a gold shield and a gun."

"Yes, I tremble in my boots just thinking about that. Truthfully, Socks, have you ever seen such an ineffectual lover?"

"And that pisses you off?"

"On the contrary. It pleases me to the top of my bent—that's the highest branch of a tree, Socks, figuratively. And it never hurts to remind Maggie of that fact—of both of those facts. Ah, here's Sterling again, and all zipped and buttoned, which can only be considered fortunate for the ladies, as well as for the rest of us. Socks, good friend, take care, and feel free to mount a raid on the kitchen pantry when you sneak in to watch movies on my plasma television machine."

"I wasn't going to . . . I wouldn't do that. Ah, damn, Alex—how did you know?"

"He knows everything," Sterling said as he opened the back door and climbed onto the high seat. "Don't you, Saint Just?"

"I do my possible, yes, thank you. Socks, you'll assist Maggie into the vehicle, if you please?" Saint Just then climbed into the front passenger seat, carefully belting himself in without wrinkling his sport coat. He did not much care for handing the reins to Maggie, and had already made a mental note to pursue a license to drive vehicles. "I may not know everything, but I know Maggie is dreading this visit with her family more than an appointment with a tooth drawer. It is our duty, Sterling, to keep her in good spirits and, most probably, away from sharp, pointed objects. Are you up to the task?"

"You know I'll offer myself as a supporting prop, and all of that. But do you really think—?"

The driver-side door opened, then slammed. "Let's get this dog and pony show on the road, okay?" Maggie said, holding the key to the right too long, so that the ignition screamed. "Oh, yeah, this is going to be a real fun trip."

"As long as you're happy, my dear." Saint Just smiled as Sterling whimpered in the backseat.

It wasn't, Maggie knew, that you physically couldn't go home again. It was that sometimes you just didn't want to, at least not to the Kelly Family home. The closer the SUV got to Ocean City, the tighter the knot in Maggie's stomach became and the more her head pounded.

Not that her passengers noticed. Sterling was happily

watching *Shrek* on the pull-down screen for the backseat, and Saint Just had, probably only to spite her, put on earphones and was listening to the soundtrack from the musical *Jekyll and Hyde*, saying he might as well have his melodrama with violin accompaniment.

Which had been a crack at her lousy mood.

"Okay, heads up," she said, giving Saint Just a poke in the ribs. "I've got to get around this circle, so you look right and I'll look left. Sterling—cross your fingers."

Ignoring the honking horn behind her, Maggie nervously eased her way into one of New Jersey's infamous traffic circles, one foot poised over the brake, then gunned it when Saint Just gave her the all clear.

"Very neatly executed, my dear, even if that truck driver did seem to have taken exception," Saint Just said, removing the headphones. "By that pinched white line around your lovely mouth, may I assume we're very nearly at our destination?"

The Ninth Street bridge was just ahead of them now, the bridge that would take them onto the island and to her doom. Hey, if Saint Just wanted melodramatic, she'd give him melodramatic. "Okay, now listen up. We're late—"

"Yes. I keep wondering, as you've made the journey from Manhattan to Ocean City in the past, how you could possibly have taken three incorrect turns."

"Don't push, Alex. I've got a lot on my mind. We're late, so that means everyone else is already there. That means Erin, along with her husband, Gavin the Neurosurgeon, all praise Gavin. Maureen lives here, so we know she's already at the house, probably kissing Mom's backside and scoring Brownie points, as usual. Tate? God knows. If there's still a red carpet on the front walk, he hasn't shown up yet."

"Sibling affection is so moving, isn't it, Sterling?" Saint Just drawled, extracting his quizzing glass from his pocket and draping the black grosgrain ribbon around his neck. "But to recap? Erin is the oldest, Tate is the only son, and Maureen is the baby of the family. Leaving you . . . ?"

"Can we all say middle-child syndrome?" Maggie said, turning right onto Wesley Avenue. "Doctor Bob says that's what made me an overachiever, so I really shouldn't complain. Now, I'll introduce my parents as Alicia and Evan, but don't call them that, not unless they ask you to. Call them Mr. and Mrs. Kelly. And maybe bow."

"Alicia Tate Evans, your very first nom de plume, Tate being your mother's maiden name, as I recall. Attempting to curry favor, were you?"

Maggie wanted to be angry, but she was too truthful to keep from smiling. "You got it, ace. And you'll be happy to know that grand gesture went over like a lead balloon. How dare I put their names on the covers of unforgiveable smut? To tell you the truth, I was kind of relieved when my historical-romance career went belly-up and I could pick another name."

"One with lots of Os, because Os look good on a book cover. Yes, I remember. And you have my sympathy, Maggie, truly you do, but it's for only three days. Surely you can manage three days. And your parents will be just as happy to see our backs, I'm sure. As the esteemed Guido Cavalcanti wrote, and as you had me repeat in one of our books, 'A guest, like a fish, has an unpleasant odor after three days.' "

"Oh, good, now I'm a flounder. Thanks, Alex." She pulled the SUV toward the curb in front of a large, three-storied, apricot-colored stucco beach house on the land side of the beach-front street. "Here we are. Home sweet home, at least for the last five years. Tate bought it for them."

"How generous of him."

"Oh, don't worry, the deed's in his name. But, yeah, it was a nice thing to do. I shouldn't always look for ulterior motives." Maggie, with some reluctance, turned off the ignition. "One more time—you're friends of mine from England. You don't live in my same building, you never lived in my condo, and we are *not* romantically involved. Clear?"

"How will you explain the coincidence of our names?"

"I won't have to. Nobody in my family reads my books. Last time I sent Mom one, she sent it back, said the family is still waiting for me to write a *real* book." She grinned at Saint Just. "So they won't know you from spit. How's that for a shot in your consequence, *my lord*?"

Maggie had been both right and wrong about her family. Maureen was most certainly a sycophant, embarrassingly eager to please, but Erin and her neurosurgeon husband had opted at the last minute for Thanksgiving in the Bahamas, a happy event that allowed Saint Just and Sterling to each have his own bedroom for the duration.

Tate, Saint Just had decided, was that most objectionable of creatures: stupefyingly boring. He spent most of his time with his cell-phone earpiece attached to his head and the rest of his time making snide remarks about effete, East Coast, left-wing liberals.

Which meant that Maggie spent a lot of her time on the front porch, with her father, as the woman seemed to have morphed into a timid mouse the moment they'd crossed the threshold Wednesday afternoon.

Saint Just, his hands thrust deep in his slacks pockets, walked the beach, his head down, reliving the high spots—actually the low points—of the past three days.

Maggie's opening comment, very badly timed, inquiring whether there was a wake going on in the house, led to Maureen dragging her from table to table, explaining that the multitude of flowers had all come from Tate: "He told Mom he has so much to be thankful for. Isn't that sweet? Look, this one's an actual magnolia tree. Isn't that something?"

Maggie's floral offering, ordered via the Internet, had been at last tracked down, located in the second-floor guest bathroom.

That had been the beginning, but there seemed still to be enough room left to go downhill from there. Saint Just shook his head, remembering . . .

They were giants, the Kellys were, or at least Tate and Maureen were. Upon meeting them, Saint Just had for a moment thought he might be able to comfort Maggie with the idea she may have been a changling. But that thought had evaporated when the patriarch of the clan, Evan Kelly, entered the room; not very tall, rather thin, and with a rather haunted look about him, he appeared much like a puppy grown used to daily beatings.

And then there was Mrs. Kelly, mother to these giants and to Maggie.

Saint Just heard her. One was always hearing Mrs. Kelly. One simply didn't *see* her, which had been made clear by the bellow from the first-floor master bedroom just as Maureen was reciting the affecting contents of Tate's card from the potted magnolia tree in the dining room.

"Margaret? Is that you, Margaret? About time you showed up! And look what you're responsible for this time. Come here, look! Last-minute guests. How could you just spring them on me like that? I told your father you always find a way to make a shambles of everything, and you've done it again. I had to put the extra leaf in the table, for your *friends*, and now my back's gone out, and I'm stuck in this bed like some invalid. Come in here! Be some use for a change. Help me to the bathroom."

It had been amazing, and quite the eye-opener, to watch as both Maggie and her father reacted to the woman's voice. They seemed to shrink in place, the pair of them.

Maggie had headed down the hallway, and Saint Just had barely been able to hear her mumbled greeting. He did, however, have very little difficulty hearing Mrs. Kelly say, "My God, Margaret, you're *fat*. How could you let yourself *go* like that?"

Nearly every hour on the hour, sometimes again on the half hour, Alicia Kelly would bellow, and someone would pay the price. Maureen seemed to do so gladly, with a smile that possibly owed something to the vial of small pink pills she kept in her pocket, and Tate was somehow excused.

But Maggie and her father were very definitely the woman's main whipping boys.

And it explained so much. Why Maggie backed away from loud voices, angry confrontations, and people who presented themselves as so very *sure* of themselves. Why she was so sure she was always in the wrong. Why physically imposing or large people seemed to turn her in on herself, leach all the spirit out of her. Why she'd been visiting Doctor Bob once a week for nearly five years, with no end in sight.

Obviously, the famous Doctor Bob hadn't been able to rid Maggie of her childhood memories, or trauma, or whatever people like Doctor Bob called such things, leaving it up to Saint Just to put some starch into the poor girl's backbone.

He had no idea how to accomplish that feat, however.

"Alex! Wait up!"

Saint Just halted, turned to see Maggie running across the sand, her hair and skirt blowing in the wind, her sea-green cashmere sweater hugging her lithe curves, her feet bare on the cold sand. Yes, she had become slightly more rounded in the past six weeks, but he liked her with fewer sharp edges. Her dark copper, chin-length hair, with its exquisite highlights, begged to be touched.

And happiness, lately so lacking in her Irish green eyes, shone from her now.

He could pen an ode to her beauty. She was fresh and sparkling, totally unaffected, and unaware of her impact on the male of the species. Not that terribly small, but in this land of Kelly Giants, a veritable Pocket Venus.

"Maggie," he said as she fell into step beside him. "Is your presence here in the way of a companionable stroll with a friend, or am I serving as a bolt-hole?"

"Both, I guess. Dad and I had another nice talk earlier—I actually feel like I'm starting to know him a little bit. He's afraid of Mom. He didn't say it, but he is. And yet, he loves her very much. Strange," she said, pushing her hair out of her face as she smiled up at him. "Oh, and I just told Tate to shove it."

"I beg your pardon?"

"I told him off, Alex," she said, dancing ahead of him into the last little wavelet to roll up onto the beach. "Oh, cold! And I'm so *hot*." A shoe in each hand, she spun around in a circle, her head back, spinning round and round, until she lost her balance, and Saint Just caught her.

"I'd say you were a tad in your altitudes, except that it hasn't quite gone noon and you rarely drink."

"I'm drunk on life, Alex! I told him *off!*"

"Really. And what, pray tell, prompted this confrontation?"

She sobered and stepped away from him. "You did, Alex. I couldn't stand the look in your eyes every time Mom yelled and I went running like some Pavlov dog. And I could see that muscle working in your jaw whenever Tate started on one of his damn lectures. I'd had enough. I mean, not coming home? Avoiding them? That's not the answer. I had something to say, and I finally said it. I'm a big girl now, all grown up, and I've got to stop reacting like some intimidated child."

"Remarkable," Saint Just said, longing to take her in his arms. She looked so *free*, so very liberated. He'd been very worried she'd suffer a backward slide, reach for the solace of Dame Nicotine while upset, but she hadn't. She'd gone on the offensive. "Would that I could have been there, my dear."

"No, no. This one I had to do on my own." She narrowed her eyes. "And I was *brilliant*. Oh, yes. *B-r-i*-double-*l*-brilliant! I tell you, I sliced him into a million pieces, and he's so thick he didn't even realize it until he tried to walk and came apart like a string of paper dolls. I think I want to go back, take on Maureen, tell her it's time she stopped being a mouse and got a life. You know, while I'm on a roll."

"Oh, I really don't think so," Saint Just said, pulling her arm through his and heading them both off down the beach. "One victory a day should be sufficient. And my congratulations. Your brother is a bit of a twit. Not enough to expend my energy on, but certainly no one who should be able to cow my own dear Maggie."

"And I was *good*," Maggie said, leaning her head against his shoulder. Then, suddenly, she sobered, this being-high-on-life business obviously a tad transitory. "Oh, boy, now I've got to go back, and Maureen will have run tattling to Mom, and all hell's going to break loose. Quick, drown me."

"I have a better suggestion, if you don't mind. You and Sterling and I could drive up the coast, to Atlantic City. I understand the trip is no more than eight miles and there are baccarat tables in every casino. Much akin to faro, I believe, or at least close enough as makes no matter."

And that's how it came to pass that after turning in the rental SUV at Philadelphia International Airport, Saint Just embarked upon his first airplane ride with a six-figure cashier's check tucked in his pocket.

He left behind a small thank-you gift for his hostess, a five-carat diamond tennis braclet hidden inside a long velvet box tied with a silver ribbon.

It was silly, a petty revenge, but he doubted that Tate's floral excess looked quite so good to Mrs. Kelly anymore. Of course, if Maggie ever found out he'd put her name on the card, the entire world would not be large enough for him to hide in—but as duels were frowned upon, and punching the arrogant fool's lights out would only upset everyone needlessly, thoroughly trumping the man's magnolia would have to suffice.

*We're on a hook, we're on a hook. The plane goes up, the hook comes out, it attaches to the line, and we're on the hook until we land. It's just a big bus, no, an old trolley car. And we're on a hook . . .*

"Maggie? Do you intend to release that death grip you have on the arms of your seat and open your eyes? We've been in the air for at least five hours. I don't think anything untoward is going to happen."

"Don't bother me, Alex, I'm meditating," she said, opening her eyes only slightly, not moving her head as she shifted her gaze toward him. "And don't look out there. I never look out there. If I look out, and down, then the plane will drop. I'm holding this thing up with sheer willpower, and you should be damn grateful. Stop it! How can you keep looking out there?"

"It's elementary, actually. I turn my head toward the window, and I *look*. But you're correct. There's nothing much in the way of a view, save the clouds below us. I once partook in a balloon ascension in Hyde Park, as you know, but that was tame indeed when compared to modern jet flight."

He leaned across her and spoke to Sterling, whose seat was on the other side of the aisle. "Enjoying yourself, Sterling?"

Sterling's grin was heartwarmingly naive, in Maggie's opinion, clearly that of a man who didn't understand the dangers of flight. "Oh, yes, Saint Just. Have you made use of the facilities? You really should. Completely fascinating . . . although one does wonder where everything, um, *goes*."

"Some of us wonder, Sterling. Others of us do not," Alex said as Maggie giggled. "I'm so gratified that you're amused, my dear. While you've been meditating, as you call it, Sterling here has been running amok in the aisles. I think we, in the role of parents, will soon be considering putting him in leading strings."

"Oh, let him alone," Maggie said, reaching over to pat Sterling's hand. "You're enjoying yourself?"

Sterling nodded. "I've located all of the emergency exits, and I know that my seat cushion serves as a flotation device, and that I should put on my air mask when it drops down, then place one on my child."

"You don't have a child, Sterling," Maggie pointed out.

"True. I'll concede that. But I am prepared." He held out a small bag. "Pretzel?"

"Thanks, but no. I think we land soon, if I adjusted my watch correctly. Now, Bernie told me Heathrow Airport is a real zoo . . ."

"With—"

"Figuratively speaking," Maggie added quickly, before Sterling, always so literal, would ask if they had monkeys and elephants. "So we stick together, find our way to the luggage carousel, look for the limo the production company arranged for us, and get the heck out of there as fast as we can. Then it's a straight shot south to Surrey and Medwine Manor, or so I'm told. Any questions?"

Sterling raised his hand. "Won't we have time to see London at all?"

"Yes, Maggie, it's unseemly to just rush about and not at least take a drive through London. I very much want to see Carleton House again. Such a magnificent grand staircase, and the Prince Regent entertained lavishly."

"Um, Alex? They tore down Carleton House sometime in the eighteen-twenties. They tore down a lot of places. We're not landing in Regency London. I'm sorry, but except for palaces and Parliament and all that stuff, you won't know this London a whole lot more than you knew Manhattan when you first got there. They've got McDonald's here now."

Alex was quiet for some moments, then said, "I think we should like to see it, in any case. And, much as you may naysay me, I most especially wish to visit a particular establishment a few steps off Threadneedle Street. As your research is always so very much on the mark and the family has been serving at the pleasure of his majesty since the sixteen hundreds, I am going to assume the shop is still there in one form or another."

"What kind of shop?"

"One devoted to the best in umbrellas and walking sticks. Very *specialized* sticks, if you take my meaning. You know I was forced to leave my cane in New York, what with the metal detectors at the airport."

Maggie sat back in her seat, blew out her breath, recited mentally: *Saint Just is Saint Just*. "A sword cane. You want another sword cane. Is that really necessary?"

"You'd have me go naked in my homeland?"

"Oh, cut me a break. Whoa!" she said, grabbing the seat arms in a death grip as her stomach lurched. "Damn it, I *hate* when they do that."

"Do what, my dear? And may I say, your usually healthy complexion has gone rather white."

"Do what? You mean you didn't feel that? The pilot's putting on the air brakes—I think that's what they're called—because we're making our descent. I know, in my head, that he's probably dropping us down from a billion miles per hour to a million miles per hour, but it feels like we're stopping. Thirty-five thousand feet up, and the guy's slamming on the brakes like he's trying to avoid a deer in the road. I *hate* that."

"Ah, the often too-fertile imagination of the writer. You're your own worst enemy, my dear." Alex patted her hand. "Close your eyes, Maggie. Meditate. Think good thoughts. We'll be on the ground soon, and shortly after that we'll be at Medwine Manor, where you'll be feted and fawned over as the great talent you are."

Maggie opened one eye, and glared at him. "Don't patronize me, Alex. I'm not going to get hysterical and start screaming or something."

"Really? I cannot tell you how gratified I am to hear that. In that case, my dear—lean across me and see the great metropolis of London spread out at our feet. Glorious, isn't it? Like something out of a picture book."

"Sadist." Maggie groaned, and slapped her hands over her eyes.

# Chapter Four

One hand on the golden knob of a sword cane that in style and quality of workmanship greatly resembled the one his fictional self had purchased at the same small shop, Saint Just was a very happy, extremely content man as the limousine rolled out of London and, eventually, into Surrey.

It was raining, nothing out of the ordinary for England, and was rather gray and damp, also not unusual, but nothing could put a damper on Saint Just's enthusiasm. Or on Sterling's.

"Oh, look, Saint Just," Sterling said now, his head half out of the window he insisted on keeping lowered, the better to take in the scenery. "That marvelous mansion, up there, at the top of the hill. The very picture of your family's estate in Sussex, isn't it?"

Saint Just leaned past Maggie. "Seventeenth century. The pediment is familiar, indeed. The same symmetrical flanking wings, most likely added in the eighteenth century. The unique bell tower. Good God, Sterling, I think you're right. That's Blake House. But here, in Surrey?"

In between them, Maggie slid down on her spine on the

leather seat. "Is there a sign anywhere, Sterling? Something with the name of the place on it?"

"I don't—oh, there's an old fingerpost." Sterling leaned even farther out the window. "It's . . . I can barely make it out . . . it's—got it! Peakely Manor. Why?"

Maggie sort of sucked in her cheeks. "Oh, okay. Thanks, Sterling."

"Maggie?" Saint Just asked quietly. "Is there something you want to tell me?"

"Absolutely not. Nope. Nothing I want to say." Then she sighed audibly and sat up straight once more. "Okay. I've never been to England until now, right? But you had to have a house, a bunch of houses. Other characters had to have houses. So . . . so I bought a few books. I think, I'm pretty sure, your Blake House is based on Peakely Manor. I just moved it to Sussex."

Saint Just was actually finding it difficult to breathe. On one level, he understood what Maggie was telling him. Yet, on another, a more visceral level, he'd just been orphaned, disenfranchised. Erased. Eliminated. "But . . . but it's *my* home. My family home."

Maggie shook her head. "Oh, cripes. Alex," she said, putting a hand on his arm as she spoke to him, quietly. "You're fake, remember? Fictional. You've never really been here. You're more real in New York than you've ever been here. I mean, you *exist* in New York. People see you, talk to you. You're evolving, just as you keep saying, and growing, and becoming more Alex Blakely, less Alexandre Blake, less the Viscount Saint Just. But I agree, this has to be a shock, seeing my imagination up against the real thing. I . . . I'm sorry."

She was wrong. Maggie was wrong. He *was* Saint Just. He would always be Saint Just. His address had changed, that was all. This wasn't his England. His England had long ago disappeared, along with Brummell; and Byron, Shelley, and Keats; Prinney himself . . . even Carleton House.

The past was the past, and he was very much of the moment. To go back would be to disappear into the pages of Maggie's books. He and Sterling both, living again in the Regency Era, but never again living *now*. He could not, would not, allow that to happen.

There was no Blake House to return to, no mansion in Grosvenor Square, no hunting box in Scotland.

In a way, this was probably a good thing. He was becoming less fictional by the day. After all, he couldn't go back . . . not if there was nowhere to return *to*.

Saint Just took a breath, let it out slowly. "My goodness, Maggie, how you're looking at me. As if I might have an attack of the vapors or fall into a sad decline. I assure you, that is far from the truth. As you say, as I've said, Sterling and I are evolving. Blake House was drafty in the winter, in any case."

Maggie was quiet for some moments before she spoke again. "You're pissed, right?"

"I am not—upset. I fully understand what you did, why you did it. However, even without home or fortune, I remain Saint Just. That, my dear, will never change."

She saluted. "Yes, *sir*. Jeez, what a grouch. Sterling? Why aren't you being a grouch?"

Sterling smiled sheepishly. "I don't want to go back," he said, then blushed. "Sorry, Saint Just, I hate to be disloyal, and all of that, but I really don't. I like Henry, and my motorized scooter, and Socks, and the television machine, and—"

"Yes, Sterling, we get the point," Saint Just said as the limousine slowed and the driver made the very tight turn between stone pillars. He had turned onto a gravel drive that led downhill rather than up, then finally leveled as the trees disappeared behind them and a parklike setting opened before them, a bubbling stream nearly encircling the large cut-stone manor house at the center of everything.

The dividing glass slid down soundlessly and the driver announced: "Medwine Manor, everyone. You just stay dry in the back while I fetch brollies for you. This is a fierce mist."

"Mist?" Maggie said as rain drummed on the roof of the limousine. "This *mist* starts looking anything more like a deluge and I'm going to ask you two to begin building an ark."

"Oh, Maggie, but I'm afraid Saint Just and I don't know how to—oh. I see. Never mind."

Saint Just smiled at his good friend, deliberately shaking off any lingering melancholy. After all, he had proven in these past months that he was nothing if not adaptable. "Have no fear, Maggie. I shall carry you over the threshold, if necessary."

"It won't be," Maggie said, avoiding his gaze, as well as his offered hand once he'd stepped out of the limousine. "There's a porch—portico. I'll make a run for it."

Saint Just and Sterling followed, taking advantage of the umbrellas the driver offered, stopping just below the curved stone steps to admire the facade of the three-story building.

"Not quite up to what we've been used to, is it, Saint Just? A bit ragged about the edges, and all of that."

"And yet, obviously being improved upon. Notice the scaffolding to your left, Sterling, in front of the west wing."

"Are you two coming, or what?"

"I do believe Maggie thinks we're lagging behind, Sterling," Saint Just said, motioning for his friend to precede him up the steps, to where Maggie waited in the open doorway.

He handed the umbrella to the driver, who also took

Sterling's, mumbling something about driving around to the back door to unload the luggage, then took a moment to inspect the foyer.

"I knocked, but no one came, and when I tried the door it was open," Maggie told him, wiping raindrops from her face. "Oh, this is big, isn't it?"

Saint Just took inventory of the large foyer, at least forty feet square. An intricate black-and-white marble tile floor shone beneath a soaring ceiling painted to look like a summer sky dotted with fluffy white clouds. A wonderfully broad stone staircase rose slowly from the open hallway, and a gallery stretched around three of the four age-darkened white marble walls that had been carved to include columns and angels and goddesses, or some such romantic nonsense.

That last wall, along the stairs, was dominated by an immense mural stretching from the ground floor up to the top of the first floor, a creation that depicted a goodly number of dancing, frolicking ladies and gentlemen being attended by rosy-cheeked children.

"I can only sigh in relief to see that as you were thumbing through books and building my various estates, you didn't pattern any of them after the interior of this pile. The decor is rather . . . flamboyant."

"Yeah, well, I think it's pretty neat," Maggie said, her head back as she turned in a slow circle, looking at their surroundings. "No wonder they decided to film here. Wow."

"The place is passable, I agree," Saint Just said, amazed to find he was feeling more and more comfortable by the moment. Then again, after all, this was his milieu, real or imaginary. "Ah, and I may be wrong, but I do believe our host approaches now. He's not rigged out well enough to be a servant."

They all watched as a fairly squat man dressed in hunting clothes that had obviously seen their share of hunts came lumbering down the stairs, one hand on the stone railing, his gaze directed at his boots, as if he'd taken a tumble once and planned never to do that again.

Not until he had safely navigated the stairs and stood on the parquet floor did the man raise his head and smile at Maggie. (Saint Just and Sterling could very well have been invisible.)

"Hullo, you beautiful bit," he said, waggling his bushy white eyebrows. "Welcome to Medwine Manor. I'm Sir Rudy Medwine, and you're gorgeous. Another American actress, I hope. We've already got one, but she's a little starchy. Don't think she likes me. She should. I'm very rich. Mine's the Medwine Marauder, best fishing reel in the world. Knighted for it, I was. Now I'm living the high life. Used to live down the road from this place, in a pokey two-up-two-down, and now all this is mine. You want to know me. Really, you do."

Maggie opened her mouth, may have said, "Uh . . ." before Saint Just deftly stepped in front of her and bowed to Sir Rudy. "Sir Rudy, how delighted and, indeed, honored we all are to be numbered among your guests. Please allow me to present to you Miss Maggie Kelly, who, writing as Cleo Dooley, penned the brilliant book that will be filmed here on your marvelous estate. I, for my sins, am Alex Blakely, Miss Kelly's personal assistant, and the gentleman just now waving to you is Sterling Balder, her spiritual advisor. We are all quite happy to make your acquaintance."

Sir Rudy pointed his finger at Saint Just. "You . . . you're English. Upper-crust English, at that. Are you all English? I wanted Americans. I distinctly told them I wanted Americans."

"For what?" Maggie grumbled.

This was certainly going well.

"Miss Kelly is very much the American woman, Sir Rudy," Saint Just told him, taking the man's arm and leading him back to the staircase. "Sterling and I are English, yes, although it has been years since we've been on this side of the pond."

"Centuries, even," Maggie groused, following the two men while Sterling brought up the rear.

The small party climbed the stairs slowly, giving Sir Rudy ample time to catch his breath, but he was huffing and puffing by the time they reached the first floor.

"I think everybody's in there," the man said, pointing to closed double doors that probably led to the main saloon. "They're not a happy bunch. The rain, you see. It's keeping them indoors. And that scaffolding has to come down before next week, for the filming. Dicey, that. I ordered a joint and pudding for dinner, hoping to cheer them up, but they haven't eaten yet, so be careful none of them tries to take a bite out of you."

"Charming," Saint Just said, turning to hold out his arm, indicating that Maggie should proceed, enter the room ahead of him. "Sir Rudy is rather unusual, isn't he?" he asked her quietly as she stopped beside him.

"I like him," Sterling said, standing on tiptoe, the better to see once Sir Rudy had crossed the wide hallway and pushed open the doors. "No airs and graces about that man. None at all."

"And I'm a toplofty prude, I imagine?" Saint Just asked him.

He should have known Maggie would answer: "If the high-topped Hessian boot fits, Chauncy," before giving him a wink and heading into the chandelier-lit expanse of the main saloon.

Left with little else to do, Saint Just followed, to be met by an odd assortment of people, some of whom lounged on green-on-green-striped satin couches, some of whom propped up the enormous marble fireplace mantel, and one who was stretched out on the floor, a long leg behind her ear, most of her backside showing, the rest of her fairly magnificent body covered in a bright-blue leotard.

"Ladies and gentlemen," Sir Rudy announced in a booming voice. "Here's more of you, come to join the party."

One of the gentlemen at the fireplace pushed himself away from the mantel and strode towards them, his rather pasty flesh sheened with perspiration, his totally bald head glistening under the light from the chandeliers.

"Must be one of the actors. He looks like a pint-size version of Telly Savalas, except he's more rubbery. I wonder if he's going to offer us a lollipop," Maggie said out of the corner of her mouth.

"I beg your pardon?"

"An actor, Alex. Played a cop on an old television series. *Kojak*. My dad was crazy about him. It isn't important."

"Indeed," Saint Just said, feeling more and more comfortable in this large room, more and more in his element. And because of the way he felt, he stepped forward, extended his hand to the bald man, gave a slight inclination of his head. "Alex Blakely . . . and you are . . . ?"

"Peppin," the man said in an oddly thin, high voice. An almost childish voice. "Arnaud Peppin, reluctant director of this grand epic, if we can ever start filming. The leads are here, so who are you? Although you already look and sound more English than that idiot over there. He wants an accent coach, like that's going to happen on our budget."

"Mr. Peppin, of course. How . . . charming," Saint Just said with another slight nod and a smile—not having the faintest idea what the man was talking about. Clearly he was going to have to correct that lapse, and quickly. He then repeated the introductions he had begun with Sir Rudy.

By now, all eyes were on the newcomers, except for those of the woman who was still on the carpet, although now she was lying on her side, her head propped in one hand, her other hand sliding caressingly down the side of her breast and onto her hip as she smiled only at Saint Just.

Nothing all that out of the ordinary there. He had been very carefully created to have that effect on women. It was a gift. Occasionally a curse.

Arnaud seemed remarkably unimpressed to learn that the author and her entourage had arrived. Saint Just knew this because the man turned his back to him and said, "Relax, people. Joanne will handle this. It's only the writer."

Saint Just immediately and quite automatically put his right arm straight out to his side, and Maggie's advancing body immediately and very predictably slammed against it.

"Only the writer? *Only* the writer? Hey, cue ball, let me tell you a—"

"Ms. Dooley! Oh, how thrilled I am to meet you! I heard you were coming. I'm Sam Undercuffler, screenwriter."

Saint Just lifted his quizzing glass to his eye and inspected Undercuffler as he scurried over to them. The young man was depressingly brown. Brown hair, brown eyes, brown slacks; brown tweed jacket with brown suede patches at the elbows. The barrel of a cheap brown pipe protruded from his jacket pocket. His brown shoes, lace shoes, were badly in need of reheeling and a good polish.

"Oh, so good to meet you, Ms. Dooley—Cleo. May I call you Cleo? I adapted your book for the screen. Well, you probably figured that out, since I said I'm the screenwriter. Oh, would you listen to me? I'm just so excited to finally meet the creator of the brilliant Saint Just Mysteries. The brilliant creator of the brilliant series, I should say. I'm playing with an idea of my own, for my own television series, you understand, but I know you wouldn't want to hear about that. Would you? Please, if there's anything you want, anything you need . . ."

Saint Just stood amused as Maggie tried to get her hand back from the screenwriter, who was still pumping it with all the enthusiasm of a dairy maid only three churn strokes away from butter. "Two writers. Together. Members of the same literary fraternity. Why, he even looks so much the writer, doesn't he? Isn't this wonderful, *Cleo*? I imagine you two will have *so* much to talk about."

Now, sometimes Maggie said *bite me*, out loud, so everyone could hear her. But sometimes she could say *bite me* without actually uttering a word. Her facial expression was more than enough. This was one of those times.

Still, when she did speak, it was to say hello to Sam Undercuffler, smile politely, ask him to please call her Maggie, and agree that it was wonderful that two writers could be here, each with their own hand in the creation, as it were.

Poor girl. That had to have been painful.

"Well, come on, come on, there's lots more to meet," Sir Rudy said from behind them, actually giving Sterling a little push so that he stumbled farther into the room.

"I'll take care of this, Sir Rudy. Thanks anyway," Arnaud said, then clapped his hands. "Okay, people, listen up. It's introduction time. Raise your hand when I call out your name, and let's get this over with. I've got things to do."

"And yet again . . . charming," Saint Just said quietly.

"Yeah," Maggie agreed. "I feel so warm and fuzzy . . . so wanted."

"Okay . . . right. Here we go," Arnaud continued, either slightly deaf or just not caring what anyone else might say; Saint Just was fairly certain it was the latter. "You met the writer. Sam, back up, you're blocking my view. Okay, over there. The tall guy who looks like an English valet? He's our English valet, Clarence. Real name, Dennis Lloyd. Raise your hand, Dennis."

The man bowed, and Sterling waved to him.

"Next up, Sterling Balder."

"Hullo?" Sterling said, his arm still raised in midwave.

"I don't think he means you, Sterling," Maggie said, squeezing his hand.

"That's me! Over here on the couch! Perry Posko, otherwise known as Sterling Balder."

Saint Just looked at the actor, then at his own Sterling Balder. They were very nearly a match, from their likewise thinning hair to their spectacles, to their pudgy waistlines, to the open, trusting grins on their faces.

"Good casting," Maggie said. "Clarence and Sterling both. That's encouraging, right?"

"I imagine so," Saint Just said, leaning closer to her. "I do have a few reservations about the gentleman in front of the mantel. Is he wearing makeup?"

"Tanning booth. Bet you," Maggie said, then shut up when Arnuad pointed to a rather tall, definitely dark gentleman who seemed to be studiously ignoring everyone.

"Evan? Over here, Evan. That's Evan Pottinger, our Lord Hervey. The villain, but you know that."

Saint Just bowed yet again. "Delighted, I assure you."

"Completely and totally unimpressed, I assure *you*," Pottinger drawled, then turned his back on everyone.

"Method actor," Arnaud said. "He's getting into the role. Everybody thinks they're De Niro. Evan wants to wear the costumes and everything. Wants everyone in costume. Pain in my ass, that's what he really is."

"How very droll," Saint Just drawled as well, amused, and certainly not ready to reveal that he had no idea what a method actor was. "I believe I should like to see that."

"Well, you won't. Period costumes cost a fortune, and

we're only renting them from the company that supplied *Sense and Sensibility*. I'm not going to have anyone dribbling gravy all over them."

"Ah, my good sir, a *true* gentleman would never dribble."

"Too bad, gorgeous. Because I could lick it all up for you," the leotard-clad beauty said from the floor, so that Saint Just had no recourse but to look at her, watch as, catlike, she uncurled herself and stood up. "Hi. I'm Nikki Campion, and I'm the love interest. Just call me Nikki."

"That would be my honor, Nikki," Saint Just said, fairly certain that if Miss Campion were to hold out her hand and he was to bow over it, kiss it, his life expectancy could most probably be measured in the minutes it would take for Maggie to get him alone and kill him.

So wasn't he lucky that Miss Campion didn't hold out her hand? She merely pressed herself up against him, went up on tiptoe, and kissed him on his left ear. "If you screw as good as you look, see me later," she breathed into that ear, then turned and walked away in a manner that left no doubt that she felt every male in the room watched her every step.

Sir Rudy made a sort of whimpering sound in his throat, turned on his heels, and quit the room.

Saint Just looked at Maggie—not that he, the perfect hero, was actually afraid of the woman—and was surprised to see her looking at him in some sympathy.

"I'd be pretty disgusted by having to watch that, and hear it—the woman obviously doesn't know how to whisper—except it wasn't your fault. And because we're down to the last man, that one very tanned and blond man has to be playing Saint Just. You want to call that nice Miss Browning with the tinkling-bells laugh and ask her to book us on the next plane home? I can't believe you want to stick around to watch surfer dude over there in action as you."

Saint Just would have blanched if he was the sort who blanched. He turned his attention to the man awkwardly lounging at the mantel just as the fellow made some sort of flourishing motion and then went to rest one elbow on the mantel, missed, and nearly came to grief before righting himself.

"I have to work with this," Arnaud said, shaking his head, as obviously he'd also seen the actor's clumsiness. "Troy? Give us a wave, why don't you, and try not to kill yourself when you do it. People, meet Troy Barlow, our Viscount Saint Just. Our blond beachboy turned dark-haired, sophisticated sleuth. Does Hollywood know casting or what?"

Sterling nearly danced in place. "I know him! That's Brick. Brick Lord. He's in one of my favorite soap operas. He's Dyson's identical twin brother, and Brittany thinks Dyson's the father of her unborn child, but it's really Brick who—oh, my!"

"I play both parts, yes," Troy said, advancing only as far as the couches, where, as Saint Just manfully stifled a wince, he sat down with all the grace of a lobster navigating an escalator. "You thought Brick and Dyson were really twins? You hear that, Nikki? I'm a working actor. A craftsman. While you're humping transmission repairs. *Now* do you understand why my name comes first on the credits?"

Nikki looked at Arnaud, pouted. "You told me last night that you'd fix that, Arnie."

"That'll teach you to screw short, bald men," a female voice said, behind Saint Just. "Like he's in charge of credit placement? I am, sweetheart. And don't bother shaking that silicone at me because I don't think you're that hot."

Saint Just stepped to one side to allow a slim woman as tall as Bernice Toland-James—as thin as Bernice, as red-headed as Bernice, presenting as powerful a presence as Bernice—to push past everyone, to pose directly beneath the main chandelier. "Joanne Pertuccelli here. In charge of production. Who the hell are you people?"

"Oh, no, not again. I'm getting bored," Maggie said in her marvelously mulish way that so endeared her to Saint Just. "Is anyone else going to crawl out of the woodwork or are you it? Because this is the last time I want to hear, 'Oh, it's only the writer.'"

"You're Cleo Dooley? Name looks pretty decent above the title. Good use of Os." Joanne frowned, fingering the large silver stopwatch that hung around her neck on a long, black, braided band. "You don't look like a writer."

"Yeah. I get a lot of that one, too," Maggie said as Sterling, a man who learned from experience, prudently stepped behind Saint Just. "Thanks heaps, Joanne. I take it you're also in charge of public relations? I mean, I was hoping for a welcome like that after a long flight and the rain and everything. Thanks so much. Really."

"I think that's probably sufficient, Maggie," Saint Just warned quietly, taking her arm and leading her across the wide expanse of faded Aubusson carpet, toward the drinks table, where Evan the Villain was already in residence, still studiously glowering and ignoring everyone.

"Touchy," Joanne called after them. "Hey, nice ass, handsome."

"Is she talking to—"

"No, Sterling, I believe not, so you can spare your blushes," Saint Just said as Maggie, always put in a good mood by the so-innocent Sterling, grinned. "Besides, as gentlemen, we'll ignore the lady's lapse into crudity."

A nervous giggle caught Saint Just's attention, and a moment later, a gum-chewing young lady with hair too blonde to be genuine pushed herself out of a chair in the farthest corner of the room. "Hi, I'm Marylou Keppel. I heard the introductions, before, but Arnaud always forgets me, unless he needs something. I'm the gofer."

"I . . . I beg your pardon?"

"You know. If somebody needs something? Gofer it, Marylou. Go-find it, Marylou. Go-get it, Marylou. Gofer. Oh, I stand in sometimes, I prompt. Tight budget on this one. But mostly? Mostly I'm a gofer."

"How . . . how wonderful for you, I'm sure," Saint Just said blankly. "Maggie? Isn't that wonderful for Miss Keppel?"

"You're dying here, aren't you, Alex?" Maggie asked, then laughed. "But, hey, you wanted to come."

"Excuse me," Joanne Pertuccelli said from behind Saint Just. "I still don't know who you two are. Who authorized you to be here?"

Maggie covered her mouth with her hand, pretended to cough as she said, "Time to turn on the charm, big boy."

As if he had to be told.

"Ah, Miss Pertuccelli, a thousand pardons," Saint Just said, bowing to the woman, taking her hand—a litte awkward, having to reach for the thing—and raising it to within an inch of his lips. "You see before you Miss Dooley's inspiration, immodest as that is to say. Her distant English relation. I am Alex Blakely, on whom the Viscount is patterned, and with me is my dear friend and compatriot, Sterling Balder. We . . . we travel *everywhere* with Miss Dooley."

"Really?" Joanne said, obviously not impressed, which was, in fact, quite lowering to the perfect hero, the irresistible-to-women perfect hero. He consoled himself with the sure knowledge that her heart must be otherwise engaged, making all other men invisible to her. "Just so you know, you're not included in her expense account.

Arnaud? Hey—Arnie! This weather is costing us big money. What are you going to do about all this damn rain?"

Arnaud stayed where he was, his back to the woman. "What do you want me to do with it? Wave my hands at the sky and yell 'cut'?"

"I think I like him, even with his 'only the writer' crack," Maggie said. "Marylou? Is showing me to the nearest bathroom outside your job description?"

"Heck, no, that's fine. This way. And there's piles of bedrooms. I know who's in each one, so we can sniff out three more for you guys, okay? The rooms are big, but the plumbing sucks."

As Joanne, Marylou, and Maggie walked away, Perry Posko moved across the room so quickly, and slid to a halt so sharply, that he nearly left skid marks. "*You're* Sterling Balder? Really? Oh! Oh! And he's right—we even look alike! Why didn't I see that? Oh, this is great. This is terrific. Can I watch you? Can I follow you around? I mean, I want to *be* Sterling Balder. I want to eat, drink, *breathe* the character. I want to *be* you!"

"Well, um . . . well, you can't," Sterling said, then looked at Saint Just. "Can he? I mean, I'm Sterling Balder. I've always been Sterling Balder. I don't want to be anybody else—why does he want to be me? Is that allowed?"

"Oh. Oh, no, no," Perry said quickly. "Not identity theft or anything like that. Gosh, I wouldn't want you to think that. Nothing strange, nothing kooky. But this part is a real break for me. If the first movie goes over, I'm set for the next five, six years. There's already talk of a series, you know. It's not like I'm ever going to be anything but a character actor, not looking like this. Um . . . no offense. I just want to get it right, and I know you could help me. Will you help me?"

"Saint Just?"

"Go, Sterling. Enjoy yourself. Teach Perry here to be

you. There cannot be too many good-hearted gentlemen in the world. You already possess your own fan club on the Internet. Perhaps Perry can bring that good heart of yours to an entire new audience."

"Well," Sterling said, blushing, shuffling his feet. "I suppose we could . . . we could talk."

"There you go, Sterling. I'll be here, praying Sir Rudy keeps a tolerable cellar as I sample his wine. Oh, and while you two are talking? Perhaps you can toddle after Maggie and Miss Keppel, and find out which bedchambers have been alloted to us. I feel the need to change out of my dirt before the dinner gong goes. There's a good fellow."

Perry pointed a finger at Saint Just. "Oh, you're *good*. Just the way you stand, just the way you said that—the accent, the way you almost threw away the line, yet at the same time it was so clear you expect to be obeyed. Troy should be watching you, taking notes."

"Really," Saint Just said, chancing a look at the man who would portray him, to see Troy Barlow chewing on a handful of nuts, his mouth open, before he wiped his salt-greasy hand on his trousers. This . . . this *buffoon* was going to play the Viscount Saint Just? "I do believe it's possible you're on to something there, Perry. Thank you."

# Chapter Five

Maggie heard the knock on the door and let the drapery slide back into place, blocking out the depressing view from her bedchamber window. Ugly scaffolding and rain. Rain and more rain.

She crossed to the door and pulled it open, then turned and headed for one of the pair of wingback chairs on either side of the unfortunately cold fireplace. "Do you believe this, Alex?" she asked as she settled into the chair. "This place is like something out of a book. Only it's the *before* picture in a remodeling book. You don't want to see the plumbing. Oh—we're sharing a bathroom, all three of us, even though we've each got our own room. Marylou said this wing hasn't been touched since the forties. She said the nineteen-forties, but I'm betting on the eighteen-forties. And we have to make up our own beds, since all the maids went home early because of the rain. Do you know it's been raining for a week?"

"I appear to be learning quite a lot since entering this room. The state of your mood being uppermost, of course."

"Sorry." She stood up again, hugging herself, rubbing

her hands against her upper arms. "I'm cold, Alex. Do you know how to make a fire?"

Alex eyed the wood piled inside the fireplace. "I most certainly do. You yank on the bellpull over there, tell whomever comes to serve you that you desire the fire lit, and *voilà*."

"Not funny. I already told you, everybody's gone home. Go look out that window, Alex. The road we drove in on? The creek, stream, whatever you want to call it, is nearly flooding it."

"And that I do know, my dear. Before I could make good my escape from the main saloon, dear Arnaud emptied his budget of woes on me. The rain, the mud, the damp, the food, the plumbing, his filming schedule. Do you recall, Maggie, that nearly half our story takes place out-of-doors? I hadn't realized I was such a devotee of nature."

Maggie, who had sunk to her knees in front of the fireplace and was staring at the wood, hoping for some spontaneous combustion, sat back on her heels and looked up at Alex. "You're too happy. Why are you so happy? Or doesn't it bother you, that *only the writer* baloney?"

"As I'm the creation, not the lowly writer, I believe I can contain my outrage, at least long enough to remind you that we measure ourselves by our own yardsticks, not by the opinions of others." Alex reached past her, lifting the lid of a small brass box. "Ah, I could be wrong, but this little pile could be called kindling. And matches as well. Aren't we the lucky ones. If you'll excuse me?"

"Be my guest, knock yourself out." Maggie stood up, backed up, watched as Alex stuck some small bits of wood beneath the logs, then struck a long match against the stone hearth. "*Only the writer*. And opinions do matter, Alex. Do you know how sick I am of hearing that line?"

"I believe I do, yes. But do go on."

"I will go on. The only reason that motley crew downstairs is even here is because I *wrote* the damn book."

"Damning your own work?"

"Don't get cute. You know what I mean. Without writers? There'd be no books, no magazines, no movies, no television."

"No commercials."

"Yes! Even commercials. Do you think they write themselves? 'When shifting gears, think Boffo.' Oh, yeah, I've seen Miss Boobs in those commercials. Somebody had to write those words. Somebody with very little talent, but still."

The flames small but growing, Alex stood up, brushed his hands together. "About Miss Boobs, as you so rudely referred to her. How can I put this? Are—"

"Are they real? Oh, yeah. Sure. And I'm William Shakespeare."

"Oh. Pity. But do continue, my dear. I believe I interrupted you in midrant."

"I'm not ranting. I was *saying* that writers are underappreciated."

"Absolutely. I couldn't agree more."

"And underpaid. *Grossly* underpaid."

"Again, absolutely."

"And we're going home tomorrow."

"Absolutely not."

"It's raining and miserable and—hey. You were agreeing with me here. What do you mean by 'Absolutely not'?"

Alex motioned for Maggie to seat herself once more, then sat down across from her. Smiled that to-die-for smile that affected its creator as much as she hoped it would affect her loyal readers, damn it.

"Arnaud—Mr. Peppin, that is, although actors and their ilk seem to be such informal creatures, so that we're all on a first-name basis. To continue—Arnaud and I had a mutually advantageous chat downstairs. He got to vent his spleen on matters of his general unhappiness, and I was most happily able to take some of the burden from his shoulders."

Alex polished his quizzing glass against the sleeve of his sweater. "I'm amenable that way."

Maggie knew his tricks. She'd *invented* his tricks. When Alex fiddled with his quizzing glass, he was either trying to deflect somebody's attention or he was just the slightest bit uncomfortable with whatever it was he had to say. Not that anyone else in the world would ever know that. "What . . . did you . . . do?"

"Volunteered my services, of course. Sterling's and mine both. And without thought of monetary remuneration, which seemed to please both Mr. Arnaud Peppin and Miss Pertuccelli all hollow. Ah-ah, don't pout. It's true. As of now, Sterling and I will be coaching our television-movie counterparts in, shall we say, the manly graces. Indeed, even Mr. Pottinger has come aboard, once Arnaud agreed to the extremely reasonable proposition that Mr. Barlow and Mr. Posko would feel more at home in their roles if they were to be allowed to accustom themselves to the proper wardrobe of two well-dressed Regency gentlemen."

"Why does everyone's last name begin with a *P*?" Maggie waved her hand, rubbing out the question. "Never mind—like you say, we're all going to be California-friendly, on a first-name basis. Whoopee . . . not. And let me guess. In order to show the actors how to behave, how to dress, how to move—all that bilge—*you* are also going to dress in costume. How the *hell* do you do it? How do you keep getting away with murder like that?"

"Never murder, Maggie. We leave that to the villains, remember? *I* am a hero."

"And I think I'm going to be sick," Maggie said, resigned to the inevitable. "Okay. So I'll pitch in, too. Sam asked me to look over the script, and I am dying to get my hands on it. You know he royally screwed it up, don't you?"

"That's my sweet Maggie, ever the optimist," Alex said, getting to his feet. "Allow me," he added, walking to the door to answer the knock Maggie hadn't heard. She'd been too busy listening to the blood rushing in her ears, playing catch-up to her perfect hero sometimes getting on her nerves more than it should.

Sterling entered the room, then stopped, gave a flourish of his arm as he bowed, and Bernice Toland-James and Tabitha Leighton swept into the room.

"Maggie!" Tabby cried, coming toward her, arms outstretched, shoulder-length blonde hair flying, a long silk scarf tied loosely around her neck and flowing out behind her. "Give me a hug. Wonderful! Now tell Bernie you're not going to change a word of that marvelous manuscript. I told her, over and over again as we flew here, as we fought Heathrow together, as we drove through this monsoon—over and over again—that the book is brilliant."

"When she wasn't telling me what a rat bastard David the Fornicator is," Bernie said, sighing. "And Tabby here really liked her manicurist, too, until she found out David was, shall we say, getting his cuticles buffed by the girl. God knows where she'll get her manicures done now. I mean, if she tries Lee Press-On Nails, she might glue herself to the bathroom sink, where she'd be stuck, now that she's tossed David out again. Yet again. Honest to God, Mags, I'm really broken up for her. Really."

"Bernie, be nice," Maggie said, trying not to laugh. She'd be upset for her agent if David Leighton wasn't such a total loss. She could only hope that one day Tabby would figure that out, too, and dump him. Like in the ocean.

"It's all right, Maggie. You know I just ignore her. Back

to the manuscript. You can't throw it away. It's brilliant. Just brilliant!"

"You haven't read it," Maggie pointed out, once more enveloped in Tabby's hug and her expensive scent. She blew at the blonde hair that tickled her nose and gently disengaged herself from the embrace. "I didn't send you a copy."

Tabby laughed her nervous laugh. "I don't have to read it, Maggie. I *know* it's brilliant. You're *always* brilliant. Tell her, Alex."

"Yeah," Bernie said, searching in Maggie's purse and coming out with the plastic case holding her nicotine cylinders and inhaler. "Ah, here it is. I left my cigarettes in my room. I'm more used to carrying a flask with me, not a pack. Anyway, you read it, Alex. You tell her."

Maggie grabbed the inhaler from her friend and pointed it at Alex. The man was *so* lucky it wasn't a dart gun. "You read my manuscript?"

"A gentleman never tells," Alex said, taking the inhaler from her and giving it back to Bernie. "You don't need that."

"Don't tell me what I need. Besides, I've got a spare," Maggie said, chin thrust out, and rumaged in her purse for the thing before turning to her creation once more. "I put a security password on my computer, Alex. To keep you *out*."

"I thought that, at first, and then dismissed the idea as beneath you. But the work was probably a healthy exorcism for you, and now you can begin again."

Maggie was seeing red. Blue. Green. All the colors of the rainbow, and they had turned into bright little stars and were circling her head. Yes, stars. Or maybe M&M's, because she sure could use some chocolate about now. She waved them away with her hand. "You read my manuscript. You freaking *read* my manuscript! Don't you feel guilty?"

Alex seemed to consider this. "In what way?"

"In what—in *every* way. About snooping, for one thing." She grabbed his elbow and all but frog-marched him over to the fireplace. "And . . . and about what was in it. How Saint Just had done something terribly wrong, and how he . . . how he felt this need to . . . to atone . . . to—oh, hell, who am I kidding. You don't feel guilty at all, do you?"

"Truth to tell, my dear, I was actually rather . . . bored. All that unnecessary breast-beating over a perfectly understandable descent into physical violence. So sorry."

"Ha! You hear that, Maggie?" Bernie said. "Clearly one third of your readers are males between the ages of twenty-five and sixty-seven. You've seen the demographics, the survey results, the focus groups. And you would have *bored* them. You had Saint Just contemplating his navel for three fourths of the story. Boring!"

Maggie lowered her voice so only Saint Just could hear her. When Saint Just had appeared in her life, he'd appeared with a bullet scar on his shoulder, a gift from a duel she'd written about in *The Case of the Pilfered Pearls*. "When I rewrite, you're getting a broken leg. Very possibly a compound fracture. Be ready for it."

"You wouldn't dare," he said, smiling his most charming smile, which she ignored. Tried to ignore.

Now she whispered. "Just tell me you feel guilty. Just a little bit guilty. And tell me you didn't realize that you could have been killed, damn it. Did it ever occur to you that you can *lose* at something? That you could have been the one who ended up on a slab at the morgue?"

"Ah, the truth. At last. You worry for me, don't you, my dear. How very gratifying."

"Bite me," Maggie said, then turned to face Bernie and Tabby once more. "Okay, okay, we trash the book. I know when I'm beaten."

"There's a reasonable puss," Alex said, and this time his smile told her that he knew how very close to the edge he was treading with that typically Regency Era lack of sensibility to the equality of the sexes. "Although I imagine Sterling would rather you kept some of it."

"Me?" Sterling piped up from the window, where he'd been looking out at the rain. "Did I, I mean, did Sterling get to do something wonderful? And what does that mean—to contemplate one's navel?"

Maggie glared at Alex, then finally relaxed. She'd fought her battle, won what she could, and nobody was going to say she wasn't gracious in defeat. "Later, Sterling. I take it you're impressed with the view?"

"No," Sterling said, pressing his forehead against the glass and turning his head so that he could, in his mind, at any rate, look at the outside of the building. "Can't really see anything, with it coming on to dark and still raining. The scaffolding's out here, Saint Just. Just like it's outside your room and mine. It must extend completely around this wing. I think if this window opens, I could walk outside on the thing all the way from one end of the wing to the other."

"Fascinating, I'm sure, only I would ask that you don't embark on that particular experiment in the dark and wet," Alex said, then bowed to the ladies. "I'm told that dinner will be served within the hour, so I'll leave you all to your toilettes while Sterling and I conference once more with Arnaud. We begin coaching exercises first thing tomorrow."

"Yeah. Right. Go away," Maggie said, collapsing into the chair again, to be closer to the fire. She looked at her friends. "Don't ask. Trust me, just don't ask. Now, tell me about your trip. I didn't know you were traveling together."

The three women talked of New York for a while, of taking off their shoes to get through Security. Tabby had brought slippers in her carry-on bag, and had held up the line while she put them on, as she had no plan of walking barefoot on those dirty floors with all their germs.

Then Maggie asked, "Did you meet anybody from the production before Sterling brought you up here?"

"Just the regulation corporate bitch," Bernie said, sitting down in the facing chair while Tabby stood in front of the cheval glass, fussing with her scarf and hair. "Joanne Something-or-other. What a horrible dye job. I wouldn't be caught dead in that shade of red. We had to slit our wrists and make a blood oath we wouldn't charge the production company for anything. Oh, and Sir Rudy. What a charmer. He pinched me. Tabby? He pinch you?"

Tabby continued to finger-comb her hair. "Who? Oh, Sir Rudy. No, he didn't. But I did have a few words with Dennis Lloyd. I recognized him immediately from something I saw on PBS a few years ago. What a handsome man. Very dignified and yet . . . approachable."

"Revenge sex," Bernie told Maggie, winking. "Our little blondie is planning revenge sex. This should be fun to watch."

"Bernie, it's no such thing! You can be so crude."

"And so right," Bernie said, getting to her feet. "Well, it's been fun, but I'm going to go unpack before dinner. We're in the completely other wing. You coming, Tabby?"

Maggie followed them into the hallway. "Marylou, the gofer, told me this wing is still pretty much the way it's been for the last sixty years or so. What are your rooms like, and why didn't I get one in the other wing? I got here first."

"Life's a bitch, isn't it, Mags," Bernie said, and Maggie really couldn't do much more than nod her agreement.

"I'm only the writer," she said as they stopped at the head of the curving staircase that was only a little less elaborate than the one that led to the first floor. "It slipped my mind for a minute. Sorry. Now excuse me. I've got to go find Alex and kill him."

"New York, England. Some things never change." Bernie kissed Maggie's cheek. "One of these days, sweetheart, you're going to open your eyes and see what everyone else sees."

"There's nothing to see."

"It's like that television show. You know. *Will and Grace*. Except that Alex isn't gay." Tabby frowned. "Well, I thought he was in the beginning. But he's not. You two were made for each other. And you said so yourself, he's a *very* distant cousin."

"Done now?" Maggie asked, willing her cheeks not to go red.

"Am I done now?" Tabby asked Bernie, who was busily inspecting the large tapestry hanging on the wall behind them. "What else did we talk about on the plane?"

"Oh, I don't know, Tabby. About being *discreet* about the thing, maybe?" Bernie grabbed the agent's arm at the elbow and pulled her toward the East Wing. "Sorry, Maggie. It's a new act. I usually work alone. But we'll get better at it."

"Please don't. I don't know which was worse over Thanksgiving: listening to my mother tell me I'm getting fat or listening to her tell me that I'm not getting any younger and need to tackle some guy when he isn't looking and get married. I don't need you two playing matchmaker."

"We'd never tell you you're getting fat," Tabby said, then bit her lips between her teeth as she looked at Maggie's figure.

"It's eight pounds. Eight lousy pounds. It was ten, now it's eight. I'll get rid of them."

"I've lost ten pounds since I gave up the booze," Bernie said, putting her hands on her hips and turning in a full circle. "Of course, I've taken up smoking again. But we won't mention smoking as a diet aid, will we?"

"Not when I'm within earshot, no," Maggie said, then she sucked in her gut and headed downstairs, just in time to see Alex entering the main saloon.

He was wearing a dark blue frock coat, skintight tan pantaloons, high-topped black Hessians (his own, she knew), and pristine white linen, complete with white waistcoat and a perfectly tied neck cloth. She saw his quizzing glass hanging around his neck, the glass itself tucked into a pocket, and he carried his new cane. He moved with grace, his posture perfect, his black hair brushed into the Windswept style she knew so well from illustrations in her research books. Beau Brummell would have wept, the man was so perfect.

"Oh, God," she groaned, leaning on the stone banister for support as her knees went weak. "There goes the libido. And he knows it, too. Everybody knows it. Damn the man . . ."

Three hours later, after suffering through Alex's total command of the dinner-table conversation, complete with feminine fawning over him, male sparring with him, and Joanne Pertuccelli's complete indifference—Maggie could like the woman if Joanne wasn't such a boring, one-track-mind person—Maggie was wondering how she could kill Sam Undercuffler without anybody noticing he was gone.

Except that nobody noticed the writers, so maybe she could get away with it.

"One more time, Sam," she said as they sat in the main saloon, "zippers weren't invented during the Regency Era."

"But there are zippers on the costumes. I checked."

"We're not talking about costumes here, Sam. We're talking about zippers. And there weren't any in the Regency. Saint Just does *not* turn his back to the lady in the bed, make it obvious he's zipping his zipper. He buttons his buttons."

"Yes, but if he turns his back and buttons his buttons, anyone looking at him from the back won't know what he's doing. It'll look like he's maybe playing with himself or something. He's got to turn, zip up, turn back. It's as close to sex as we can get with this movie, since it's network, not cable."

"Okay, okay, I understand. I can be reasonable. We just rewrite it a little, have him standing beside the bed, looking down at Marianne, smiling wickedly as he buttons his shirt. The viewer gets the same idea, right?"

Sam started scribbling on his copy of the script. "That's good. That'll work. Gives Troy more face time, too, so he'll like that. But then Nikki's back is to the camera. She won't like that."

"Oh, for God's sake. What do you do, keep score on who gets the most face time?"

Sam looked at her. "Oh, yeah. Sure. You didn't know that? No, I guess you didn't. That's why you need a screenwriter to adapt your stuff from the book. It's a whole other ball game when it's on the screen."

But Maggie wasn't listening. She was much too busy looking at the guy who was standing just at the entrance to the main saloon.

Tall. Slim. Blond. Green eyes she could see from twenty feet away. Knife-creased camel slacks, a camel cashmere pullover sweater, a second black cashmere sweater draped over his shoulders and loosely tied. A young Peter O'Toole in Ralph Lauren; as gorgeous as any of Lauren's models. Slightly aloof, faintly bored, enticingly detached.

As she stared, Bernie came up behind her, bent down to

whisper in her ear. "Can I keep him, Mommy? Huh, huh, can I, please?"

"We'll see, sweetheart. We don't know who he is, let alone where he's been," Maggie whispered, her gaze glued to the man as he spied Sir Rudy, waved, and walked over to him. She lifted the script and began fanning herself with it. "Oh, God. I'm too young to get hot flashes. Who *is* he?"

"Not your problem. I've got dibs."

Sam Undercuffler sighed as if he knew he'd become invisible, gathered the pages of the script, and wandered off to talk to Marylou.

Sir Rudy and the new arrival shook hands, and then the older man called out, "Everyone? My nephew, Byrd. Byrd Stockwell. He's a model for the magazines. But he's not queer. He can't be queer. He's m'heir. Not that he's supposed to be here."

"Thank you, Uncle," Byrd said with a slight shake of his head. "I'm sure everyone will remember me now, won't they? Unless someone would want me to strip and maul that lovely lady over there to prove my masculinity?"

Nikki Campion, the lovely lady in question, hopped to her feet and broke all land speed records in getting herself to Byrd's side, almost coming to grief over the hem of her Regency Era gown, which barely contained her boobs. "Hi. I'm Nikki."

"And the rest of us are dog meat," Bernie said, sighing. "Oh, well, I'm too old for him anyway. Even if I wasn't off men, which I am, considering my track record. We're getting to be quite a crowd, aren't we?"

"*Shhh*," Maggie said, leaning forward to listen to the introductions, and to watch Alex as he watched Byrd Stockwell.

Nothing. No reaction. Obviously Alex didn't look at

the man and think *competition.* How did men *do* that? She looked at Nikki Campion and saw competition. Women *knew* competition when they saw it. Alex couldn't care less.

Man, she'd made him secure. And, sometimes, that really pissed her off.

"I almost didn't make it, Uncle," Byrd was saying after the introductions were completed. "I told you to dredge that stream. Much more rain, and we'll be cut off here." Then he looked down at Nikki. "Not that that's entirely a bad thing . . . Nikki."

Maggie groaned. "Oh, never mind. He's a jerk. The handsome ones always are."

"Except for Alex. But you already knew that, or you wouldn't have modeled Saint Just after him. The perfect hero."

Oh, if Bernie only knew the truth! Maggie closed her eyes, thought for a moment, then said, "Bernie? Can you keep a secret?"

Her friend laughed. "*Me?* How long have you known me, Mags?"

"Yeah, right. Never mind, stupid question." Maggie reached for her nicotine inhaler even as she wondered why Sir Rudy kept looking at his nephew as if he wished the handsome man was on the moon.

# Chapter Six

Saint Just stood at the mantel, observing the room and his companions.

He felt good, extraordinarily good. In his element. Relaxed, in charge.

Perhaps even a tad smug.

"Don't look so damn happy."

Definitely a tad smug. He smiled at Maggie. "I admit to being very nearly giddy. But am I being that obvious?"

"You're wearing Regency clothes, standing in a room that could be a Regency Era drawing room. You're surrounded by adoring fans who have spent the night hanging on your every word. Yeah, it's obvious. It's also sickening. I feel so out of place with all you *Regency folk*."

"Tabby and Bernie and Arnaud and Sir Rudy aren't in costume," Saint Just pointed out reasonably. "Nor is Joanne, our resident harridan, nor our resident scribe, present company excepted, nor our little gofer. Oh, and the robin."

"The who? Oh, wait a minute. You mean Byrd. Ha! And I thought you hadn't noticed. Jealous, Alex?"

"Of precisely what, my dear? The man is a hopeless poseur."

Maggie pushed slightly against him. Once, twice. "You're jealous. Jealous, jealous. Because he's gorgeous. In an asexual sort of way. I imagine, though, that he's the kind that would appeal to both sexes. Bernie's already asked me if I had an idea as to which way he swings."

"I beg your pardon?" Saint Just asked, cocking one eyebrow. "And I say that with the fervent hope that you and I can both pretend that neither of us knows to precisely what Bernice referred."

"Don't worry. She only said that because he isn't paying her any attention. Not that he's shying away from Boffo girl. Want to bet where she spends the night?"

"I'm going to pretend I didn't hear that one at all. Why this fascination, though, may I ask?"

Maggie shrugged. "I don't know. Sir Rudy said there's no television because Arnaud made the workmen take down the antennas or dishes or whatever because of the outside shots, and I don't feel like reading. I can't work because somebody talked me into leaving my laptop in New York. So, this is by way of entertainment."

"You're easily amused. No television machines? Ah, now we really are being thrown back in time, aren't we? I know, let's have a real Regency evening, shall we? Tabby can play the piano, and Sterling can sing for us."

"Let me see, how can I say this? Okay—*no*. We are *not* having a sing-along. How about cards? We could play cards."

"Or another game," Saint Just said, watching as Joanne shot visual daggers at Byrd Stockwell's back. Odd, that. Was she afraid he'd ask to be put on this thing called an expense account? "Let's the two of us figure out why our keeper of the expenses is so put out with the nephew, shall we? The looks she's been sending in his direction all evening are enough to curl the man's toes in his tasseled shoes. Have they met before tonight, do you suppose?"

Maggie watched as Joanne, with one last searing look at Byrd, who was busily romancing a very willing Nikki, grabbed up her notebook and all but flounced out of the room. "Maybe. I don't know. How long has everyone else been here? No, wait, that doesn't matter. Sir Rudy introduced Byrd to everyone. He wouldn't have done that if Byrd had been here before tonight. And Sir Rudy doesn't seem to be very happy he's here now, if you ask me. Anyway, Joanne's boring. What else have you got?"

"Not a whacking great deal, I'm afraid. I rather enjoy Sir Rudy. Now, he has previously met Joanne, in London, I believe, which is how we all got to be here rather than in California. He offered his estate at no charge, and Joanne jumped at it. The woman does seem to enjoy pinching pennies for her employer."

"So that's how they got to be shooting the film here? I didn't know that. And Sir Rudy offered this place for free? Why?"

"That one, my dear, I can answer. He wishes to rub elbows with American actresses. Daresay, more than his elbows. He's quite put out that Nikki isn't living up to expectations. I believe the man was expecting, indeed, looking quite forward to, nightly orgies."

"Disgusting," Maggie said, sucking on her inhaler.

"I quite agree. Put it away. That contraption is no more than a bad habit now, you know."

"And this bothers you how?"

"I'm not quite sure," Saint Just admitted. "Perhaps I am perplexed over how a woman of such strong will in other matters could be so weak when it comes to this nicotine addiction of yours."

"Ha. A lot you know. I don't even have a cartridge in this thing."

Saint Just struck a questioning pose, one hand to his mouth. "And yet you're holding it, using it? Why?"

"I don't know, okay. You've got your cane, you've got your quizzing glass. I've got my unloaded nicotine inhaler. We've all got crutches, Alex. You saw Joanne with her stopwatch. Keeps it around her neck, is always touching it, fingering it. Bernie's always got a glass, even now that she's not hitting the hard stuff anymore. Tabby fusses with her scarves—she'd feel naked without her scarves."

"Hmmm. We are a pitiful bunch, aren't we? In fact, Sterling seems the most normal of us all, which you will admit is rather mind-blowing."

"Sterling is pure of heart," Maggie told him. "He's real. He doesn't need anything artificial, doesn't need to hide behind anything or use it to deflect others. He has no personal agenda. Sterling's—what *is* he doing over there?"

Saint Just looked across the room to where Sterling stood with Perry Posko, the two of them sitting down in unison, then standing up, then sitting down again.

"I think that's self-explanatory. Sterling's teaching the man how to sit. As we are all aware, you can tell a gentleman by the way he splits his coattails as he takes his seat. Look over there, Maggie, at our lamentable Viscount as he poses with our villain. Evan, for all his other sins, still appears pristine. But our Viscount? His coattails are sadly crushed and pleated, the result of the man's propensity to both slouch and to simply *drop* himself into his seat. The man has a lot in common with the good *left*-tenant, except that Wendell, bless him, also has a brain."

"But you're going to work with Troy, right? Because I agree with you. That guy is no more the Viscount Saint Just than Sir Rudy of the fishing reel is Prince Charles."

"I've made a beginning, yes, while you and the scribe had your heads together. And I've discovered something. The man is a monkey, but one with what he calls a photographic memory. Which, alas, explains how he's come to learn a string of rather unfortunate cant he found listed somewhere on the Internet. And which he repeats at the drop of a hat."

"I don't understand."

"I know, neither did I. His lordship—I'm to address him as his lordship whenever he's in costume, you understand—took it into his head to do his own research for the character, and that research began and ended with this list. So far, I've been called a knotty-pated flapdragon, a rough-hewn moldwarp, and—oh, yes, my personal favorite—an unmuzzled, guts-griping rampallion. He reported happily that he's memorized three entire pages of this sort of drivel, and he's quite proud of himself."

"But . . . but those are Shakespearean insults, aren't they? I'm pretty sure I've seen that list online. Sort of mix-and-match insults, Will Shakespeare style. He's in the wrong freaking era."

"Yes, but reciting the words, according to his lordship, has helped to refine his accent. Although I have already prevailed upon him to refrain from dropping his *H*s like some Cockney."

"Really?"

"No. Not really. Not even close. For the most part, our dear Viscount sounds like a chimney sweep. We begin our lessons in earnest tomorrow, at which time I fear I may just have to choke the man, although not with one of these wretched neck cloths. They're ready-fashioned, you understand, and fasten with Velcro. I'm nearly too ashamed to wear mine. Oh, dear," he added, lifting his quizzing glass to his eye as he noticed another bit of intrigue taking place near the drinks table. "Excuse me, my dear. I believe I'm needed."

Maggie followed after him as he approached Dennis Lloyd and Evan Pottinger, who were at that moment glaring at each other. Dennis, clad as Clarence, the Saint Just valet, in rather badly fitted burgundy-and-gold livery, stood in a most belligerent posture, one definitely unbecoming to a valet.

Evan, looking dangerous in unremitting black, his expression equally dark, seemed faintly amused even while poised to strike. Very much the villainous Lord Hervey.

There were moments when Saint Just could almost believe the magic of moviemaking had opened the pages of Maggie's book and let everyone out for their moment upon the stage. Then again, there was Troy Barlow. The fellow certainly helped Saint Just remember that reality and fiction were miles and miles apart.

"Gentlemen?" Saint Just said, stepping between the two men. "Clarence? Lord Hervey? Is something amiss?"

"Step aside, fool," Evan bit out imperiously—really rather good, clearly a man immersed in his role, which is what being a method actor, Saint Just had learned from Arnaud, was all about. "I demand this man be sacked. I ordered him to pour me a drink, and he refused. I'll not suffer insubordination from a mere servant."

"Why, you miserable excuse for a thespian," Dennis countered, and Saint Just put his palm against thc older man's chest, holding him back from the fray. "Who do you think you are? *Servant*? I'm not your bloody servant. That's it! I'm getting out of this ridiculous costume, and you can all just go hang if you think I'm going to play this stupid game. Americans! You're all insane!"

Saint Just watched the Englishman storm off, then cocked an eyebrow as Tabby quickly excused herself from Bernie and trotted after him into the hall. Then he turned his attention back to Evan. "Taking this playacting business just a step too far, perhaps, my lord Hervey? I do believe you've insulted the man."

"And I do believe you and I have nothing to say to each other. I'm not your *student*," Evan said, looking down his nose at Saint Just . . . which meant he had to raise his chin a good three inches. Still, what the man didn't possess in height, he most certainly made up for in his show of villainous arrogance. "Now, out of my way. I'm through with you."

Saint Just stepped back two paces and bowed. "I look forward to your untimely end, your lordship," he said cheerfully. "Something to do with a fall from the rooftop and landing on the spines of an iron gate, I believe? Messy business."

"A lot you know. That's being rewritten," Evan said, and now it was time for Saint Just to put out his hand and hold Maggie in place.

"Whatdoyoumeanrewritten?" Maggie asked, all in one breath. "That's the big ending. Saint Just and Hervey dueling on the ramparts, Hervey lunging, Saint Just neatly sidestepping, Hervey going down. Do you know how long it took to choreograph that scene in my head? Sam? *Sam*! Where is he? I'll *kill* him!" And she was off, in search of the screenwriter.

"Writers," Evan said, taking out his snuff box. "A curse and an abomination." He tapped the lid of the box twice, then frowned when it didn't open, dropping out of character to say, "Cheap junk."

"Not necessarily. Sir Rudy was kind enough to supply snuff boxes from a not-at-all-shabby collection I discovered displayed in his study," Saint Just said, taking the box from the man. "Observe, if you will, and learn."

He then balanced the box on the back of his bent left wrist and tapped the box twice, upon which the lid opened. He withdrew a lace-edged white linen square from his waistcoat (his own fine Irish linen, in point of fact), then neatly pantomimed, complete with flourish, taking a small pinch, lifting it to his nostril, and sniffing delicately. "I'd now sneeze, but I am not a playactor, so I'll refrain. Here you go, old fellow—catch."

Evan swiped the box out of midair, said something decidedly nasty, and retreated to the mantelpiece, where he stood and scowled in fine villain fashion.

Well, that was fun, Saint Just decided. For the most part. What else could he do?

Pouring himself a glass of wine, he debated about approaching Byrd Stockwell and Nikki, but decided against it as the young woman pulled a small pink barbell from beneath the couch and began doing curls while begging Byrd to feel her biceps.

There was something about a woman in ankle-length sprigged muslin lifting weights that destroyed whatever remained of Saint Just's illusion that he was immersed in a true Regency Era evening At Home.

As for Byrd Stockwell? That gentleman didn't interest Saint Just at all, although he might have wished to confer with the man's tailor, had he the time.

Left alone, Saint Just lifted his quizzing glass to his eye and surveyed the room and the remainder of its occupants, his gaze alighting on Maggie.

She and Sam were seated at a table in one of the corners, Maggie furiously paging through the blue pages of the script. He'd leave her to it.

Shifting his gaze yet again, he saw that Sterling and Perry were now practicing bows, which left nothing much for Saint Just to do save approach Troy Barlow, attempting to not see that the idiot was tossing shelled peanuts into the air and trying to catch them in his mouth.

"My lord?" Saint Just said, even if it made his jaws ache. "Are you perhaps ready for another lesson?"

Troy leapt to his feet as a peanut hit the floor and bounced away. "Tiptop! Ready-o! I'll be a gleeking jack-a-nape if I'm not!"

"A-hum. Yes," Saint Just said, squelching a sigh. "Do you think, marvelous as all of that is—and your pronunciation, your accent, are improving veritably by leaps and bounds—that we can dispense with the self-taught for the nonce?"

"Huh?"

"Cool the slang," Saint Just said, taking the man's arm and leading him over to the fireplace now that Evan had abandoned that post in order to take up another in front of the pier glass, watching himself as he struck various poses.

"Still not good enough?" Troy asked, clearly crestfallen.

"No, sadly, not quite. You are not, good sir, a scamp from the bowels of Piccadilly. You are Alexandre Blake, the Viscount Saint Just. The epitome of good taste, fashion, and breeding. Um . . . and perhaps you might not wish to wipe your greasy fingers on your pantaloons? Arnaud, I am convinced, would not approve."

"Wouldn't want to upset the cue ball." Troy looked down at his fingers, grinned, and lifted his hand to wipe the grease and salt on his neck cloth. "Better?"

"Not measurably, no," Saint Just said, aware that it would take more than a few days to turn this sow's ear into anything even vaguely resembling a silk purse. "Perhaps it would be a better use of our time if we were to go over the script, concentrating on the scenes in which you appear?"

"Oh, yeah, right. I know just the one. Arnaud wouldn't swing for more than two sessions with Ignatz, and he's only a stuntman, not a fence man."

Saint Just attempted to decipher this. "A fencing master?"

"Yeah. That. I've got this scene with Evan—Lord Hervey—where we fence each other. It's the very last scene."

"I remember," Saint Just said, stroking his chin as he envisioned Troy Barlow on the Medwine Manor roof, nimbly dancing about on the parapets. No, the vision wouldn't form. What did form in his mind were recent memories of Troy: his nearly coming to grief as he attempted to lean a casual elbow on the mantelpiece, missing five out of six peanuts he tried to toss into his mouth.

Then there was Evan's remark that the scene had been changed. Saint Just wanted to know how it had been changed. After all, what Maggie knew, he also should know. "I would say we cannot begin too soon. There are a pair of quite good foils in Sir Rudy's study. Shall we adjourn?"

"You really can do it? Fence? Oh, boy, did Arnaud ever get a bargain with you. Free for nothing, right? Hey, you know what?" Troy said as he followed after Saint Just, who had the sinking sensation that he was off on a fruitless exercise.

"I imagine I don't. Tell me."

"Well, I was just thinking. If you're really good, you could double for me in that scene, just the shots from the back, when I'm supposed to be winning. You'd need a blond wig, but we've got one. You know, in case I have a bad hair day? We could just jam that down on your head, and from a distance? It could work. Because Evan's been practicing with a coach, and I just know he's going to try to make me look like a jerk."

"A man with low expectations," Saint Just said, pausing as Maggie called his name. "I would think he'd be aspiring to run you through, at the very least."

"Oh, he can't do that. They're not real, you understand. The swords."

"Épées," Saint Just said, his sympathies suddenly very much with Maggie, who had been wise enough to foretell the fiasco that was becoming more and more apparent when it came to translating the brilliance of Saint Just to the small screen. "And what do you mean, they're not real?"

"They're fake. You know. I mean, like I'd let Evan come at me with a *real* sword? As if! So, you know, I think maybe we should ask Marylou where the fake ones are and use those. In case you're really good at it. Besides, I just remembered. The sword I use is inside my cane. You have to see it. Looks like a cane, feels like a cane, but there's really a sword inside."

"Sword stick," Saint Just said, but his heart wasn't in the correction. "I happen to have one of my own, as a matter of fact," he said, inclining his head toward his cane, which was, at that moment, resting against the arm of a chair.

"No. You've got one? A *real* one. Let me see," Troy said, already heading for the cane.

Nearly succeeding in remaining graceful, Saint Just beat him to it, taking up the cane and giving the handle a neat twist before extracting the thin blade with a theatrical flourish meant mostly to keep the sharp thing above his head, out of Troy's avid reach.

"You can't do that, Alex," Maggie said from behind him, her tone amused. "They'll just send for another actor. And next time, he may be a redhead. Who burps."

Saint Just lowered the weapon. "May I be of some assistance, Maggie, or have you only toddled over here to watch as I reach the end of my own rope and dangle here by my fingernails? Unless I'm wrong, and you and Sam are getting along swimmingly?"

"You don't want to know. That way, when they discover the body, no one will blame me."

"That bad, hmmm?" Saint Just said, then looked at Troy. "You're still here? Go fetch your toy sword cane, why don't you."

"And have you use a real one? Do I look nuts to you?"

Maggie coughed into her hand, warning Saint Just to be silent, which was probably prudent of her, for he was beginning to feel himself fraying about the usually sharp edges of his composure.

"I know. I'll get Evan's, and we'll practice with props at

both ends," Troy said, grinning madly, as if suddenly struck by inspiration. "And then I'll cut you to ribbons, thou reeky, sheep-biting pumpion!" Then he clomped off in his Hessians, looking much like he was on his way through a stable yard and had just stepped in something.

"Oh, good grief," Saint Just said, lowering the stick. "The man is beyond useless."

"And you've become the center of attention, in case you haven't noticed," Maggie pointed out just as Evan Pottinger and Byrd Stockwell approached, both of them eyeing the sword stick.

"An amusing toy," Evan said with his best Lord Hervey sneer. "But in more talented hands, a formidable weapon. Give it over, and allow a real man to show you how it's done."

Saint Just knew himself to be mean, but if Evan Pottinger wished to sacrifice himself as a target to ease a bit of the tension he felt, Saint Just wasn't going to naysay him. "How very droll. My lord Hervey, am I to consider your words a challenge? Or do you attempt only to amuse me?"

"Not a challenge. An insult, pretty boy, and an opportunity to employ this thing with the expertise it deserves."

"Really? And how do you propose to do that, my lord Hervey? Hold the *thing* in both hands, then insult me to death?"

Byrd, whether sensing a fight or hoping to avoid one, retreated to Nikki's side once more, to watch from a distance.

"Hoo-boy, an old-fashioned pissing contest. Just what this night needed. You know, this is where I've always wanted to be able to twitch my nose and be somewhere else," Maggie said, sighing. "Somebody says something dangerously stupid, and all I want is *out of here*. Alex, cool it, please. And Evan, old sport? Zip it. Trust me in this, you don't want to go there."

Evan shot Maggie a hard look. "I do not recall applying for your advice, madam. Oblige me, if you will, and shut . . . up."

"And now, good sir, you have passed beyond the pale, even though you've just parroted one of Hervey's best lines from Maggie's book. However, that said, surely you can't believe I will stand by while you verbally attack the lady," Saint Just drawled, his pulses thrumming quite enjoyably, which Maggie had to know, for she had given him both his love of adventure and his appreciation for the ridiculous. And his cool, measured temper.

Evan struck a pose that Saint Just nearly suggested could use some more practice in front of the pier glass. "Show me a lady in this room, and I'll promise not to insult her. But I don't see any."

"Oh, brother," Maggie said, sinking into the chair behind her. "Here we go. Don't say you weren't warned."

"Maggie?" Saint Just said, holding out his now-sheathed sword cane. "If you would be so kind as to take possession of this for me, as our own aspiring Viscount has just returned with what I believe are the imitations."

"Props," Maggie managed, grabbing the sword cane she'd told Saint Just, at least twice, she never wanted to see again, let alone touch, after his last use of such a contraption as a weapon. "They're called props. Are you two really going to fight?"

"Not at all, my dear," Saint Just said, his gaze never leaving Evan Pottinger's face. "I promised Troy a lesson, but I am not averse to giving one to Evan here, as well. I'm magnanimous that way."

Evan grabbed one of the sword canes from Troy and uncovered the ersatz blade. "We'll see who gives whom a lesson! *En garde*, you swine!"

Saint Just, careful to hide his amusement, stepped back a pace, then turned himself in a full circle, so that when he confronted Evan again it was with the tip of his unsheathed ersatz sword stick, which just happened to now rest an inch from Evan's Adam's apple.

"Wanna see that again, *Lord Hervey*?" Maggie asked, bouncing in her chair.

"Maggie," Saint Just said, quietly maintaining his pose. "It's not polite to gloat. But you could applaud if the spirit so moves you."

"Oh, splendid, Saint Just!" Sterling called out as he and Perry Posko clapped. "Sterling, did you see that?"

"I certainly did, Sterling," Perry replied, still clapping.

"So cute! Tweedledum and Tweedledee come to England. Right down to their matching yellow waistcoats," Maggie said, but also quietly.

"Now we've got two Sterlings? Who's on first?" Bernie asked, leaning over the back of the chair to ask Maggie her question. "And, after you tell me that, explain to me again why you haven't jumped Alex's bones by now."

Saint Just, who'd heard the comments of both women, ignored both. Except for a small smile. He was, after all, at least for the past few months, *human*.

"You cheated!" Evan accused, pointing a shaking finger at Saint Just before he threw down both pieces of the sword cane rather like a child about to launch a tantrum.

"And you, Lord Hervey, are dead," Saint Just said, neatly sliding the blade back into the cane he still held. "At least, theoretically. Lessons, dear Lord Hervey, Viscount Saint Just, begin at ten tomorrow, in Sir Rudy's study."

"Yeah. Be there or be square," Maggie said, getting to her feet. "God, that was fun. Better than television."

"Wait a minute, wait a minute," Troy said, frowning. "You said *Vee-count*. Isn't it *Viss-count*? Aren't I the *Viss-count*? I don't like that. *Vee-count*? That can't be right. Arnaud! Arnaud!"

Maggie went on tiptoe, to whisper in Saint Just's ear.

"As exits go, I don't think you're going to be able to top this one, Alex. I'm betting we can get a flight out of here by tomorrow afternoon. You game?"

"I'm beginning to see the wisdom of the suggestion, yes. But—"

"But you don't want to give up showbiz. I know. Besides, I still have to kill Sam. I just saw the last scene, Alex. Remember the duel on the roof? Gone. All gone. Insurance squawked at it as too dangerous and threatened to pull coverage if Troy was put on the roof. Evan, I'm guessing, is more expendable, but I'm not the one who's going to tell him that."

"So, where will the duel take place?"

Maggie grinned, one of those close-mouthed grins that boded no good, Saint Just was sure. "Oh, you're going to love this. In Marianne's bedroom, so our Nikki can be in the scene, sitting up in bed, sheets drawn up *almost* completely over her breasts as she shrieks at appropriate moments and gets her face time. That's big, Alex. She's got to get a minimum of five close-ups or they're in violation of her contract."

"You're fashioning this charade out of whole cloth simply to depress me, aren't you?"

"No. Oh, no. I'm not fibbing. Fight, fight, Nikki screams, close-up, fight, fight, fight, Nikki yells, 'No! Don't kill him!' Fight, fight, fight. Saint Just and Lord Hervey go chin to chin with the swords crossed between them and curse at each other—standard stupid swordfight shot. Close-up, close-up, push away, fight, fight. Etcetera. Then Lord Hervey grabs Nikki, who almost but not quite loses the sheet, and holds her as a shield as he backs toward the door."

Saint Just was appalled. Truly appalled. The sword fight with Lord Hervey had been an inspiration, quite the highlight of the book. "He escapes? He doesn't die?"

"Oh, yeah, he sure does escape. But first Saint Just

makes a stab at getting him, by reaching down and pulling on the sheet that's dragging on the floor and—"

"Why on earth would I do any such thing?"

"Not you, the Viscount—and keep your voice down. I'm explaining here. You—he—pulls on the sheet, which only serves to bare Nikki's naked body—we don't see that, but we do hear her shriek—while the camera zooms in on Saint Just, who says something like, 'Ah, well, I'll get him next time,' before he tosses the sheet and his weapon aside, and begins unbuttoning his shirt. Fade to black, the end. So? Ready to vomit yet?"

Saint Just searched his mind for words, something to say that would express what he felt, and came up with, "They can't do that."

"Oh, yes, they can—or maybe you haven't noticed the steam that's been coming out of my ears for the past hour. Sam's going to write the sequel, a completely new story with the same cast, and if that works, then they'll use the rest of our books to launch a series with interchangeable villains."

"Lord Hervey is finally apprehended?"

"In the sequel, yes. Sam says so. Villains are a dime a dozen. It's Troy and Nikki they want to hold on to."

"Good God, why?"

"Who cares? And it's all in my contract, so once I'm done killing Sam—just on general principles because he refuses to believe facts have anything at all to do with good fiction—I'm going to kill Tabby. And then I *am* going home, whether you go with me or not. I mean, if I want abuse, I can visit my mother. At least then I can go up on the boardwalk and get more chocolate fudge."

# Chapter Seven

Maggie sat at the ancient dressing table and giggled as she remembered the end of last night's more-than-a-little-bit-weird evening.

After the fiasco with Evan Pottinger, Alex had suggested that those remaining in the room indulge in a game of forfeits, a Regency Era amusement.

He'd described forfeits as a game in which a player needs to give up some small personal possession after breaking one of the silly rules—and the rules definitely were silly—and then had to perform some stupid stunt in order to retrieve the item.

"Oh, kind of like strip poker," Nikki had said. "I like that game, except I always lose." Then she'd looked at Byrd Stockwell and winked. "*Always*."

"And on that note, I'm out of here," Bernie had declared, lifting Sir Rudy's hand off her knee, kissing him on the cheek, and then leaving the room while the man was still blushing.

Joanne had come back for a while, but stomped out again after Sir Rudy told her that Nikki and Byrd had left the room together a half hour earlier, and Tabby and Clarence the valet had never shown up again, come to think of it.

Sir Rudy's Little House of Pickups, that's what Medwine Manor was, except that Maggie had, as usual, spent the night alone.

Not that she cared. She didn't care. Really. Not at all. So what if she had to write love scenes from memory. No biggie. Life did not revolve around sex.

She made a face at her reflection. "It doesn't spin too darn fast around abstinence, either," she told herself, putting down her hairbrush and getting to her feet.

She walked over to the window to pull back the heavy drapes and look out at . . . rain. Is that all it did in England? Rain?

Remembering Sterling's interest in the scaffolding, she pressed her forehead against the cold glass and tried to see what he had seen. She saw wet metal scaffolding and wet boards. Nothing to write home about, that was for sure. And beyond the scaffolding, all she saw was water. Lots of water.

"The driveway's gone," she said out loud. "For crying out loud, the driveway's gone! How are we supposed to get out of here?"

She was gearing herself up for a major meltdown—which was *so* unlike her—when someone knocked at her door.

"Maggie? You in there?"

"*Undercuffler*," she gritted out from between clenched teeth in her best Jerry Seinfeld imitation of "Hello-o-o, Newman." "Good. Now I can kill him."

She opened the door, and the writer just stood there, waiting for her to invite him in. Which she might have done, if it weren't for the thick manila envelope he was clutching to his chest. "I said, no."

"Ah, come on, Maggie. It's a script. Dialogue, stage directions, and some of my best work, really. I've been working on it for two years now. I know it can sell, but I just want you to read it. Won't take you an hour, honest. All I want is your honest opinion."

"Liar, liar, pants on fire," Maggie shot back, wondering if she'd slipped a gear somewhere between dealing with the lumpy bed and the lousy plumbing. "You want me to say I love it. You don't want the truth."

She slipped into Jack Nicholson mode: "You can't *handle* the truth. I know writers, remember? You just say you want honest criticism, then get all bent out of shape if I don't tell you your stuff is the greatest thing since sliced bread."

Sam held out the envelope with both hands. "I rewrote the final scene of *Disappearing Earl* last night after everyone went to bed. Got rid of that business with the sheet. I got rid of the whole bedroom thing, and now they're going to duel on the main staircase. Perfect for filming, you have to admit that. Arnaud already gave me the okay. It's all in here along with my script, if you want to see it."

"That's blackmail," Maggie said, but she took the envelope, then tried to close the door.

"Wait—I've got news."

"You still can't come in. If you come in, you'll sit down, and you'll stare at me the whole time I'm reading your script."

"That's okay. I just wanted to tell you that we're . . . well, we're sort of cut off from civilization until the rain stops and the creek goes down. The stream, the whatever they call it in England. Sir Rudy says the place always gets soggy, but this time it's really flooded. None of the village people—ha! Village People! Get it?"

"Yeah, I got it. Har. Har. Go on." Maggie lowered her chin and looked at Sam from beneath her eyebrows.

"Oh, sorry. Anyway, none of the people from the village who work here made it to work this morning. We're on our own. Oh, and the lights went out last night sometime, so we're on the generators now. Sir Rudy has five of them, but they're all in the same place in the basement, and the basement's starting to flood. You should see Arnaud. He's having a cow, and Joanne's screaming so loud I'm surprised you didn't hear her up here."

Maggie was upset by all this bad news, but didn't want to let Sam know that. After all, it was only rain. Only a monsoon. And the possibility of no electricity. No food. No escape. "Anything else?"

"No. Just the ghost."

Maggie chewed on the inside of her cheeks for a few moments. "Oh. Only the ghost. Okay. *What ghost*?"

"Um . . . Uncle Willis? At least, that's what Sir Rudy calls him. Nobody knows his name. But he's here. Some old guy who didn't want to leave. Supposedly there's a small book about him in Sir Rudy's study." Sam scratched his head. "Do you know Sir Rudy bought this place just the way it is? Furniture, books, even the household staff. They all came together. Those aren't even his ancestors on the walls in the portrait gallery. They came with the place. I love that. It's *so* Hollywood."

"I think I'll go back to bed now, if you don't mind," Maggie said. "Unless you've got more good news?"

Sam frowned. "Nope. That's about it. Oh! The Sterlings? They've mounted a ghost hunt. Your friend Alex told them that if they find Uncle Willis they're not to touch him, just leave him where he is, and most definitely not to invite him down to luncheon. That's what he called it—luncheon. I really want to follow that guy around with a notebook. He has some great lines."

"Thank you," Maggie said, then mentally slapped herself upside the head. "I mean, thanks for all the news. Maybe I'll go downstairs after all, see what's in the kitchen. Or did somebody make breakfast?"

"Marylou did. Arnaud put her on kitchen duty until the

housekeeper and everyone can make it through. She's a pretty good cook."

"Wonderful. I'll read this later, I promise." Maggie put down the script, refusing to acknowledge Sam's small moan of protest, and stepped into the hallway, just in time to see Sterling and Perry come down the hall.

Sterling was carrying a large, moth-eaten butterfly net. "Hello there, Maggie. Wonderful day, isn't it?"

Perry held up a small camera. "We're off to find Uncle Willis, since there's nothing else to do."

Maggie smiled weakly, waggled her fingers at them, and watched them as they headed for what she supposed must be the servant staircase to the third floor.

"What's up there, anyway?" she asked Sam as they both made their way to the grand staircase.

"Attics, I guess, but I'll bet there's some really good stuff up there. Maybe even valuable stuff. We're not filming up there. Just in the main rooms and on the grounds, although with the rain, maybe Arnaud could do something with the attics. Are you sure you don't want to go back and get my—I mean, the changes to the final scene? You're the reason I changed it, you know. You should be grateful."

Maggie stopped on the bottom step and turned to glare at the man. "Grateful? You've all totally screwed up what was a damn good story, and I'm supposed to be grateful? How do you figure that, Sam?"

And then something unexpected happened. Sam of the plain, round face and the affable if cloying demeanor turned into a not very nice man. Standing two steps above her, so he was a good foot taller all of a sudden. His face going red, his hands balling into fists, he said, tight-lipped, "You're such an ungrateful New York bitch. I kiss your ass, and what do I get? Do you know how hard it was to take your mess and whip it into something worth anything? So don't you condescend to me. You're just a hack who got lucky, that's all you are. Read my stuff, don't read it. I don't give a damn, because *my* script is going to be produced if I have to do it myself. I'm better than you'll ever be on your best day!"

Maggie stepped back, nearly fell down the last two steps. What had just happened? It was like Barney the Dinosaur had suddenly morphed into a T. rex, and Maggie's body couldn't make up its mind whether it wanted to go into fight or flight mode. "I . . . uh . . . that is . . ."

"Yeah, right. That's what I thought. East Coast women. All balls, no brains. Give me a break. You want to know competition, you come to Hollywood. It's dog-eat-dog out there, and I'm on the brink, even if I have to do shlock like your pathetic little mystery movie. Well, you know what? This is the last time. I don't need you. Nobody wants you here anyway. I mean, come on, sister, buy a clue."

He was being loud. He was hovering over her from his place on the stairs, menacing as a vulture.

All Maggie's usual defense mechanisms shifted into overdrive. Experience had long ago taught her that you can't win with someone who thinks arguments are won with the loudest voice, that the field goes to the physically intimidating.

She went into full retreat, heading across the landing and for the stairs to the ground floor. Where she'd go after that she didn't know. Out into the rain? Maybe that was a good idea. Anyplace. Anyplace but here.

Keeping her gaze on Sam Undercuffler, who really looked as if he might follow her, Maggie reached for and grabbed the wide stone railing and raced down the steps . . . cannoning into Alex, who caught her easily.

"Well, hello there," he said, neatly holding her at the shoulders. "Is there some sort of emergency?"

If she told him about Sam, he'd go into Hero Mode.

That, she definitely didn't need. "Is there . . . I just . . . no." She took a deep breath, let it out in a rush. "No, no emergency. I just . . . I was just going to go outside and see how flooded the drive is—it looks flooded from my room."

He didn't believe her. She'd created him, she knew his skeptical look, and he didn't believe her.

"I've just come back from indulging in much the same exercise," he said, turning her about and offering his arm so that they climbed the stairs together. "A rather abbreviated exercise, as one look was more than sufficient to tell me that we are rather cut off from civilization at the moment. As a matter of fact, when you, um, stumbled into me, I was amusing myself by inspecting the artistry on this wall."

"Big, isn't it?" Maggie said, stopping to look up at the romping figures, as stalling appealed to her more than going upstairs to see Sam waiting for her. "Who's the guy in the center?"

"Ah, that I do know, although I have yet to discover the name of the artist. The gentleman riding so triumphantly through the posies in his chariot is none other than Sir Willard Gainsley, the fellow who originally ordered construction of this pile. His great-grandson commissioned the painting shortly after the wing additions were completed."

"And everybody else?" Maggie asked, sneaking a look up the stairs, relieved that Sam Undercuffler wasn't still there, maybe dressed in the suit of armor that stood on the landing, ready to split her head with the battle-ax held in one metal gauntlet.

"Sir Willard's family. Four generations strong at that point."

"Sir Willard," Maggie said, remembering Sterling's pursuit of the estate's ghost. "Uncle Willis?"

"No, not at all. Uncle Willis was the oldest son of a second son, somewhere along the line, and quite put out to find that a poor relation is just that, never to inherit more than his own father's debt. He came to a rather bad end, I understand, and then decided to haunt the place. Supposedly, there's a complete history in Sir Rudy's study, if you're interested. Marvelous research for you, since you seem to be in need of an alternate plot for our next adventure."

"There's an actual history of this place? You know, I think Sam already told me that. I'll think about it—and ignore the sarcasm about needing a new plot because I know that's just you being you. Besides, ghosts are so overdone in mysteries. I'd rather look at the whole history, not just at Uncle Willis. Except I'm really not in the mood."

"As you wish," Saint Just said once they were in the upstairs foyer. "And, now that we've had our idle chatter, exactly what sent you racing down the stairs that way?"

"I told you. I wanted to look at the driveway."

"So being called a no-talent hack by that insufferable brown pup had nothing to do with your haste?"

"You heard? Oh, that's lousy, Alex. And why didn't you come rescue me? I thought Sam was going to take a swing at me. I really did."

"Cowards never hit first, my dear," Alex said, stepping ahead of her to open the double doors to the main saloon. "But I assure you, I'll deal with the man directly."

"No!" Maggie stopped, figuratively dug in her heels. Covered her sudden fear with bravado. "That's the *last* damn thing I want—you protecting me. We've been there, done that, remember? And it didn't work out all that well. I'll fight my own battles, and I would fight this one except Sam Undercuffler's not really that important, okay? I got spooked for a minute, I'll admit that, but I'm also over it. I'll handle him. Besides, the rain stops and we're out of here, end of story. In the meantime, I'm going to go scope out this study everybody's talking about and find a good book. Even a bad book. And then I'm locking myself in my room."

"Very well," Saint Just said, shooting the cuffs on his Regency costume; today he was wearing a bottle-green morning jacket and tan pantaloons. "I suppose Tabby and Bernie can amuse themselves without their friend, whom they've come to England to support in this possibly trying time spent watching her magnificent book reduced to ninety minutes of film minus commercial breaks."

"Bite me."

"Ah, there she is, the Maggie I adore. Now, come along. Evan has a question for you. He asked me, actually, but I knew you'd rather answer him."

Maggie looked around the main saloon, wondering when she'd before seen such a motley-looking crew of unhappy people. "Oh, this is going to be another fun day. Where's Tabby?"

"With the also-absent Clarence, one could suppose. More than that, I don't believe either of us wants to know."

"I'll drink to that," Maggie said, pouring herself a glass of orange juice from the pitcher on the coffee table, then snatching up a piece of rather cold, hard toast. "Some breakfast."

"There were eggs and ham earlier, but I'm afraid you missed them, as did Bernie, who is still in her room, in case you were about to inquire as to her whereabouts. Ah, but here's our Lord Hervey now. One meets the most insufferable people in Society."

"You want to punch him, don't you?" Maggie asked, feeling a little better, especially since Sam Undercuffler was nowhere to be seen. "A wisty castor, then watching when his nose begins leaking claret."

"Not really, sorry to disappoint. He, like Undercuffler, really isn't worth the effort of more than a brilliant, cutting, verbal set-down, which both will receive soon enough if I'm pushed beyond my endurance. A gentleman must have his standards. Now, sending a few of my servants round to administer a well-deserved beating? That does hold some appeal."

"Shhh, he'll hear you," Maggie said, trying not to giggle. "Ah, Mr. Pottinger, hello. You wanted to ask me something?"

"Lord Hervey, if you please, madam," Evan Pottinger said, his bow barely a cursory nod in her direction. "But, in point of fact, I have been reading over the scene in the gazebo, and I can't seem to find my motivation. Why am I so set on killing this servant girl?"

Maggie rolled her eyes. "Oh, come on, you don't know why? Didn't you understand when you read the book?"

Evan blinked. "Read the book? Why would I do that?"

"Because you're a method actor?" Maggie suggested. "Don't you guys *immerse* yourselves in a role? Or do you just like to dress up and act like you know what's going on?"

Evan produced his snuff box and did a pretty darn good job of taking imaginary snuff. "Ah. I see now why Sam entertained us all during breakfast with his rather colorful comments about you, Miss Dooley."

"Kelly. Dooley's my pen name. And what did he say?"

"Now, Maggie, you wouldn't want his lordship here to stoop to repeating gossip, now would you?" Alex asked, stepping into the breech. "Come, Lord Hervey, ask Miss Kelly exactly what you want, then be a good fellow and go away."

Evan glared at Saint Just, who glared back. "Not worth your effort, remember?" Maggie said quietly, then addressed Evan once more. "You want to know your motivation for being an unmitigated bastard? Is that it? But you don't have time to read the book?"

"No. I don't have the *inclination.* Just synopsize it for me, please?"

Maggie wanted to scream. "Okay. Sure. Lord Hervey is your typical jackass sociopath. Let's see, what sort of background did I give him in my mind when I was creating him? Oh, yeah. Pulled wings off butterflies, likes to set fires, screwed his half-sister, beats his valet—you know, the usual stuff. You kill, *Lord Hervey*, because you bloody well *like* it. Good enough?"

Evan lifted his chin, his eyes bright, dancing. "Oh. Oh, yes. I can see it now. Pent-up rage at an unfeeling mother. Years of abuse at the hands of the father. Jack the Ripper, but in better clothes and operating in a better neighborhood. Oh, this is perfect. This is wonderful. Meaty."

He held his balled fists up in front of himself. "The hatred and loathing for his fellow man that lies beneath the urbane, witty surface. I can *feel* the rage now, the incredible anger beneath the fashionable facade. Now all I have to do is *channel* it as my hands slowly close around the servant girl's neck and I squeeze . . . *squeeze*."

Maggie watched, bug-eyed, as Evan turned and walked away, his hands still in fists. "Yeah, right. So glad I could help. The guys in the white coats will meet you at the front door in an hour, okay?" She turned to Alex. "Jeez Louise, that is one scary guy."

"Not half as frightening as our Saint Just. Look at him. God's teeth, I believe I'm experiencing my first failure."

Maggie looked across the room to where Troy Barlow and Nikki Campion stood close together, each holding a copy of the script as they read lines to each other. "He looks all right to me, and his coattails aren't wrinkled, either. What's your problem?"

"Let me count the ways. His accent. His posture. His expression, which reminds me most of a stunned sheep. I worked with him for an hour, earlier, in the breakfast room, trying to explain the proper use of cutlery. Ah, but here comes our host. Sir Rudy? Any news on the state of the cellars?"

"Not good, not good," Sir Rudy said, shaking his head as he clomped into the room in thigh-high black rubber waders held up by bright red suspenders. "I used to watch this place all but float away when I was a lad from the village. Thought it was funny then. Not so bloody funny now."

"I know I'm not laughing." Maggie smelled the expelled cigarette smoke before she saw Joanne Pertuccelli. "I just called Stateside to warn everyone off until next week. But that doesn't mean we're going to waste time, people. I've already got Arnaud blocking out interior scenes for some of the stuff that was supposed to take place outside. Sam's helping with that, scoping out possible locations. We can do this, people. We're Americans. We've got ingenuity. We've got innovation on our side. We've got a budget, damn it. We can do this!"

"Yay, team," Maggie grumbled in disgust.

"We'd damn well better," Evan called out imperiously from his place in front of the mantel. "I talked to my agent this morning, and I'm up for a voice-over part in *The Simpsons* Christmas special."

"Oh, now there's a huge career move, Evan," Troy Barlow said, his sneer pretty good for a guy Saint Just seemed to consider a total write-off. "*I* may start filming December fifteenth on *Celebrity Jeopardy*."

"Oh, he is not," Maggie said, probably louder than she should have, but she was laughing too hard to be subtle. "What's the first category—*Spelling of Three-Letter Words*?"

But nobody was listening because everyone was talking—yelling, actually—the actors all playing out a scene in what was probably a long-running show of one-upmanship.

"I don't think I like Americans all that much anymore,"

Sir Rudy told Maggie. "Present company excepted, of course. I think."

"Thank you, Sir Rudy. I think," Maggie told him. "Is it true we could lose power?"

The man shrugged. "It's definitely getting wet down there. But it's not all horrible. Dearest little Marylou has the kitchens well in hand. Very amenable girl. I think she likes me. The redhead—not the one over there, screaming, but the other one, the tall one? She said I was sweet, so I know that's not going anywhere. But Marylou. Well, she's a dear."

Maggie smiled as gently as she could. "That's nice, Sir Rudy. But do be careful, won't you? You wouldn't want some fast American girl to turn your head, now would you?"

"I'm not completely against it, no," he said, then excused himself, telling Maggie he wanted to return to the kitchens, as Marylou had promised him a peach pie. He passed behind Maggie, and she gave a small yelp when she felt him pinch her bottom.

"He pinched me," she told Alex, who was watching as Troy Barlow attempted to perform an elegant leg—a particularly deep, sweeping bow. Luckily, the well-muscled Nikki caught him before he fell. "Sir Rudy *pinched* me."

"Callous as this sounds, Maggie, my dear, we all have our problems," Alex said, then left her where she stood. Before she could make good her own escape, Joanne stomped in her direction.

"I want to make it clear, Ms. Kelly, that while you may have somehow managed free air flight for yourself and your companions, there *will* be a ten-ninety-nine sent to you at the end of the year, and you *will* have to report the fares as income."

"Really," Maggie said, wondering if the water outside was deep enough for her to just go drown herself in it and put herself out of her misery. “There’s no such thing as a free ride, is there, Joanne?”

“Not in this business there’s not.” Then Joanne lost her eagle-eyed look and asked, “Have you seen Mr. Stockwell?”

“Who? Oh, Sir Rudy’s nephew. No. I can’t say as I have. But you could ask Nikki, I suppose. Last night they seemed . . . pretty chummy.”

“Looks can be deceiving, Ms. Kelly,” Joanne said, and once more Maggie was alone. She was being talked at, talked to, and then left alone much too much for one morning, so she decided to hunt down Sir Rudy’s study.

Once there, and after admiring the dark paneling and the walls crammed with books, she found a small stack of *People* magazines she hadn’t read yet. And, wow, there was a small fire in the grate. She could make herself comfortable here for a while. Dragging a cashmere afghan over her legs as she curled up in one of the chairs flanking the fireplace, she was enjoying a review of Harlan Coben’s latest book in two minutes, sound asleep in ten.

She awoke some time later with a stiff neck and in the dark, for the fire had burned down to a few embers and the velvet draperies were shut tight over the windows.

It took her a few moments to get her bearings, remember where she was, but the sound of hushed voices kept her in her chair.

She didn’t know who was in the room with her, and because they were whispering, she couldn’t figure it out. She was able to understand only every second or third word.

“You said *mumble-mumble* knew.”

“I *mumble* I know. But that’s *mumble-mumble-mumble* same as having *mumble* in my hands.”

“I *mumble-mumble* everything to—”

“There’s no risk *mumble-mumble* person who only happened to *mumble; squared.*”

“Oh, shut up. And I don’t like that now he’s *mumble-*

*mumble* on it. When do we *mumble* for the *mumble-mumble*? Today?"

"No power *mumble* nobody *mumble* us. *Enough mumbles to make Maggie want to scream* . . . our friend."

"I'm your *mumble* friend. Don't *mumble* that or *really nasty-sounding run of mumbles*. And I mean it."

"*Mumble-mumble* avoid suspicion *mumble* be silly."

And then nothing.

Maggie heard the study door open and close. She quickly threw off the afghan and raced to open the door, look out into the hallway. But it was nearly pitch black in the hallway.

One of them had said something about the power, right? Yeah, something about the power.

She felt her way across the room and pushed open the drapery on one of the huge windows. It was brighter outside than it was inside, not that there was a measurable difference.

Using that faint light, Maggie located a table lamp and quickly switched it on. Off. On. Off. On–off–on–off.

"Oh, great, the generators are floating. This is just perfect," she said, possibly whimpered. "I'm in a haunted house, with no power, no household staff. I'm surrounded by wackos, and at least two of them are up to something. Alex is going to love this, damn him."

If she told him.

That thought hit her about the same time her shin collided with the leg of a chair as she fumbled her way toward the hall once more.

"I don't *have* to tell him," she said out loud. "He can't go sticking his nose into anything and playing the hero again if he doesn't *know* there's anything to stick his nose into, after all. And there's not. There's not! I just heard two people talking, that's all. So I'm going to forget the whole thing ever happened. I'm going to forget it, and I'm going to ignore Sam Undercuffler, and I'm going to look the other way while Tabby screws around with an actor, and I'm going to find Bernie and stick close to her because she's the most sane person here. And just saying that shows how desperate I am."

Maggie stopped, leaned against the wall. "And I'm going to stop talking to myself. That's first on the list. I'm going to be calm, cool, collected. Right after somebody feeds me."

Following her nose to the kitchens, she turned down a piece of freshly baked pie and instead made two ham sandwiches, one for herself, the second for Bernie. Grabbing two cans of soda from one of the huge, stainless-fronted refrigerators, she thanked Marylou—who'd been telling her how "cute" Sir Rudy is—begged a flashlight, then headed up the servant's staircase to find Bernie's room.

"Knock, knock," she said, opening the door to each room and cautiously sticking her head inside. Three rooms were empty, including the one she knew was Tabby's because of the red-paisley silk scarf carefully draped over a lampshade, probably to give the room a sexy ambiance. The only good thing was that Tabby and Dennis weren't in the room at the moment.

Figuring she was getting closer, with only two rooms to go, Maggie repeated her "Knock, knock" routine and opened the door to see . . . "Oh, God. Sorry!"

The image of Nikki Campion "riding" bareback on Byrd Stockwell would probably burn holes in her retinas before it disappeared.

"There are just some things people shouldn't know," she said, rubbing her face in hopes of dispelling the image, and immensely grateful that Nikki and Byrd were so involved that they had neither heard her enter nor apologize. "Okay. Last door. What do I get, the lady or the tiger?"

Maggie knocked, entered, then stood for a moment

until her eyes became accustomed to the near darkness. "Bernie? You here?"

"*Mmmmmpff.*"

"I'll take that as a yes," Maggie said, closing the door, then crossing to the window to push open the drapes. "It's cold in here. Why didn't you light a fire? And why are you still in bed? It took me forever to find you, and you won't believe what I saw when I opened the—Bernie? Honey, you don't look so good."

Bernie pushed herself up against the pillows, then quickly dragged the covers over her shoulders. "It's cold as a morgue in here," she said, then glared at Maggie. "And thanks for the compliment. I'm sick. My head hurts, my nose is all stuffed up, I've got a scratchy throat, I'm achy, I'm sneezing, I—"

"Sound like a NyQuil commercial," Maggie said, hopping up to sit on the side of the high bed. "You probably picked up some cold germ on the flight over. Dirty air. What have you taken?"

Bernie sneezed, then blew her nose in a crumpled handkerchief. "Taken? Why should I take anything? Nothing helps, except booze, and you won't let me have that. We can put a man on the moon, Mags," she said, sniffling, "so why can't we cure the common cold? Huh?"

"I don't know. Because everyone's too busy inventing new and improved erectile dysfunction drugs?"

"Yes!" Bernie sat up straight, her red hair a tangled mess, her nose a nearly matching red. "That's it! And tell me why the world needs three or so different drugs for erectile dysfunction. Are that many guys having trouble getting it up? Bull! They just all want to feel nineteen again, when all it took was waking up in the morning to get themselves in the mood."

Maggie nodded furiously, willing to tackle any subject, as long as it had nothing to do with Medwine Manor or the movie. "I know, I know. And then they show these commercials where the guy comes up behind his wife—we know it's his wife because she's washing dishes, and girlfriends don't wash dishes. That keeps it G-rated or something. Anyway, the guy comes up to his wife, who's washing dishes, or digging in the garden, or making supper. He's *ready*. So, of course, *she's* just overjoyed to drop everything she's doing and be a freaking *receptacle*. Those commercials make me *so* mad."

Bernie sneezed again, laid back against the pillow. "You do know that if they came up with a guaranteed-orgasm pill for women, no ads would be allowed on the air. We'd never see a bunch of housewives and young mothers bursting out of their suburban homes, dancing, and singing 'It's Raining Men.' Or that song from *Jekyll and Hyde*. 'Bring On the Men.' Yeah. That's a good one."

"Or 'Girls Just Want to Have Fun,' " Maggie agreed. "Okay, so now that we've settled that one, and before you start on world peace or the price of Jimmy Choo boots, I've got some bad news for you."

"Nothing could be worse than this cold. And, speaking of cold, why is it so cold in here? And why are you holding a flashlight?"

"That's part of the bad news. The power cut out, and the generators are under water in the cellars—Marylou told me some fool left the service doors open and water was pouring down the stairs into the basement. We're completely surrounded by water from the rain, the ornamental pond, the stream, wherever it's coming from, so nobody goes in, nobody gets out. No household staff, no cook, nobody but us'uns. Oh. And it's still raining."

Bernie was quiet for some moments, then said, "A helicopter. We can call for a helicopter rescue. I've seen those on TV."

"I don't think so, no. According to Sir Rudy, this happens all the time. Nobody's coming to the rescue. We just wait until the rain stops and the water goes down. Besides, I can't really see you in a harness, being pulled up over the rooftops, can you?"

"Not sober, no. I'm starving. Feed a cold, right?"

"Oh, I forgot. I brought us lunch, but I left everything on a table in the hall. Hang on, I'll go get it."

"No big hurry. I'm just dying here."

"Right," Maggie said, heading for the hall, only to quickly close the door when she saw Byrd Stockwell and Nikki Campion standing in the open doorway across the way, lost in a lip-lock.

"What's wrong? Is the flood up here now? Are we going to drown? Tell me, Maggie. I can take it."

"Shhh," Maggie said, heading back to the bed. "I'll get the sandwiches in a minute. First . . . you're never going to believe this one . . ."

# Chapter Eight

It was amazing to Saint Just how, in such a very short space of time, he could become so bored with his Regency costume (tailoring was an art, one that obviously had not extended to whatever cow-handed buffoon had fashioned this coat).

He was equally disenchanted with the company (most of whom would cheerfuly murder each other for an extra moment on film), Medwine Manor (cold, drafty, soon to be dark), and England in November (for no particular reason save that there was no television machine and he was certain to miss the New York Giants on *Monday Night Football*).

Already unclasping the crudely fashioned, prefabricated neck cloth with one hand while unbuttoning his waistcoat with the other, Saint Just stopped dead just inside Sterling's bedchamber and stared at his friend and compatriot.

"*What* are you doing?"

Sterling, who had pulled up his shirt, exposing his bare belly, quickly pulled down his shirt and smiled at Saint Just. "I'm not sure. Remember yesterday? When you were all talking about Maggie's latest manuscript?"

"And you were admiring the scaffolding? Yes, I recall the moment. What of it?"

"Well, everyone kept talking about what was wrong with Maggie's book, and somebody—I forget who—said the story had you contemplating your navel for several hundred pages. And I've been wondering exactly what that meant, and why anyone would want to, because I've been looking at mine for ten minutes now and—and now you're laughing at me, aren't you?"

"Never, Sterling," Saint Just said, keeping a straight face only with difficulty. "I believe what was meant was that Maggie wrote me as examining my life—who I am, what I am, where I'm going, where I've been."

"Why would anybody want to do that?" Sterling asked. "A person could discover things about himself best left alone, and all of that."

"Very true, my friend. You look nearly incomplete, Sterling. Where's the other Sterling?"

"Perry. He's really Perry. He's only pretending to be me. And he's having a small lie-down in his room, if you must know. He thought he saw Uncle Willis, but it turned out to be nothing more than another suit of armor we found in the attics. The lightning flashed and lit it up, and Sterling—that is, Perry—screamed like a young girl, then backed up and fell over a small chest. Landed square on his rump. He's taking a restorative rest, but then we'll be off again. We have an entire other wing of the attics to search."

"Are you quite convinced there is a ghost, Sterling? In any case, it will be coming on to dark soon, so I'd rather you and your friend weren't stumbling about in the attics."

Sterling nodded sagely. "In case Uncle Willis shows up."

Saint Just smiled. "Exactly. And now, if you'll excuse me, I believe I'd like to retire to my own room, to bathe with what may be left of the hot water and attend to my toilette, then return these costumes to Marylou. Yours, too, Sterling. I think we've had enough of playacting."

"You're returning the costumes? But why? I thought these clothes suited you down to the ground."

"If the tailoring were better, perhaps. But possibly even not then. I wouldn't wish for Maggie to hear me, but modern clothing is immeasurably more comfortable. And, of course, everyone else will look the fool once I'm in my own impeccable wardrobe again."

"Except Byrd Stockwell. He cuts a rather dashing figure, don't you think?"

"The robin? I can't say as I'd really noticed," Saint Just said, avoiding Sterling's gaze. Because in truth, Byrd Stockwell annoyed him most thoroughly, even if he didn't want to believe the man's wardrobe and bearing had anything to do with that dislike. There was just something vaguely *false* about the man, and Saint Just knew he would feel more comfortable if the man wasn't in Armani while he was stuck in pantaloons and neck cloths, as if numbered with the actors.

Once refreshed and clad in black slacks and matching shirt, Saint Just went on the hunt for Maggie, who had been conspicuous only by her absence after telling him that Bernie was feeling poorly and that Tabby was still among the missing. As Dennis Lloyd also had not been seen since breakfast, this had come as no great surprise.

The cast had dispersed after a cold luncheon of meat and cheese, as Sir Rudy had suggested they all consider bringing blankets and pillows to the main saloon and prepare to spend the night sharing body heat—a suggestion that had been met with considerable derision and a snort or two from Evan Pottinger, who had said he'd much rather suffer hypothermia in his own room, thank you very much.

What a jolly gathering, one to which Saint Just would be more than happy to wave his farewells the moment the rain stopped, which it showed no signs of doing.

In the meantime, however, he would have liked a word or three with Sam Undercuffler, to take the fellow to task about his appalling lack of manners, and to point out to him that such boorish behavior toward Maggie would not be countenanced in the future. In other words, Saint Just planned to scare the clod spitless, which would serve to help him pass an enjoyable quarter hour.

But Sam Undercuffler hadn't been seen in the past several hours, not even appearing for supper, which had consisted of unhappy people . . . and more cold meat and cheese.

Indeed, most everyone seemed to have decided to give supper a skip, as most of the guests of Medwine Manor had bolted themselves in their rooms for the duration . . . doing Lord only knew what with Lord only knew whom.

Saint Just was only interested in Maggie.

So, after checking the empty study, the equally empty morning room, the likewise deserted main saloon, Saint Just climbed the stairs again, carrying a lovely silver candelabra that suited his mood as well as the architecture, and prepared to knock on Maggie's bedchamber door.

He heard music coming from under the door, which stilled his hand as he was about to knock. Music? But there was no electricity. Ah! Of course! Maggie's battery-powered CD player. Maggie could no more exist without music than she could breathe without air. And, when she wanted the world gone, she just turned the music louder.

Today, the music was blaring. Oh, dear.

Opening the door slowly, Saint Just smiled as, with the aid of several branches of candles lit around the room, he saw Maggie dancing to one of her favorite songs, Linda Eder's "Never Dance."

She moved gracefully to the story within the song, of

that night in Rio and the man she would never forget. Arms high above her head, Maggie's body told its own story as the pulsing beat throbbed through the room. Somehow happy, somehow sad. Never dance . . . never kiss . . . never love. And yet . . . feel the passion . . . the heat of desire. Just to dance again.

Saint Just couldn't resist. Who could possibly resist?

He put down the candelabra and moved to stand in front of her. Watched for a few mind-blowing moments as she swayed in front of him, her eyes closed, an expression of bliss on her beautiful face.

And then he slipped his arm around her waist, took her hand in his and brought it down.

And guided her into the dance.

She opened her eyes, goggled at him, even as she moved with him. "What . . . what do you think you're—"

"Shhh. This is the best part."

"Yes, but—oh, hell."

Hip to hip. Thigh to thigh. Moving to the rhythm.

He was a marvelous dancer. Maggie had written him so. He was so very good at so very many things.

He watched her as they danced, watched her watching him. Spun her out. Brought her back. Laughed as she finally grinned, as the devil peeked out from behind her eyes, as she gave herself up to the sensuous beat, the *heat*, the *passion*.

The *desire*.

One last whirl, one last dip, and the song was over. But not the dance.

Saint Just knew what came next on the CD. "Vienna." Love remembered. Love lost. Slow, sad . . . yet soaring. He drew Maggie close, tucking her right hand in his left, then folding them together against his chest as he held her, as they moved to the poetry that had been love in Vienna.

And Maggie allowed all of it.

Of course, being Maggie, she was not content for them to drift together silently.

"You never knock," she said as he pressed a kiss against her hair.

"I'm a bad man."

"Yes, you are. And it's embarrassing, being caught like this."

"Dancing? I vow I wouldn't know why."

"No, you wouldn't. You're never embarrassed. I was just trying to, I don't know, blow off some steam?"

"I see." Saint Just lightly traced his fingertips down the back of her neck. "I could help with that."

"Yes, I'm sure you think you could. This . . . this isn't going anywhere, you know."

"I know." He stroked her back, shoulder to hip. "Dear Lord, how I know . . ."

The song began to soar, and he moved with it. They moved with it.

"You could disappear as quickly as you showed up, you know. I couldn't . . . it's not possible for me to . . . oh, hell."

"There is such a thing as the *moment*."

"Like 'Vienna'? Love followed by regret? No, I couldn't do that. I just couldn't, Alex."

"And yet, ''tis better to have loved and lost than never to have loved at all.' "

Maggie stopped moving, pushed slightly away from him even as they continued in the dance. "Tennyson? He wrote too late for the Regency Era. I'm very careful to use only quotes written before your time in history. So how do you know Tennyson?"

"Noticed that, did you?" Saint Just rolled his eyes, smiled at this change of subject. Dearest Maggie, so transparent. But he was getting to her, and she had begun to weaken. He could afford to be patient. "My Maggie, the nitpicker. What? I cannot attempt to improve my mind?"

She shook her head, walked over to the portable CD player and shut it off. "I suppose not. But you could have used Congreve. He wrote before the Regency. Remember? You said it in *The Case of the Pilfered Pearls*, right before you gave your mistress her walking papers. 'Say what you will, 'tis better to be left than never to have been loved.'"

"And got my face slapped for my pains. Yes, I recall the moment. There are times, dearest Maggie, when I believe your mission in life is to deny me pleasure."

"Bite—never mind. And that's not true. I've written a couple dozen love scenes for you and—oh, no. I'm not going there. I don't want to talk about the books. I most especially don't want to talk about the love scenes. Do you have any idea how *difficult* that is for me since . . . since you got here?"

She looked so lovely when she was flustered. Saint Just couldn't help himself. He pushed. "No, not really. Tell me."

"Oh, right. You'd love that, wouldn't you? Forget it." She ran her fingers through her hair, which settled again most becomingly, which it should, for the price she paid for a silly man with scissors to snip at it once a month. "Okay. This has been a long time coming, and it's not going away without talking about it, is it? So let's get this over with, why don't we?"

"Perceive me as amenable to your every wish, if the *it* you're referring to is our, shall we say, mutual attraction," Saint Just said, fingering the ribbon holding his quizzing glass. "Shall I put the music on again?"

"That was *not* what I meant, and you know it. God! This is like arguing with myself—you know all the snappy answers, probably even before I ask the questions. Do me a favor, Alex, and get out of my head."

"Done and done, my dear. Sterling and I both. Not that it wasn't enjoyable there, but I so much prefer our present situation. Although, after seeing Dennis Lloyd in the Saint

Just livery, I must say I still do lament that you have yet to make him a fully well-rounded character, so that Clarence might join us here. He had such a way with boot black. I vow, I'm soon to shed a tear, feeling so very nostalgic for the man."

"Shut up. Just shut up." Maggie began to pace, yet another of her fortes. For a woman who detested exercise, she was quite the accomplished pacer, some days going for miles in her own living room-cum-office when one of her stories was first percolating in her brain.

Saint Just watched her for a few moments, then broke the silence. "Maggie. My dear, dear girl. We are destined, you know. The *left*-tenant is a mild diversion, nothing more, poor man, and we both are aware of that, also. When you created me, the perfect hero of your dreams, there was nothing else for it but for me to appear in your life."

She stopped dead to glare at him. "Oh, really. Really? Boy, you're a piece of work. You're telling me you've ruined me for other men? Of all the arrogant, self-serving, miserable excuses I've ever heard, that one—"

"Hits closest to the mark?"

"The hell it does." Maggie pressed her palms to her forehead, whether in pain from a dose of the headache or in a vain attempt to push him back inside her head, he didn't care to ask.

But because he knew her so well, and because he was who he was, Saint Just advanced on her slowly, took hold of her hands, and gently pulled her into his arms.

"The hell it does, yes. I am everything you both love and loathe in a man, Maggie. I appeal to you physically, as well as to your mind. You are attracted to my strengths as well as to my foibles. I attract you even as I sometimes frighten you, as I did when you and Sterling were in danger, and for which I apologize yet again, even as we both know I would do the same again. I am your imagination, all of it, come to life. And even more, now that I have been here for a while and have—and I know how you loathe the word—*evolved*. Now, do you wish to know what I think of you? How I am attracted to you? How I was attracted to you from the beginning and am more so with each day that passes?"

"No," she mumbled against his chest. "No . . . no. I was wrong. Let's not do this. I'm not ready for this."

"Yet, sad to say, even your reluctance attracts me. Your determined obstinance in the face of all that's reasonable. But there is so much more. You're also a loyal friend in the face of all obstacles. You can be rather funny at times, most often when you are not aware of that fact. You're intelligent and most remarkably human. Genuine, even in your faults—your very few faults. You're endearingly vulnerable and yet courageous and strong. You are totally unaware of how very beautiful you are. And, of course, you had the splendid good sense to invent me."

Maggie pushed back fractionally and looked up at him as he held her in the cradle of his arms. "Oh, that was *so* Saint Just. There are times, lots of them, when I feel like Doctor Frankenstein after his monster ran amok in the village. Now let go, okay?"

"You're afraid of me? Of yourself? Of *us*?"

She pushed a little harder, but he wasn't letting go. Not this time. "Cut that out. I am *not* afraid of you. Then again, I'm not nuts. You're a fictional character. My fictional character."

"All yours, my dear," Saint Just agreed, trying not to smile. She was weakening. He could sense it.

"Yes, but I don't write fantasy. And you're fantasy. A real fantasy."

"Also all yours, my dear. Have you ever wondered about that? About the need I might have filled in your life ever since the day you first dreamt me? Could *I* be the explanation for your reluctance to become seriously involved with other men?"

"Stop that! You're fiction. There's nothing magical or . . . or kinky about a writer's imagination. It's not my fault you're here."

"No, but was it your *wish* that got me here. After all, we'd all but lived with each other for five years before I made my existence known to you."

"Since you *poofed* into my living room. Right. I remember. How can I forget? It's been months, and you're still here." She opened her mouth to say something else, then shut it again.

"But how long will I be here. Yes, I know."

"No. That's just it. You *don't* know. You don't know, I don't know. We've been in *woo-woo* territory from the moment you and Sterling showed up, and nobody knows how long you'll be here. I . . . I can't take that chance. I won't let myself be—oh, forget it!"

This time when Maggie tried to free herself, Saint Just let her go. Time, it would seem, was his enemy. He'd not spent enough of it here, with her, for her to believe he would always be here. Then again, time was also on his side. Every day that he spent with her, she would feel safer with him, until the day she felt secure enough to really *be* with him. Be his. As he was hers, as he had been hers, even before he'd admitted as much to himself.

They were two halves of the same whole.

Sterling, bless him, was in the way of a bonus. Sweet, gullible, all-that-is-wonderful Sterling. The best of both him and Maggie, with no shadows. Childlike, in many ways.

Saint Just smiled at the thought, but prudently decided not to share that conclusion with Maggie, who was once again prowling the room, all her pent-up energy looking for a release.

He could have told her where she'd find it, but that would only get his face slapped. Pity.

"And another thing," Maggie said, just as if there had been no break in their conversation, which there hadn't been, Saint Just understood, at least in her mind. "This mess we're in. I mean, really. No heat, no hot food, no electricity. Cut off from civilization. Trapped here with a bunch of Hollywood hoo-hoos. Undercuffler and his asinine script. Joanne and her stopwatch and her penny-pinching—*don't* say it! I am *not* that bad. Tabby's shacking up with the valet—sort of—and I'll never be able to look her miserable husband in the face again, not that I can look at him now without wanting to smack him one. Bernie's sick, poor thing, and about an inch away from hunting for a bottle. My book stinks, and I have to start it over from scratch when we get back to New York. I'm *fat*, and I have to go see my mother again in less than a month, for Christmas. I mean, my life just keeps getting better and better."

"That is quite a thick budget of woes, I agree. Have you considered, as I've heard you say on occasion, going out into the garden and eating worms?"

"Very funny. Besides, all I could do around here is go out in the garden and *drown*." She stomped over to the nearest window, pulled back one side of the drapes even as she turned to him. "Look! Look at it out there. Did you ever see such a mess?"

"Um, Maggie?" Saint Just said, his smile thin, his tone, he hoped, merely conversational. "I have a splendid idea. What do you say you and I toddle off downstairs and find Sterling? He's been ghost hunting, you know, and he has the most amusing story to tell you. Really." He held out his hand to her. "Come along. You've been sulking up here long enough."

Maggie glared at him, then took a single step backward.

"What? What's wrong? You're talking to me, but you're looking *past* me. You're looking at the window. What's—" She turned around before he could stop her.

"Well," he said a moment later as she fainted and he caught her, "God knows I wanted the woman in my arms again." Then he tipped his head to one side and considered Sam Undercuffler, who was hanging by his neck from the scaffold on the other side of the window, his body swaying slowly in the wind and rain.

# Chapter Nine

Maggie sat propped up by pillows on one of the sofas in the candlelit main saloon and watched out of one slightly open eye as a rather low-keyed mayhem unfolded around her. She'd been back among the living for some twenty minutes or so, but had been "floating," not really awake, not really paying attention.

She could get away with that only for so long, however, because reality kept coming back to hit her in the face.

That reality was that Sam Undercuffler was dead. In an old English manor house. With its inhabitants cut off from civilization. In the dark. While a storm raged outside. It was all so cliché.

*Ten Little Indians*. Sort of. Maybe the Three Stooges version . . .

Arnaud Peppin appeared not to want to participate in directing that mayhem, having taken to a corner of the room, where he sat with both hands on his blue beret, which he was audibly sucking between his teeth.

Nikki Campion was weeping into the hem of her Regency gown, when she wasn't checking to make sure everyone *noticed* her weeping into the hem of her Regency gown.

Evan Pottinger, also still in Regency costume, hovered at the mantelpiece, clipping his nails, flipping the clippings into the fire. *Yeech*.

Dennis Lloyd, out of his Clarence the valet costume, but unfortunately having misbuttoned his shirt in his haste to get to the main saloon, a nervously grinning Tabby in tow, was busily explaining to anyone who would listen that he and Tabby were very sorry for Sam, but they'd heard nothing, seen nothing out of the ordinary about the man. After all, they'd been together the entire time, mostly in his bedchamber. All day in his bedchamber, as a matter of fact.

"And what would be the entire time, sir?" Alex asked the man, sticking his quizzing glass to his right eye. "After all, we have no idea how long poor Mr. Undercuffler has been hanging outside Maggie's window, now do we?"

"Well . . . um . . . it doesn't matter. Tabby and I have been together since last night, first in her room, then in mine, because nobody would bother us there. Haven't we, Tabby?"

"Shhh, Dennis," Tabby said, her cheeks going red. "No one was supposed to know that."

"Oh, yeah, right," Bernie said from her seat on the facing couch before blowing her nose quite noisily into her handkerchief. "None of us knows the two of you have been banging each other senseless, Tabby. Not us. Jeez. Nope. Totally clueless."

Maggie believed she should step in before her friends came to blows, but when Tabby put a hand to her mouth and ran out of the room, scarves flying, Dennis chasing after her, Maggie decided the two would sort themselves out in time. They always did.

Sterling—both Sterlings—leaned over the back of the couch, which for a moment had Maggie believing her faint had left her seeing double. "Maggie?" Sterling asked her.

"Are you all right now? When Saint Just came down the stairs like that, carrying you, I had quite a fright. Didn't I, Sterling?"

"Oh, he did, he did," Sterling *redux* said, nodding furiously. "But you're all right now, right? Right?"

"Yes, I'm fine, thank you. Both of you."

But they didn't take her word for it and go away. They just leaned over the couch some more, still staring at her. As if she might go *pop* at any moment.

"Um . . . so, have you guys found Uncle Willis yet?"

Both Sterlings frowned, shook their heads. "We thought we heard him earlier on, while we were poking about in the attics, but we didn't see anything."

Ah-ha! As Alex would say: *a clue*. Perhaps even the beginning of the reason Sam killed himself. *Please let him have killed himself.* Maggie pushed for more information. "You heard something? What did you hear? When? Which wing of the attics? The wing where Sam was hanging?"

"Is something amiss, Maggie?" Alex asked, for he was a man who missed nothing.

She looked up at him in mild disgust, and with a fleeting nervousness as she remembered their earlier interlude. Oh, bad word, *interlude*. Much too romantic a word. "What do you have, anyway? Built in radar? And not amiss, Alex, no. But the Sterlings—I mean, Sterling and Perry—said they heard some noise in the attics. Earlier." She turned to the Regency Twins. "When earlier, Sterling?"

The two exchanged looks.

"After the suit of armor?"

"Definitely after the suit of armor."

"But before the bat?"

"Most definitely before the bat."

"Gentlemen? Can we be a tad more precise, if you please."

"Let them alone, Alex. They're trying," Maggie said,

then finished the rest of the water someone had brought her and sat up straighter. "What bat?"

"The one in the attics, of course," Sterling said. "We heard the squeaking, the wings flap-flapping. One bat. Maybe more. In any case, we concluded that we didn't wish to stand about and wait for the thing to get tangled in our hair."

Maggie looked at the nearly identical, both partially bald men. Best casting of the whole movie. "No. You wouldn't have wanted that to happen, would you? So, you heard the bat, but you didn't see the bat. Or bats. But when?"

They looked at each other, then said in unison: "Before dinner."

"Just before," Sterling added. "Sorry we can't be more precise, Saint Just. I know how you like things precise, and all of that."

"Not to worry, Sterling. So, shall we say at approximately five o'clock? Once it was already dark? Very well. Thank you, gentlemen," Saint Just said, and the two retired to a corner of the room where Marylou had set up a small dessert table consisting of the pies and cakes she'd so industriously prepared in the, thankfully, gas-powered ovens.

Sir Rudy, still in his waders, entered the room, wiping his forehead with a large red handkerchief. "So sorry to report this, but the telephones won't work. Checked them all, I did, and it surprised me how many I've got. Upstairs, downstairs. Don't know why I have so many. But they're all those portable types, you understand, and we need power for them to operate. We'll have to find a way to get to the constable in the morning, if the water dissipates. Not that it makes much difference, for the constable couldn't get to us tonight in any case, and the poor boy is still dead. Oh, peach pie. Smashing! Excuse me!"

"Nice to see him so concerned," Maggie said, getting to

her feet. "Poor Sam commits suicide, and our host cares more about peach pie."

"If it was suicide," Alex said quietly. "Which I very much doubt."

Maggie closed her eyes, took a deep breath. "Why did you say that? Why did I know you were going to say that? Why do I know that Sam's ego was way too big for him to kill himself? Do the others know? Damn it. Alex, we could be stuck here with a murderer. *Do* something."

"I am doing something, my dear. I'm observing. Have no fears, we'll have this settled before dawn."

"You wish."

"I promise," he corrected, chucking her under the chin, so that she swiped his hand away, which was less revealing than throwing herself into his arms and screaming, "Protect me!"

"The police can't get here? Nobody can come take away the body?" Troy Barlow, still in his Regency costume, spoke from the drinks table, where he'd been dedicatedly depleting an entire carafe of wine, one glass after the other. "So Sam stays here all night? Oh, no. We can't have him here all night. He could start to *smell.*"

"No more than you do, you imbecile," Evan Pottinger said on his way out of the room. "I'm going to go get changed. Suddenly, this costume feels silly. Troy? Did you hear me? You look silly. You, too, Nikki."

Nikki interrupted her grief for Sam to stare down at her gown in sudden horror. "Oh!"

Maggie looked at Alex as Nikki ran past them, then picked up two of the many flashlights on the table and pointed toward the hallway. Even with Evan and Nikki gone, there were still too many ears in the main saloon. Not to mention too many imbeciles.

Once the two of them were sitting side-by-side on the

stairs leading down to the ground floor, Maggie asked, "Sam's in the house? When did that happen?"

"While you were still playing the die-away heroine who'd had a tremendous shock to her sensibilities, I imagine, my dear," Alex told her, carefully wiping his hands together as if to rid himself of any lingering feeling of having touched the dead screenwriter as he hauled him in through the open window.

"You pulled him in? You *touched* him? Boy, that took guts. I couldn't do that."

"We could hardly leave him where he was, with his nose pressed against your windowpane as if begging entry."

"Oh, please. It was graphic enough the first time. Don't re-run it for me."

"My apologies. Arnaud assisted me in the retrieval, which may explain why he's on his third Scotch at the moment. We placed Sam in the morning room, on the table there. He—Undercuffler, that is, was already in rigor. Stiff as the proverbial board. We discovered the body at six this evening, but I'd say he'd already been deceased for several hours as a body goes into rigor in about three hours. No one can remember seeing him since shortly after the two of you had your argument this morning."

"Then the Sterlings did hear a bat in the attics, not Sam, at five o'clock. Okay. It's probably good to establish some sort of time line. So you cut Sam down, then laid him out in the morning room? Boy, there goes breakfast," Maggie said, closing her eyes. "I didn't know you knew about rigor."

"The Learning Channel," Alex explained with a slight bow of his head. "Which is where, coincidentally, I also gained my incomplete but at least serviceable knowledge concerning lividity."

"Well, bully for you. What's lividity? Oh, wait, I know that one. I saw that on *CSI*. Someone dies, and the blood pools inside the body at the lowest points of gravity, right? So Sam's blood," she hesitated, swallowed down hard, "was probably in his face, because of the rope, and maybe in his feet and legs?"

"One would assume so, wouldn't one?"

Maggie turned the beam of her flashlight on him. "You're smiling. One of those Saint Just supercilious smiles. I hate when you do that because it means you know something I don't. Still, I'll bite, as it's the only way I'm going to learn anything. One *wouldn't* assume so?"

"Not once one had stripped the poor fellow of his soggy clothing and looked, no. Sam Undercuffler's lividity was, excuse the crudity, almost entirely behind him."

"His back? But . . . but that would mean he was killed, left to lie somewhere, and then later . . . hung up?"

"To be discovered with only a slight, secondary lividity in the areas you mentioned. Ah, the blessings of forensic science as imparted by commercial television programs. We're all experts now save, I think we can safely deduce, our murderer. Yes, Maggie. The hanging was for effect and after the fact. Hours after the fact, I believe. Entirely unnecessary and definitely overdone."

"And that bothers you, doesn't it?" Maggie thought about this for a moment. "Not at all your sort of thing, right? Not an English, understated sort of thing? Which makes it an overdone *American* sort of thing?"

"I would say so, yes. Possibly. But not definitely. It's equally possible the murderer had simply wanted Undercuffler out of the way—assuming he was murdered in the attic—and that's why he hung Sam out the window."

"Because the Sterlings have been poking around in the attics and might have stumbled over the body?"

"Precisely. In that case, the murderer slipped back upstairs to the attic and hung Undercuffler out the window. Without—once again proving we are not dealing with a genius here—checking to make sure Sam wouldn't be visible from the floor below."

"So we weren't meant to find him?"

"No, I don't think so. At least not until several hours after we'd noticed he'd gone missing. Would you, for instance, have asked about his whereabouts?"

"Are you kidding? I was trying to avoid him all day."

"But he would have been missed at some point, so all the murderer stood to gain was time. I wonder why."

Maggie thought about this. "Time for the rain to stop and the water to go down? Time for a getaway?"

"Hmmm, possibly. We'll consider that later, if we might? For now, I would like to concentrate on the how, not necessarily the why. And most definitely the *who*. Lifting a stiff, dead weight, having the strength to tie that dead weight to a length of heavy, braided drapery cord knotted to the scaffold, then pushing that same dead body out an attic window? I believe we can rule out the ladies, don't you?"

"Nikki lifts weights," Maggie said, then shook her head. "No. That's pushing it. Unless there's two people involved."

"Yes, I've considered that possibility as well. Irregardless, the lividity certainly squashes Troy Barlow's theory, although I allowed him to run with that notion for a while, if only to keep him occupied. Unfortunately, you see, he heard me when I took Sterling aside outside the morning room to inform him that we might be dealing with a murder."

"Oh, good going, Alex."

"It was an unfortunate lapse, yes, with my only excuse being the dim light in that hallway, even with all the candles lit in their sconces. But I did impress him with the fact that Undercuffler's death could also be a suicide. That nobody has ruled out that possibility, even as we consider alternate possibilities. Which," Saint Just ended with a small smile, "set him off quite nicely with a theory of his own."

"Troy? He has a theory? Okay, this should be good.

What's his theory? Murder or suicide? You said suicide, right?"

"Suicide, of course, as Troy's first choice was that Undercuffler did indeed do away with himself. Provoked by your cruel rebuffs, by the way, your constant harping on the very reasonable improvements he made to your book. And then you crushed him—totally destroyed his spirit—by refusing to read his own script."

"I was going to read the damn thing," Maggie protested. "Eventually."

"Yes, I'm sure you would have, thanks to your lamentable inability to say no and mean it when others encroach on your good-heartedness. But to continue? Undercuffler, opined our Troy, hanged himself from the scaffold, making sure you would be the one who eventually discovered his body. In other words, Sam Undercuffler killed himself to upset you. Rather like slicing off one's own nose to spite one's face, but it has been done before. Shame on you, you cold, heartless woman. Or, to quote our trumped-up Viscount Saint Just, you 'bawdy, artless harpy.'"

"He's blaming *me*? Reasonable improvements? *Harpy*! Oh, for the love of—you're kidding, right? I pass out after seeing Sam swinging outside my window, which was more than reasonable, damn it, and now you're making up stories for when I was out cold. That's mean, Alex. Really mean."

"If that were true, which it is not, believe me when I tell you that my joy would not be unalloyed. But I will, at least somewhat, relieve your mind. Casting you in the role of hard-hearted female to Bernie when we met her in the hallway was a short-lived theory on the man's part, one she squashed both effectively and with some rather inspired profanity."

"That's Bernie. And she's feeling sick, too. What a pal. Now tell me why your joy wouldn't be unalloyed."

"Again, the Troy Toy—Bernie addressed him that way, several times, and I believe the title has a certain ring to it. He only moments ago confided in me that if Undercuffler was the victim of foul play—his words, not mine—he, as the Viscount Saint Just, is the obvious person to step in, solve the dastardly crime. As a matter of fact, he's off now, hunting up Joanne Pertuccelli and the robin, as he insists that everyone be gathered in the main saloon when he renders his verdict."

"Oh joy, this is going to be good. Evan Pottinger I can see as a method actor, believing himself in a part. But Troy? He couldn't ask someone to pass the salt without a script in front of him. Wait a minute. Joanne and Byrd? They aren't here? There's been a freaking murder, Alex. Why are people just *wandering* around? Where are they?"

"I'm sure I shouldn't know," Alex said, helping Maggie to her feet. "After all, I am nothing save an interested bystander, having been firmly put in my place the last time I attempted some sleuthing, and only now slowly climbing back into your good graces. In other words, using your modern vernacular, I believe that other than the observations I have already made, I'm going to sit this one out."

Maggie laughed, and not kindly. "Oh, sure you are. And as a true Regency character might say, pull the other leg—it's got bells on. You could no more sit out a murder investigation than you could wear stripes with plaids."

Saint Just gave an exaggerated shudder. "Oh, very well. If you insist."

"If I—cute. Real cute, Alex. Now I'm *asking* you to investigate Sam's murder?"

Alex swept her an elegant leg. "Your wish, as ever, is my command. Now, shall we return to the others?"

"So Troy can play at being you and try to declare me guilty again, this time for murder? Oh, yeah, sure. I can't wait."

"Well, the deceased was dangling outside your window,

remember? Troy's original deduction was very nearly reasonable, and it's only a small step from provoker of suicide to murderess."

"But if I killed Sam, why would I want him hanging outside my own window? Is Troy nuts, or just stupid? Never mind. Rhetorical question. Besides, if Bernie shut him up once, I don't think even Troy could be dumb enough to try to go there again. I'm safe," Maggie said, reluctantly taking Saint Just's arm. "But you are going to tell everyone about the lividity, right?"

"Only if you'll not nag at me to limit myself to no more than that, perhaps. In for a penny, in for a pound."

"Nag? Now I'm a nag? You know, Alex, I fainted. I had a shock. A big one. So maybe you could ease off a little, huh?"

"You're not fully recovered?"

"Of course I am," Maggie said, bristling. "And damn you for knowing that. With Steve, I could have milked that faint for days. Weeks. With you?"

Alex pulled out his pocket watch, the one that had been his fictional grandfather's. "Fifty-seven minutes," he supplied affably. "Ah, and here come Joanne and our Robin Redbreast. Neither looks particularly happy."

Joanne saw them first and headed straight for Maggie. "Do you have a cell phone?" she asked, wringing her hands in front of herself while Byrd switched off the large flashlight he was carrying. "Do either of you have a cell phone? I've got to call California, let them know what's happening."

"So sorry," Alex said. "I have one, yes, but the battery has run down. And since there's no power . . . ?"

"I've got one," Maggie said, sensing something wrong about the studio representative's appearance, but unable to put a finger on just what. "You don't have one, Joanne? I'm sure I saw you with one yesterday."

"That was yesterday," Joanne said in clipped tones. Angry tones. "I don't have one today. And neither does Byrd. We just checked his room. Didn't we, Byrd?"

"It's true. My cell has gone missing. Joanne here thinks that's odd. Do you think that's odd?"

Maggie looked at Saint Just. "I think mine's in my room. I'll go get it."

"Yes, do that, and I'll check with the others. Someone's bound to have one," Alex said, heading for the main saloon.

Five minutes of intensive searching later (while wondering how Alex could have let her go upstairs alone, with a murderer in the house), Maggie joined him in the main saloon, shaking her head when he first saw her. "Any luck here?"

"Considerable, and all of it bad," he told her as Troy paced the carpet in the center of the room while everyone ignored him. "The flooding, the lack of electricity, and now all the cell phones have gone missing. No one kept their phone with them while in costume."

"And now they're all gone? Wonderful."

"Yes, it is, isn't it? A clumsy ploy, yet effective. It doesn't take a brilliant detective to conclude that we are stranded here quite effectively, with a killer who intends to use that isolation to his or her own benefit—whatever that may be. Whatever, I imagine we shall know before morning. Care for a ham sandwich? Marylou has prepared several more, bless her."

"Gee, it's nice to know you're still calm," Maggic said, reaching into her pocket for her nicotine inhaler. "This is all beginning to feel like a bad murder mystery. If the lights weren't already out, I'd expect them to cut out at any moment, then come back on so we all could see the knife sticking out of somebody's back."

"A charming mental picture, thank you, although there's

as yet no good reason to suppose Undercuffler's murder wasn't an isolated incident," Alex said, pressing a hand to his forehead as if his head ached. "Still, pressing on with your theory of imminent danger to all of us, would you mind terribly if the next victim were our dear Troy?"

"Why? He's still at it? Gee, and I missed it."

"Yes, my fears have all been confirmed, as Troy does have a new suspect I have not yet shared with you," Alex said, guiding her over to the table, now piled with sandwiches. "Thus far, unless he's been holding court during our absence, he's seen fit to confide his latest theory only to me."

"Lucky you. The guy works fast, I'll give him that." Maggie peeled back the bread from one of the sandwiches, made a face at the mustard smeared on the bread. "No mayo?" She took a quick peek over her shoulder to make sure no one was watching, then did a fast shuffle with the bread, making her own sandwich with two plain slices. "So, don't keep me in suspense—who's the new winner?" she then asked around her first large bite of the dry sandwich.

"Uncle Willis."

Maggie coughed as Alex soundly slapped her back until the bite of ham dislodged from her throat. Wiping her streaming eyes with her sleeve, Maggie choked out, "The ghost? He's blaming the ghost? I'll be right back. I gotta hear this one for myself."

Troy was still pacing. He was the only one still in costume, his handsome face scrunched up as he attempted to keep the quizzing glass stuck to his eye even as he kept his hands clasped behind his back.

"Troy—I mean, *Viscount*?" Maggie said. "I hear, my lord, that you have a suspect?"

The actor threw back his head and stuck out his chest. "I do that, madam," he pronounced carefully, then swore as the quizzing glass fell from his eye.

"Having a spot of bother, my lord?" Maggie asked facetiously, mentally casting Troy in her next book as the too-blond, dandified, totally ineffectual twit. Talk about your typecasting.

"Yes, I am. Damned thing. I'm going to have Sam write it out of the—oh. Well, whoever's going to take his place, that is."

"Saint Just's quizzing glass is an integal part of his personality, Troy," Maggie told him, no longer quite so amused. She looked at the actor's blond hair. "Just like his black hair. I've been afraid to ask. What are you guys going to do about that, anyway? You're going to wear a wig? Because my readers expect a Saint Just with black hair."

"That doesn't matter. Readers don't watch television. And television viewers don't read. Everybody knows that."

Maggie felt her temper rising. "I don't. I watch television *and* I read. I even chew gum and walk at the same time. Most of America does."

"Whatever. I only know that the American public will be tuning in because of *me*. I'm the draw—not your story. Definitely not Nikki, who's only famous for being famous, or Evan, who always plays the villain. But I really like being Saint Just. He's cool. So now, exactly like in the script, I'm going to gather the suspects together and ask a few questions before I unmask our dastardly murderer. *Dastardly*. Great word."

"Yeah. One of my all-time favorites. Go on, please."

Troy swept his right arm out in front of him, as if spreading his words across a screen hung in the air. "I can see the headlines. Troy Barlow, as the Viscount Saint Just, solves writer's murder on location. Barlow saves the day!"

He dropped his arm to his side. "Well, something like that. It'll make great publicity for the movie, might even guarantee a series. My agent's going to love it. I love it. Do you love it? And now, if you don't mind, I believe I'm on."

"No, no, wait a minute. I think it's a brilliant plan. Wonderful," Maggie said quickly. "I think it's really . . . really *cool* that you've decided to take charge this way. As Saint Just, I mean. Great publicity, I agree. But we don't want any mistakes, do we? After all, Saint Just is my creation, remember. So I want to hear about this suspect of yours. I know you want to tell everyone, but could you just give me a hint?"

Troy lifted the quizzing glass once more, then seemed to think better of it and let it fall back to his chest. "Oh, okay. But only a hint." He looked to his left, his right, then motioned for Maggie to lean in close. "Uncle Willis," he said, then paused for effect. "You know. The *ghost*. He did it."

Maggie couldn't see Alex from where she was standing. She couldn't hear him. But she knew he was laughing.

"Really? Uncle Willis, huh?" she said as Troy straightened again, struck a pose, one hand on his hip. "What was his motive?"

Troy frowned. "Motive? I . . . well . . . I imagine Sam, um, bumped into him in the attics while he was searching out a new spot to shoot the gazebo scene, since the gazebo's under water. Ghosts don't like to be disturbed, you know. When I played in *Teen Screamfest Twelve*—a small part, but memorable; I was the second Chess Club member—I met my end when I opened the wrong door and disturbed the ghost. Bam! Ax straight through my head. You saw me in *Screamfest*? The flick was a bomb, but I got noticed, let me tell you."

"I'll bet you did. And look at you now. A real star," Maggie said, squeezing her folded hands until her knuckles turned white as she forced herself to look serious. Interested. "But that was a movie, Troy, remember? I don't think ghosts actually kill people. Actually, I don't believe in ghosts. So, a ghost killed you in that movie?"

Troy frowned. "Gosh, now I'm not so sure. Maybe it was a mummy?" He spread his hands, shrugged. "Well, that's one more down. This isn't as easy as I thought. No script, you know? I'm great with scripts. My phonographic memory."

"Photographic," Maggie corrected, but quietly, because the guy's train of thought was already half off the rails and she didn't want to lose him completely. Just as quietly, she made another mental note for his character in her next book: blond, dandy, brick-stupid, speaks like Mrs. Malaprop. Oh, she was going to have fun with this character—and how great was it that, even with Sam dead in the morning room, she was feeling the urge to write.

"So that's two down, huh? But, hey, you're the writer. Help me out here. Who else have we got?"

"Just look around, Troy," Maggie told him, also looking around the room, counting heads. One little, two little, three little Indians. "Why don't we two try to narrow down the numbers? Let's deduct you, me, Alex, both Sterlings. Tabby and Bernie, of course."

Troy narrowed his eyelids as he looked at her. "That was quick. All your friends. And you included me, just to trick me into agreeing with you." Picking up his sword cane, which had been propped against a chair, he looked down his nose at Maggie, once more playing Saint Just. "Oh, I don't think so, madam. Everyone is a suspect. Every last damn gleeking, dizzy-eyed scallion!"

"Scullion," Maggie corrected numbly. "You mean scullion. A scallion is a kind of onion."

"Whatever." Troy tucked the cane under his arm, turned away from her, then clapped his hands to call the occupants of the room to attention. "Now hear this! Sam Undercuffler is dead, murdered. He did *not* kill himself. Murdered, ladies and gentlemen, and everyone in this room is a suspect. *Everyone*! So . . . so . . . *so nobody leaves town*!"

Everyone began talking at once, denying their own guilt, then the sudden noise subsided as everyone began looking at everyone else with suspicion. Great. Now they had a room full of people who were suddenly afraid of each other.

"Wine?" Alex said, handing Maggie a glass.

"What, no hemlock, to put us both out of our misery?" She took the glass, downed half its contents in one gulp. "Did you hear that idiot?" she asked. "Nobody leaves town? But, hey, don't worry, be happy, at least Uncle Willis and yours truly are off the hook as suspects."

"You said 'yours truly' because you don't know if the proper pronoun is 'I' or 'me,' didn't you, my dear?"

"Sometimes I really hate how well you know me," Maggie said, allowing him to distract her because she knew him well enough to know that's what he was doing. Unfortunately, in this case, his attempt didn't work for more than five seconds. "Oh, God, Alex, you'd better keep to your promise about solving Sam's murder before dawn because, to paraphrase Will Shakespeare, this is going to be one flap-eared, boil-brained, *long* night."

# Chapter Ten

"Saint Just? A word, if you don't mind?"

"Certainly, Sterling," Saint Just said, patting the empty seat beside him in the study, where he had retired for a space, to cerebrate. "You know I am always interested in whatever you might have to say to me."

Sterling bowed his head and studied his folded hands. "Perhaps not this time. But I promised Perry. Saint Just? Do you think Uncle Willis might have taken all of the cell phones?"

Saint Just eyed his friend carefully. "What do you think, Sterling?"

Appearing to be caught between nervous disbelief and equally nervous apprehension, Sterling shook his head. "I don't know. I don't think I really believe in ghosts. Specters. All of that. But Perry was adamant, telling me all about his childhood home in a place called South Dakota. His family had a ghost, in their barn."

"Really? Did Perry see this ghost?"

"No, he never did. But he heard him, more than once, as a child. Several times. Moaning, groaning, and then some hay would sort of *sift* down from the loft above his head and he'd run off."

"Perhaps someone was *in* the loft, Sterling. Someone *real*, that is. Did Perry consider that possibility?"

"Oh, yes, he did. In point of fact, one time he saw his sister and her friend leaving the barn some minutes after he'd heard the ghost, but they told him they hadn't heard anything."

Saint Just smiled, happy for the diversion from all his heavy thinking about the method of Sam Undercuffler's messy demise and what, if anything, to do with the quite workable cell phone in his pocket. "His older sister, I imagine. And her male friend?"

"He didn't say," Sterling said, frowning. "Shall I go ask him?"

"No. No need. But I shouldn't worry overmuch about your friend Perry's experiences with ghosts if I were you. Mr. Undercuffler's murderer is very much a living, breathing person. I'm quite convinced of that."

"Working in league with Uncle Willis?"

"No, I don't think so. I doubt ghosts, if they exist, take on worldly partners in crime. But since you're here, why don't you tell me more about your experience in the attics. Did you hear any other noises, other than the bats, that is?"

Saint Just realized at that moment, or possibly at the moment Joanne had asked him about his cell phone, precisely why he hadn't offered the thing to her. He dearly wished to solve this crime himself, without interference from the local constabulary. Selfish, perhaps, but very much in his nature. Back in Manhattan, the good *left*-tenant was always so dreadfully in the way. Helpful, occasionally, but still—Saint Just, not Steve Wendell, was the hero.

"Sterling? Was the question difficult? Shall I rephrase it?"

Sterling scratched his head. "No, I don't think so. I'm just attempting to be thorough. What did we hear? Not much, if anything, in the first wing we searched. Nothing much there but small empty rooms, probably once the servant quarters. Sir Rudy has only daily help, from the village. I asked him. The attics over our wing? Above our bedchambers? Those are more open, Saint Just, with only a few divisions. There is a multitude of old furniture, much of it under dust sheets. I admit to being quite nervous in those attics. And then the bats, of course. That's where we heard the squeaking."

Saint Just considered all of this information for several moments. "The bats. Yes. About the bats, Sterling. So you didn't hear or see any in the other wing of attics?"

"No, I don't think so. And we were there a long time, poking about. Not so long in the attics above our chambers. Not more than a minute, to be truthful about the thing. Are the bats important, Saint Just?"

"I'm not sure, Sterling. I'm merely collecting information." He got to his feet. "I'm assuming everyone is now congregated once more in the main saloon?"

"I think so, yes. We all went upstairs in pairs, to gather more clothing and some blankets. I'm sure we'll be cozy enough, all of us together, although I'm fearful we won't be quite that jolly a gathering. Shall I go upstairs with you, Saint Just? You really shouldn't be alone, not with a murderer in the house."

"I think I might manage, thank you anyway, Sterling," Saint Just said, picking up one of the oil lanterns Sir Rudy had brought from the pantry. Thanks to the many flashlights—torches, according to Sir Rudy—the oil lanterns, and a multitude of candles, Medwine Manor was fairly well lit; a consequence of frequent loss of both power and the cellar generators.

"Very well, Saint Just," Sterling said, picking up his own lantern. "But I'll walk with you as far as the stairs outside the main saloon, if you don't mind. I know ghosts don't exist. A part of me knows that. But the other part of me wouldn't mind some company."

Maggie met them in the hallway, having just descended the stairs, dressed in slacks and a heavy sweater, and dragging two pillows and a satin comforter along with her.

"You went upstairs alone?" Saint Just asked her, taking the comforter from her.

"You sent me upstairs alone earlier, remember? What I could do once I could do twice." She looked at the closed doors to the main saloon. "Do we really have to go back in there? Joanne's cracking the whip, and it isn't pretty."

"Cracking the—oh," Sterling said, his cheeks flushing an embarrassed pink. "You meant that figuratively, didn't you, Maggie? Although, with Miss Pertuccelli, anything seems possible. So sorry."

"You don't like her, Sterling?" Maggie asked. "You like everybody."

Sterling looked behind him, as if to be sure no one would overhear, then said, "Perry has told me a few not-very-nice stories about the woman. She's, um, she's quite the taskmaster. And she hangs things over people's heads, and demands favors, and would be unkind to her own mother to save a penny. That is, so Perry told me. Although he didn't say 'unkind.' I can't repeat what he said, not in front of you, Maggie."

Saint Just and Maggie exchanged smiles before he asked her exactly how Joanne was cracking the whip.

"She's making them all run lines," Maggie told him. "Rehearsing. She said that as long as everyone's staying awake all night, there's no reason not to work. And you know, in a way, she's probably got a good idea. If they're working, they can't be speculating about the murderer, getting themselves all bent out of shape."

"Bent out of—I'm doing it again, aren't I?" Sterling

asked. "Sorry. But for a moment, all I could think was how uncomfortable that might be and—do go on."

Saint Just took pity on the man. "Sterling? Why don't we go inside, all together, to protect each other, and warm our hands at the fire? It's getting quite chilly here in the hallway."

"Oh, yes, good idea, Saint Just. Capital. Warmer inside. Safer, too, as nobody would think to murder anyone with all of us watching."

"He's really scared, isn't he?" Maggie asked Saint Just quietly as Sterling opened the doors and walked inside. "Poor guy. I don't think he's gotten over being kidnapped, not that I blame him. He's much more used to being on the sidelines than in the action."

"I agree. He told me after the incident that he was going to make a valiant attempt to never be a hero again, and I believe we should grant him that wish." Saint Just extended an arm toward the main saloon. "Shall we?"

"Only if you stick close and tell me if you've come up with any great ideas in the past half hour. Because I haven't."

"So sorry to disappoint, but no, I've yet to be brilliant, I'm afraid. Oh dear, look at this sad clutch of hens and cocks. I thought they were rehearsing."

"If they're rehearsing a staring match, they are," Maggie said, heading for the refreshment table, which was the only area of the large room that wasn't occupied with unhappy-looking people. Besides, their friends were there, munching on peach pie. "Tabby, Bernie. What's up?"

"My temperature, I think," Bernie said around a mouthful of pie. "But Tabby made me some tea. I'm trying to convince her it'd be better if she'd let me pour some brandy in it."

"She's only saying that to upset everyone," Tabby said, sighing theatrically. "She won't really do it. She's come too far to falter now, haven't you, Bernie?"

"Only if you shut up, Twinkletoes," Bernie said, looking past Saint Just. "Oh, brother, here we go again. I don't know who our murderer is, but he killed the wrong guy. Can't somebody put a muzzle on the dumb blond joke over there?"

Saint Just turned around to see Troy, still in his Regency costume—the only one who was, which made him look dashed silly, actually—standing in the center of the room, the sword cane clutched in his hands.

Saint Just blinked, looked again. Hmmm. Interesting. And perhaps helpful at some point? One never knew when serendipity could be twisted about, worked to one's own advantage.

"Has the Troy Toy been a bad boy in my absence, Bernie?" he asked.

"You mean a stupid boy, Alex. I'm an editor. I know which is the right word, the more descriptive word. 'Bad' is too vague. 'Stupid'? Perfect choice. Simple, yet effective. He went from person to person a few minutes ago, demanding each tell him where they were all day. Gave us all sheets of paper to write down the details. Evan ripped the paper in half right in front of him. I could like that guy if he wasn't such a prick. Sorry, pardon my French, Sterling."

Sterling, who had joined them, blushed and nodded, then took himself off to sit beside Perry on one of the couches.

"So nobody gave Troy a listing of their activities?" Maggie asked. "Bummer. That actually could have helped. Except that I was pretty much alone for a good part of the morning, so I don't have much of an alibi."

"True, but you weren't alone for the entire day," Saint Just reminded her, earning himself a quick, sharp nudge in the ribs from her talented elbow. "But what is he up to now?"

As if to answer Saint Just, Troy tucked the sword cane under his arm and clapped his hands three times. "Once more, people. If you won't write down what I've asked you to write down, which was what you were doing all day, if you'll remember, then we'll just go around the room and, when I point to you with this cane, you'll tell me what you were doing. Understand?"

Joanne Pertuccelli stood up and grabbed the sword cane, which Troy had begun to wave about his head. "I told you before, Troy, knock it the hell off. You aren't Charlie Chan. Nikki! Get over here, and bring those scripts." She glared at Troy, then let go of the sword cane when it appeared that if she didn't, Troy was willing to play tug-of-war with it. "Page forty-seven, Troy. And remember, the word is 'perambulate,' not 'percolate.' Armand! Time the scene."

"Time your own damn scene," Arnaud said in his strangely thin, high voice. "I quit. This project is cursed, anybody knows that. Jinxed. First the flood, then Sam goes and gets himself killed. It can only get worse, not better, and I'm bailing as soon as I can phone my agent. I'm not working on a jinxed project."

Sterling turned around on the couch to look, wide-eyed, at Saint Just, who simply shook his head and smiled, hoping to allay his friend's fears.

"That's it," Maggie said suddenly, turning her back to the room as she spoke quietly out of the side of her mouth. "Alex, that's it. That's what was wrong about her. Joanne's missing her stopwatch. She's always got it around her neck. Always touching it, the way you touch your quizzing glass. Talisman. Good luck charm. Worry stone. Whatever. But it's not there."

Saint Just fingered the grosgrain ribbon on his quizzing glass. "Very observant of you, Maggie. I hadn't noticed.

However, now that I have, and when I consider what the missing stopwatch might mean, I believe you and I need to view the body."

Maggie stiffened next to him. "You want to run that one by me again?" she asked as Joanne and Arnaud descended into a screaming match that lent nothing to the atmosphere save a covering noise so that he and Maggie could speak without being overheard. "No, never mind, I got it. You expect me to go with you to look at Sam's body? Thanks, but no thanks. I'm going to be way too busy twiddling my thumbs or something. Nope. Not me. Not going there. I gave you the clue; you run with it."

"Ah, but there's something I neglected to tell you earlier, my dear," Saint Just said smoothly. "You being a woman. Squeamish and all."

"Squeamish?" Maggie turned around, grabbed him by the elbow. "I'll show you squeamish. And don't think I don't know you're manipulating me, because I do. But come on, let's get on with it. We both know I was going to go."

How he adored this woman. "If you insist," he said, then bowed to the ladies and begged their leave before he and Maggie headed out into the hallway once more and off to the morning room.

Maggie matched him pace for pace, until they got to the closed door to the morning room, at which time she put on the brakes with a vengance. "Tell me what I'm going to see. You did dress him again, didn't you? I mean, I see bodies on autopsy tables all the time on *CSI*, but I know they're plastic. The actor reaches into the body and pulls out the heart, no big deal. Plastic and rubber and fake blood. I can handle that. This is the real thing."

"Maggie, I didn't scour the kitchens for a sharp knife and make a Y-cut in the man's chest," Saint Just said, amused. "And Undercuffler is covered most modestly, above and below, with quite lovely tablecloths Sir Rudy sacrificed to the cause. Although I doubt Undercuffler is too worried about his modesty."

Maggie took a deep breath, let it out slowly. "Okay. Okay, okay. Let's do this."

"That's my girl. Pluck to the backbone," Saint Just said, extracting a key from his pocket and inserting it in the lock. "We wouldn't want Undercuffler to get up and wander away, would we?" he asked, pushing open the door.

"Very funny. You're a real barrel of laughs," Maggie said, holding up her oil lantern as Saint Just did the same.

They entered slowly, just as lightning flashed outside the windows, lighting up the room—and the body—for a few seconds before thunder crashed overhead. "Oh, great, that's just what I needed—special effects. And yup, there he is. How about I stay over here, and you just tell me what you think I should see?"

"Two reasons, my dear, the first being that I wasn't quite sure I saw what I saw the first time I looked. But by now, postmortem bruising may have helped define what I saw."

"So now it's postmortem bruising. Who the hell do you think you are, Alex? A forensic scientist or something? You watch television, that's all."

"And I read books, as a true devotee should always seek to increase his knowledge," he said, putting a hand on her elbow and guiding her closer to the table, which was easily accessible now that all of the chairs had been lined up against the walls. "Some marks on a body become more intense after death. Please don't ask me to explain why, but I do believe I could incorporate some of the more elementary conclusions in our future stories, as a body is a body, no matter in which century death occurred, yes? I should like us to be more technical in future. Expand my horizons, as it were."

"Captialize on the current forensics rage to increase readership, you mean, don't you?"

"Yes. That, too. Am I so transparent?"

"I'm not even going to answer that. But it's a good idea, actually. Okay, we're here. Sam's here. Show me what you want to show me so we can make like shepherds and get the flock outta here."

"Charming." Saint Just retrieved a pair of bright yellow rubber gloves from the tabletop and put them on. "Marylou offered them to both Arnaud and myself, having found them in the kitchens. Good girl, Marylou. Always eager to help."

"You look ridiculous," Maggie said, shaking her head. "Like you don't want dishpan hands. I wouldn't be caught dead in those things."

"Really? In that case, would you be so kind as to put your bare hands under each side of Undercuffler's jaws and help me lift back his head?"

"Yeah. That's going to happen. And you've made your point. Go ahead. Show off. And then let's get out of here. This is really creepy, as if you don't already know that."

Saint Just walked to the short end of the table and grabbed hold of Undercuffler's jaw, lifting the head up and back only with considerable effort. The body was very cold, cold enough for Saint Just to feel that cold through the gloves. "He moves even less easily now. Hmmm. Now, if you'll hold up the oil lantern, please, and take a close look at our friend's throat?"

"Oh, God." Maggie stepped closer, lifted the lantern just as another round of lightning and thunder added their bit to the scene. "What am I supposed to be looking at? I can see the bruising where the rope bit into his neck. Even ripped the skin. And some—are those scratches?—that are vertical, not horizontal. Wow. That had to hurt."

"I'm convinced it did, yes. Now look higher, to the very

top of his throat, at the back of the chin. Do you see more bruising?"

Maggie glared at Saint Just for a moment, then stepped closer, looked. "Yes. Wow, Alex, there's a second bruise. Not as bad, but it's there. Wider, a little bumpy—like it hit harder in places. How did that get there?"

Saint Just lowered Undercuffler's head and stepped away from the body. "The drapery cord—braided silk—was softer. And the second bruise was much higher on the throat, much in the way it would be if someone were hanging from a makeshift noose. I have the length of drapery cord that was around his neck here somewhere, and I believe if I were to now compare it to the two different lines of bruising, it would fit the second one. The postmortem one, as it were."

"I'll take your word for that," Maggie said. "So what caused the first one? And, yes, I think I already know where this is going. But I still want to hear you say it."

"Very well. The other line of bruising, the thinner line, the cut skin, is much lower, actually a fairly straight line across the Adam's apple, indeed, around the entire neck. Not at all the sort of line you'd expect from a noose. Now, as you say you already know, what does that tell us?"

Maggie walked over to the line of chairs, sat down. "Okay, I'll play. We'll start slow, since you seem to want to build the suspense, although I have to tell you, being your straight man isn't all it's cracked up to be. I'm going to be nicer to Sterling in your next book."

"Maggie? Please stay on point, if you will."

"Bite me. All right, all right. It tells us, oh, great and learned Saint Just, how Sam died. He was strangled. Choked with something. Something thinner than the drapery cord. Gee," she said, rolling her eyes theatrically, "I wonder what it was. Oh, and wrapped around his neck with a lot of force, too, right? No woman did that."

"Thank you. I concur. Undercuffler was most likely surprised from behind, as someone looped the murder weapon over his head and *pulled*. Twisted. Undercuffler had to have put up a struggle, but to no avail. It's difficult to struggle for long when one's airway is being impeded. Still, the exercise had to have taken considerable time, at least three to five minutes, as this was not your typical garrote, where a knot is placed in the weapon and pressed against the Adam's apple—or two knots are placed along the length to correspond with the carotids—either ploy considerably shortening the exercise. No, not a quick or pleasant death, Maggie, but definitely a determined murderer."

"I don't know if I'm glad or disgusted that we both know so much about this stuff." Maggie sat back, folded her arms, rather hugged herself. "I don't like doing this, but okay, let's imagine it. The killer sneaks up behind Sam, throwing the rope, string, whatever—since you're still holding onto the punchline—over his head, twists, pulls back hard. Sam is surprised. Shocked. Scared. He reaches up with both hands, scratches at his skin trying to get the rope off. But the other guy is stronger. Sam kicks, flails, is maybe even lifted off his feet—that's a deep cut in his neck."

"Yes. Undercuffler can't cry out, but he can make noise. We've a rather full house here, so somebody could have heard him. Unless, of course, he was in the attics at the time of death."

"Right up above my head," Maggie said. "Except I wasn't there until after four o'clock or so because I stayed with Bernie all afternoon, and then I was playing music pretty loudly, and then you came in and—okay, okay, so nobody heard him. I'll buy that theory. Keep going."

"Sterling and Perry heard bats," Saint Just said. "But I don't think that means anything, unless what they actually heard was the squeaking of hinges as the murderer returned to the scene of the crime and opened a window in preparation of hanging Undercuffler outside on the scaffold. That's all you would have heard, Maggie, as the murder itself had to have taken place much earlier, perhaps shortly after you two argued. Other than the murderer, you may have been the last person to see the fellow alive, in point of fact. In any event, I believe we may consider Sterling's fear of bats a lucky escape, if the murderer was busy with Undercuffler's body at the time."

"Oh, man, don't tell Sterling. But that would explain the bats, too, wouldn't it? It was already dark. A couple could have flown in the open window. If the killer left it open, that is. Do bats fly in the rain? Birds don't, I don't think. So I don't think we can be sure about the bats." She slapped her hands on her thighs and stood up. "Okay, upstairs, right? We have to check out the attics."

"And discover, as we search, Joanne's stopwatch?"

Maggie sat down again. "And there it is, the punchline. I almost forgot that part. You're saying the cord on her stopwatch was the murder weapon? But Joanne isn't strong enough to keep the cord tight around Sam's throat long enough to kill him. Is she?"

"I doubt that highly," Saint Just agreed, stripping off the yellow gloves and placing them back on the tabletop. "Which does not, however, explain why she is no longer wearing said stopwatch, does it?"

Maggie stood up once more. "She probably has a reasonable explanation. Hell, I would. Maybe the same person who took our cell phones also took her stopwatch. Although I wouldn't know why he would. Besides, I don't think the cell phones were taken until *after* Sam was dead. That screams crime of passion and a clumsy cleanup and follow-up, neither of which can *hold* up for long, and the killer—killers—have to know that. This isn't getting any clearer, Alex, and if that flood out there starts receding, we're also running out of time."

Saint Just felt a pang of guilt over keeping secret the fact that he still possessed his cell phone. But that pang both came and left quickly. "Yes, I know. But perhaps a visit to the attics will make everything clearer. Shall we?"

"Since I don't see any way out of it, sure," Maggie said, leading the way back out of the morning room, then turning left.

"Where are you going?"

"The servant stairs are at the end of the hall on our floor, so it has to be the same on this one. I saw Sterling and Perry heading that way earlier. Sterling was carrying a butterfly net. Somehow that's not so funny now as it was then."

"I agree. But I believe we might check on the others before continuing our investigation. Just to know that everyone is where they should be?"

"Going to count noses are you? Sounds like a plan," Maggie said, following him.

As they neared the main staircase, Evan Pottinger stepped out from the main saloon. "Going somewhere? If it's anywhere but in there," he said, hooking a thumb over his shoulder to indicate the large chamber behind him, "I think I'd like to tag along."

Saint Just considered this. Perhaps the man was truly bored with the company in the main saloon, or perhaps he was interested in what was happening outside the main saloon. After all, what did anyone know about Evan Pottinger, save that he was an annoying person who thought very highly of his acting skills. "We're going to investigate the attics at the spot where Undercuffler was lowered from the window."

"Oh. Someone said there's bats up there." Evan shrugged. "There's bats down here, come to think of it. Okay, I'm game, I'll go."

Maggie led the way up the stairs, holding one oil lantern, while Saint Just brought up the rear with the other.

"Is Troy still trying to get everyone to tell him where they've been all day?" Maggie asked as they paused on the landing.

"He was, but everyone ignored him. Just the way everyone's ignoring Joanne and her insane idea that we should forget there's a murderer among us and get in some rehearsing. Somebody has to remind me why I slept with the bitch to get this part. I could play rings around Troy as Saint Just."

"I believe you could, yes," Saint Just said as they made their way along the landing and into the unrenovated wing of the building. "You actually made love with the woman?"

"Made love? Buddy, nobody makes love where I come from. Sex is a commodity, and we buy it and sell it and lend it and borrow on it. Joanne was offering a part, I needed the work—there's the couch, try not to take longer than ten minutes, and don't mess my hair. I figured I'd be doing stud duty for the whole shoot, but she cut me off the minute we got here. She's banging somebody, though. She always is."

Saint Just stopped at the door that opened onto the servant stairs. "And who do you suppose that someone might be, Evan?"

"I dunno. Could be anybody. Well, not anybody. I overheard her yesterday arguing with somebody—unless she was talking to herself. Didn't see either one of them, though, as I was on my way upstairs and I'm not sure where the voices were coming from—the way sounds bounce off the high ceilings and all this marble, you know? Joanne should have thought of that. The soundman's going to have fits with the echos in here. Anyway, Joanne was having a cow about bringing her diaphragm through customs for no reason, and he'd damn well better keep his pants zipped unless he was unzipping them for her."

"Thank you," Saint Just said, very much aware that Maggie had heard every word. "I think we now have a general understanding of Miss Pertuccelli."

"Your ears are red, Mr. Urbane," Maggie teased, slipping past him up the stairs. Once at the top, she bent down, picked up the butterfly net. "Sterling and Perry must have left the attics in a hurry."

"The bat. Or bats," Saint Just said, holding up the oil lantern and looking toward the many-eaved ceilings of the quite wide, yet more-than-twice-as-long attics. "None here. Shall we push on?"

Evan Pottinger stepped past Saint Just, wiping at a cobweb that had gotten caught in his hair. "This is where Sam thought we could do the bit where I kill the servant girl? The crew would have a hell of a time lighting the scene." He turned to Maggie. "I used to work lights. Sound, too. Played stunt double a couple of times, did anything I could, until I got my first part. But I can tell you, there's no way we could film up here, not on our budget."

"And Undercuffler would have known that almost immediately?" Saint Just asked. "He would have known that with only a cursory examination from, shall we say, right here?"

"He should have. One look's enough. So, where's the window someone hung him out of?"

Saint Just pointed away into the darkness. "According to my rude calculations, Maggie's bedchamber windows are some sixty of my usual walking paces that way."

Evan shook his head. "Nope. No reason for Sam to go all that way. There's not even any lightbulbs up here. No electricity. So why would he stick around?"

"He heard something?" Maggie suggested, hanging onto

Saint Just's sleeve. "He heard something, or saw something, and went to investigate? It's not a clear shot from here to the end of the wing. I mean, I can't see that far, but I think there are a couple of rooms up here."

"That's a couple more than I want to see," Evan said, heading for the stairs once more. "Have fun, don't take any wooden bats. Ha! Wooden bats—get it?"

"You don't have a lantern, Evan," Maggie reminded him. "Besides, aren't you afraid of being alone, with a killer in the house?"

Saint Just watched the man's expression closely, then mentally scratched the fellow off his list of suspects as Evan's complexion paled slightly. Hardly the hero all of a sudden, and most definitely not the villain. "You'll be staying with us?"

"If you don't mind, yeah, I will. Not that I'm afraid. But I'm not stupid, either. Then again, I'm also not Lord Hervey. He'd be too bored to care, right? Believe me, I'm not bored. I'm just me right now, Evan Pottinger, a man intending to stay very much alive, thank you. Okay, what are we looking for, exactly?"

"Clues, dear man. Clues. Maggie, why don't you hand Evan your lantern while you stick close as mustard plaster to me as we initiate our search. Oh, and although I'm convinced you and I have come to the same conclusion, allow me to say that Evan here is of no worry to us."

"I was wondering if you picked up on that," Maggie said, handing over the lantern. "Here you go, Evan. Welcome to the wonderful world of amateur sleuthing. Look high, look low, don't touch anything, and give a yell if you see anything you shouldn't see."

"Like what?" Evan asked, starting off toward the left side of the attics, while Saint Just and Maggie kept to the right side, under the eaves.

"If we knew that, my good man, our search would be infinitely easier," Saint Just said, counting off steps as they passed by each low, dirty-paned dormer window.

The sound of the rain was much louder up here, and there were puddles here and there where the old roof had failed to hold back the water. A smell of damp was everywhere, the few bits and pieces of dust-sheeted furniture made more obvious, and more ominous, each time the lightning flashed.

"You notice something, Alex?" Maggie asked, speaking quietly as she pointed to the floor.

"Yes, I have. No footprints in the dust after those first few, which could have been from Sterling and Perry's aborted visit. None of the puddles disturbed. Don't mention either to Evan, if you please. I think the man is close to making a cake of himself as it is."

"Yeah, if he was method acting now," Maggie whispered, "he'd be dressed as the Cowardly Lion."

"I beg your pardon?" There were times, too many times, when Saint Just became aware that his knowledge of the modern world, although growing each day, was at times still lamentably lacking in scope.

"Never mind. Are you still counting?"

At forty-two paces, the rooms began on either side of the attic. Each had its own door, and each door was closed, including that of the second room on the right.

"This is it?" Maggie asked, pointing to the door.

"I believe so. Evan? We could use an extra lantern over here. Ah, that's better. Shall we?"

Maggie motioned for Saint Just to go first, and he did so, holding the lantern high as he stepped into the room, then quickly ducked as several bats flew past him out into the main attic.

"Oh, cripes. Oh boy. Oh—*oh!*"

"It's all right, Evan," Maggie said. Of course, she said

that as she wrapped herself around Saint Just, all but cutting off his respirations.

"I'm so very fortunate to have two such stalwart assistants," Saint Just said, peeling Maggie off him. "The chamber is larger than I'd supposed. What do you say we inspect the area outside this window, and then shut said window?"

"Good plan," Maggie said, still holding onto him as, together, they sort of shuffled across the floor toward the window. "Really good plan. Except, how will the bats get back out again?"

"That, I believe, is a dilemma we'll leave for Sir Rudy," Saint Just said, holding his lantern out over the scaffolding. "Ah."

"Ah, what?" Maggie asked from behind him, her head pushed into his back. "Ah, I see? Ah, there's the scaffolding? Ah, the murderer left a clue? What *ah*?"

"Ah, it's still raining, actually," Saint Just said, stepping back and winding the casement window shut, noting the squealing sound made by the old, unoiled hinges. Yes, Sterling and Perry may have had a lucky escape.

He pulled a handkerchief from his pocket and wiped his wet face. "Other than that, all I see is the remainder of the drapery cord blowing in the wind. We cut it from below, you understand, Arnaud and I. However, this does establish as fact that Undercuffler was hung from this room, and that he very possibly was killed here as well."

"Right, Sherlock," Maggie said quietly. "Now tell me how Sam and his killer *got* here."

# Chapter Eleven

Maggie figured she jumped, oh, a good three feet in the air when Sir Rudy said from the doorway to the attic room: "Hullo, everyone! Find anything interesting?"

"Nothing yet, Sir Rudy," Alex said, squeezing his fingers lightly around Maggie's upper arm. Like she needed the warning?

"What brings you climbing up to the attics, Sir Rudy?" Maggie asked, before Alex could—because she was positive that would have been his next line.

"Me? Oh, nothing. I was just nosing about as head of the household, making sure everything was right and tight, and saw the door open to the stairway. Made me remember the leaks. I'd forgot them, you see. Mrs. Wimbles and the girls usually take charge. We've got the other wing all fixed—cost the earth, roofs—but I had my worries about this wing. So. Why are you all up here?"

"Good question, Sir Rudy. We're investigating," Evan said, lifting one corner of a dust sheet off a large chest, then dropping it just as quickly. "The murderer hung Sam out that window over there. Did you know that?"

Sir Rudy went up on tiptoe, sort of leaned in the direction of the window. He did not, however, step farther into the room. "That so? Interesting bit of happenstance, wouldn't you say? You see, I've been hacking about in the history of the family, you know, since the last of the brood cocked up her toes a year ago—ninety, they say she was, but she was ninety-five if she was a day—leaving this entire pile open for my purchase. I'll bet she's spinning in her casket out back in the mausoleum, poor old biddy, to think someone in trade is walking these halls now, sleeping in her bed, eating fish and chips off her fancy china. Still, I used to help my Da with the landscaping around here as a boy. Makes me very sentimental about the place, so maybe that's all right with her."

"I'm convinced the dear lady is resting comfortably knowing that you are restoring her family home to its former glory. Although," Alex added, "the change of name may ameliorate some of that joy."

"Yes, well, I'm Sir Rudy now, and it's no wonder I wanted to put my stamp on the place. Besides, Medwine Manor has a certain . . . ring to it, don't you think? At any rate, it would be a shame to just heartlessly evict them, all those hatchet-faced portraits and such. Thought I'd sort of adopt them, take them as my own, seeing as how all the family I've got is m'brother, Henry, who emigrated to Australia to marry a bassoonist with the Sydney Opera, if you can believe that. Oh, and there's Byrd, of course. He'd gone off with Henry for some months, but that didn't work out, so now I've got him again, right down to his quarterly allowance."

"You don't sound all that choked up about that, do you, Sir Rudy?" Maggie asked, remembering the not-exactly-warm greeting Byrd had received from his uncle. "You two don't get along?"

"Occasionally we do. Runs hot and cold, my nephew does. Sort of jumped-up, thinking how he'll one day have all my money. Bigger than his britches, as you Americans say. Doesn't even seem to remember I threw him out last time he was here, my heir or no, telling him he'd not be welcome anymore. At least, not until he owned up to the missing silver candlesticks in the dining room."

"He *stole* from you?" Maggie asked. "I wouldn't have let him back in, either. Not unless he crawled here from London on his hands and knees. Maybe over broken glass."

"Yes, yes, thank you, Maggie," Alex cut in. "We are all aware of your more bloodthirsty inclinations, along with your tendency to believe a punishment should outstrip the crime by at least double."

"Only when I'm feeling magnanimous," Maggie corrected. "My favorite is more a three-to-one retribution. I'm not proud of that, but I'm not giving it up, either."

"As we also all well know. But, if we may be allowed to get back to the point? We seem to have been drifting, haven't we? Sir Rudy, you appeared to be slightly amused to hear that Mr. Undercuffler was hanged in this room. Is there a reason for that?"

Sir Rudy nodded furiously. "Oh, right. Lost my train of thought there for a moment, didn't I? Very well. I've been reading all those dry histories in the study, getting to know my new relatives, as it were. Anyway, I'm certain that this is the very same room where they found Uncle Willis. Our resident ghost, although I've yet to hear him scream or make anything go bump in the night. This was his bedchamber, you understand. Banished, he was, to the attics, for a nasty thing he'd done. At least, that's the story. Hanged himself, too. Odd that, don't you think? I wonder if I'll have two ghosts now? That could be confusing."

Everyone looked up. "He hanged himself here? Where?" Maggie asked. "There aren't any open beams or anything."

"Oh?" Sir Rudy rubbed at his chin. "Probably some

chandelier that's long gone. Couldn't have been jolly, being stuck up here. Not even a fireplace. Just some holes somewhere in the floor, some pipes that lead off one of the main chimneys, or so I was told. Pretty modern for the seventeen hundreds. Some little trick conjured up by the fellow who added this wing. He's the one who did most of the prettying up around the place. But nothing I'd like, as the heat couldn't have been that strong, although I imagine the smoke made up for that. Well, I believe I'll push off to the kitchens and find some pots to catch that rainwater in, or it'll be down to the next floor, putting paid to the plaster."

Maggie waved weakly as Sir Rudy left the room, followed by Evan Pottinger, who said he'd had enough of attics, then turned on Alex. "Sir Rudy sure does like the sound of his own voice, doesn't he? But did you hear that? *Two* hanged men in the same room, even centuries apart? Well, Alex, I'm waiting. Tell me that's a coincidence."

"Coincidence? Possibly. Or inspiration," Alex said, bending over to right an overturned chair. "Would you call this a sign of a struggle?"

"Maybe. Or a messy attic." Maggie held her own lantern high and turned in a circle. "This is pretty big for an attic room, although this whole place is fairly immense. And cold. And damp. No central heat back in those days. No fireplace in here. Uncle Willis must have been a very bad boy. I wonder what he did. Oh, look, wallpaper. What there is left of it." She touched the wall. "I think it might have been red, once upon a time."

"And from that you conclude?" Alex asked, poking about in one of the corners of the room.

"Not a lot, sorry. Just that, maybe, once upon a time, this room wasn't all that bad. Wallpaper. Maybe a chandelier. But still the attic. And did you notice the size of the lock on that door? Maybe Uncle Willis was off his trolley, and they stashed him up here. People used to do that with mentally ill relatives because the madhouses were pretty awful. Then there's *Jane Eyre*, and Mr. Rochester's wife—that was later, and fiction, but still? Do you think we should go read up on Uncle Willis?"

Alex straightened, began looking around the entire room again. "Not unless you and the Troy Toy wish to join forces on the theory Uncle Willis murdered Undercuffler."

Maggie stuck her tongue out at him. "Thanks, but no thanks. I guess I was just curious. Doesn't the whole coincidence thing make you curious?"

Alex paused in his inspection of the large chest Evan had looked at earlier and turned to her. "Yes, yes, I thought I'd noticed that when Pottinger moved the dust sheet. Hmmm."

"Noticed what? And you didn't answer my question."

"Oh, very well. Indeed, people are curious about ghosts, black-sheep relatives, all that sort of thing, aren't they? And with Sir Rudy so proud of and eager to share his knowledge about his newly acquired heritage. And all those histories he talks about. Maggie? How long has everyone else been here?"

"I don't know. A couple of days? Maybe five? And it's been raining for, like, three or four of them. Definitely long enough to get bored enough to maybe pick up one of those histories, read about Uncle Willis. Okay, I give up. Where is this going?"

"Nowhere that I can think of at the moment, I'm afraid. In fact, all it does is enlarge the number of suspects. If only Sir Rudy and, possibly, his nephew knew about Uncle Willis, this room, the method of the man's demise. But we've just proven that it's possible everyone knew."

"Gee, thanks. That helped. What are you looking for? What did you see?"

Alex dropped the dust sheet back over the chest, and wiped his hands together. "Dusty, dusty. Of course, we've all been tramping about in here, so there's no helpful trail of footprints to follow."

"Yeah, yeah, yeah. What did you see?"

He lowered the lantern to the floor. "This."

Maggie stepped closer, peered down at the floor. There were drag marks in front of the legs of the chest, for only an inch or two, in the dust. "Somebody tried to move this chest?"

"And gave it up as a bad job, yes. Lovely old piece, and quite heavy, I imagine. Would you care to give it a go?"

"Not in this lifetime. Besides, there's an easier way." Maggie dropped to her knees, pushed her hair behind her ears, and leaned forward until her cheek touched the floor, then peered under the chest. "Move the lanterns a little closer . . . yeah, good. I can't see . . . wait a minute, I may see something."

Still with her cheek against the floor—and convinced Saint Just was having himself a high old time watching as her backside stuck up in the air—she held out her arm, snapped her fingers. "Get me something I can slide under here. Where's your cane?"

"Interesting question. But we'll leave that for the moment, even as I tell you that the cane is downstairs, in the main saloon. How about this?"

Maggie felt something against her palm and closed her hand over it. "What's this? What did you give me?"

"I can't be sure, but it could be the handle of what was once a bedwarmer. Is that important to the exercise?"

"I'm cold, I'm getting filthy down here, and you're being sarcastic. Typical," Maggie said as she maneuvered the handle under the chest. "I'm close to whatever it is now. I'm going to sweep it to the left, okay? Here goes!"

By the time she'd gotten to her feet, brushing herself

down in case a pregnant spider had decided to nest in her hair, Alex was standing at his ease, Joanne Pertuccelli's stopwatch swinging from the thin, black lanyard he gingerly held between two fingers.

"Bingo! Our murder weapon," Maggie said, grinning. "And shame on me for having so much fun, but—damn, we're good!"

"We are that, as far as this goes, yes," Alex agreed. "Shall I recap? Undercuffler was murdered here, Joanne Pertuccelli's stopwatch the murder weapon, which was probably flung aside when the deed was done, only to be searched for, in vain, by our killer, and therefore left here for us to discover. Our murderer, perhaps thinking—correctly—that the now missing stopwatch would easily be seen as the murder weapon once Undercuffler's body was found, tippytoed back to the attics some hours later, searched once more for the stopwatch, once more fruitlessly, then—remembering the story of the late, unlamented, and possibly not-yet-gone-from-the-premises Uncle Willis—improvised by hanging Undercuffler outside from the scaffold, thus hopefully covering the tracks of the true mode and cause of death. How am I doing so far?"

"Well, the sentences were a little long—Bernie would have broken them up on line edit—but, basically, that's really good. Really, really good. Now tell me how Sam and the murderer got here, leaving no footprints in the dust from the steps all the way *to* here."

Alex sighed as he tucked the stopwatch into his pocket. "Always the nitpicker. And no footprints in the dust *beyond* this room, in case you belatedly might have considered the possibility of yet another staircase closer to the center wing of the mansion. Shall we go join the others and think about that particular question in the warmth and light, preferably over a glass of wine?"

"That's got my vote," Maggie said, heading for the door.

"Oh," she said, turning to face him for a moment, "a hidden passageway! Alex—there's a hidden passageway somewhere in this room. Why didn't you think of that one?"

"I did, my dear, but a cursory search showed nothing of interest. I'm also having trouble believing Undercuffler would have casually stumbled onto a secret passageway as he wandered about the manor, hunting up shooting locations, as I believe they're called. Sir Rudy certainly doesn't know about any secret passage. If he did, dear man, the whole world would know by now. He might have given tours. As I said, this will take more thought."

He pulled his pocket watch free and held up the lantern. "Eight o'clock. My, how time keeps ticking away. What say we briefly adjourn downstairs to your bedchamber and I'll stand guard while you freshen up. I loathe saying it, but you do look rather as if you've been dragged through a hedge backwards."

"Oh yeah, right. We're on the trail of a murderer, who probably knows by now that we are on his or her trail, by the way, but hey, let's keep up appearances."

"Always, my dear," Alex agreed, flicking a finger at her cheek, probably because she was all dusty and smudged. "Shall we go?"

Maggie turned on her heels and led the way back to the stairs, grumbling under her breath as she went.

Saint Just had just finished rapping on the wall around the fireplace when Maggie came back into her bedchamber dressed in yet another pair of blue jeans, another rather lovely sweater, red this time. She slammed the door behind her.

"Do you know what's worse than trying to wash with cold water? I'll tell you. *Nothing*. I don't know how permanent-press clothes stand it."

"I'm sure that means something," he said, striking a casual pose as she tossed a damp towel onto the bed, then appeared to think better of that particular resting place and picked up the towel again, threw it on the carpet instead. "But don't you look . . . bright and shiny, my dear."

"Funny. Real funny," Maggie said, rubbing at her cheeks. "But if you think I'm going to put on makeup because of that crack, you are *so* wrong." She rummaged in her suitcase and came out with a gray hooded sweatshirt with "New York Mets" emblazoned on the front in large, fuzzy letters (he'd bought the thing for her, as a gift, from the nicest street vendor, who swore to its authenticity), and struggled into it as she mumbled something.

"I beg your pardon?"

With one last tug on the bottom of the sweatshirt, Maggie popped her head out of the neck and said, as she ruffled her hair with her fingers, "Never mind. I shouldn't have said that word anyway. You ready to go downstairs?"

Saint Just walked over to her and dropped a kiss on the tip of her shiny nose. "You're a quite adorable hoyden at times, you know."

"Yeah. That's me. Adorable tomboy. And just when I was feeling so frail and feminine. Thanks. Now come on, it's cold as a tomb in here. I can't believe anyone lived in this pile and didn't die of hypothermia."

"Ah, but the architecture is beautiful, you must admit," Saint Just said as they returned to the main saloon.

"I've seen some pretty good-looking mausoleums, too," Maggie told him as she trailed one hand down the stone banister, then hesitated once they were looking at the closed doors to the main saloon. "Okay, once more into the breech, my friends, once more—and all that crap."

Chuckling at her determined belligerence, Saint Just opened the doors, then bowed as he indicated that Maggie should precede him into the large chamber.

"Oh, dear," he said as everyone ignored their entrance. "There may be candles in their holders and a roaring fire in the grate, but I believe it may be colder in here than in the attics. Not precisely a *cheery* group, wouldn't you say?"

"What did you expect? They'd all be playing charades and laughing their heads off? Come on, let's get some wine. I'm freezing. Maybe it will warm me up."

Saint Just followed her to the drinks table, where Bernie quickly joined them.

Bernie pressed her hands together in front of herself, as if in prayer. "One. Just one short Scotch. Please? Just to take the chill off. Come on, quick. Tabby's not looking."

"Bernie, you know you can't," Maggie told her as Saint Just poured two glasses of wine, then filled a third glass from the carafe of water.

"I can too," Bernie said, taking the glass Saint Just offered her, and throwing back a look that told him that he was not, at this moment, her favorite person in the universe. "I had a Scotch last week while I was out to dinner with Sid. My accountant. Sid. You remember him? I had a Scotch with him, and nothing happened. One Scotch, Maggie. I'm not an alcoholic. Now that I'm over the hump, understand I can't drink to excess, I can go back to enjoying an occasional drink. I'm a . . . I'm a—well, there's a name for what was wrong with me, but I don't remember it."

"Try *liar*," Maggie said, and for a moment it looked as if the two women might square off.

"Now, ladies," Saint Just said, stepping between them. "Bernie? You really had a drink last week?"

Bernie nodded furiously. "I did. One. And it was nice. I *enjoyed* it. But I didn't have another one. And it *wasn't* a double, Maggie Kelly, before you open that mouth of yours again."

"Maggie?" Saint Just asked, looking at her, as he was

quite out of his depth here. Drinking during the Regency Era had been more or less the accepted thing, no matter that one might stagger home blindly every night or be able to brag of not being sober in thirty years.

Maggie frowned, shrugged, then sighed, all in short order. "Okay." She spread her arms, shrugged again. "Okay, okay. You want a Scotch, have a Scotch. Maybe you can drink occasionally instead of constantly. Who am I to judge? Besides, I'm not your keeper."

"Exactly! Quick, Alex, get a pen and paper, and write down the date. We've got a major breakthrough here. Maggie is *not* my keeper."

Saint Just sighed as Maggie, her lips pressed together firmly, turned and walked across the room, to sit down between Sterling and Perry, who probably felt a new, distinct chill as she did so. "Bernie? I know you're not happy. None of us is happy at the moment. And I know you're feeling poorly, under the weather as it were. But that was rather cruel of you, as you know Maggie well enough to be sure exactly where to place your darts."

Bernie put down her glass and stabbed the fingers of both hands through her stylishly messed mop of red hair. "I know. Maggie's my best friend, and I'm a bitch. But I feel like hell, Alex. My nose burns, my throat burns, my eyes burn. Tabby's having a good time, damn it. *Tabby!* If anybody should have been in bed with Dennis, it should have been me. It's *always* me. Not Tabby, with her rotten husband and her ungrateful kids and her *scarves*."

Saint Just gave her a sympathetic hug. "So? Did you really have a Scotch last week?"

Bernie shook her head as she leaned against his chest. "Shirley Temple. Four cherries. That's ginger ale and no booze, for you English. It was pathetic. I'm pathetic. I don't know what to do with myself, you know? I can't even smoke right now, my throat's so sore."

"Perhaps I can be of some assistance. Would you like to help solve a murder?"

Bernie looked up at him for some moments before a small smile played around her wide, currently unpainted mouth. Poor thing, she did feel bad, didn't she? He couldn't remember ever seeing her without full paint. "You think you know who did it?"

"No, unfortunately. But I know you didn't. So? Would you like to help?"

"Hey, good thought. For once, I'm not a suspect." Bernie's smile turned into a grin. "Yeah. Yeah, I would like to help. What've you got so far? You got anything?"

"How about I call Maggie over here, and she can fill you in?"

Bernie's smile evaporated. "Right after I apologize for being an ass, right? Oh, you're sneaky, Alex. But effective. Okay. Call her back over here."

Once Bernie and Maggie had hugged, and sniffled a time or two, and gone off into a corner to talk, Saint Just, feeling rather proud of himself, dared attempt to extend his winning streak by having another converstion with the Troy Toy.

The actor was sitting near the fireplace, sucking on the knob of the sword cane, and looking depressingly like a spoiled child about to explode into a tantrum.

"Hello there, Troy. Any luck with narrowing down the list of suspects?"

Troy looked up at Saint Just, then got to his feet, nearly coming to grief over the sword cane until Saint Just relieved him of it, careful not to touch the gold knob on top. He hefted the thing a time or two, not so much that anyone would notice, then offered it to the man once more. "Here you go. Be careful not to injure yourself."

Troy grabbed the cane at the middle. "I know how to handle props. And, no, I haven't been lucky. I can't be, not when nobody will even talk to me. It would have been so great if I could have solved Sam's murder, you know? Now it's like he died for nothing, you know?"

He narrowed his eyelids, an action that, for some, made a person appear more intense. For Troy, alas, the resultant expression made him seem only like a confused cocker spaniel. "Do you think it could be Arnie?"

"I beg your pardon? Who?"

"Arnie. Arnaud Peppin," Troy whispered as he took hold of Saint Just's arm, pulling him closer. "Only he used to be Arnie Peeps. Porno flicks. Not many people know that, but I do. Second-rate porn, too, in Toledo, of all places. Sam might have known. Arnie would want that kept quiet, don't you think?"

"Very possibly," Saint Just agreed. "Although, if we are considering Arnaud's sadly checkered past as motive—wouldn't *you* be the person we found hanging outside on the scaffolding?"

"Oh. Right." Troy waved a hand in front of him, as if erasing Arnaud's name from some blackboard visible only to him. "Scratch Arnie, huh?"

"That isn't something I'd wish to do, but please feel free to indulge yourself if you must," Saint Just said, as enjoying this idiot definitely held less stress than attempting to reason with him.

Troy blinked vacantly, and Saint Just could have sworn he'd seen his small sarcastic indulgence actually wing—*pfffpft!*—straight over the actor's head and disappear.

"Well, anyway," Troy went on, "nobody's rehearsing. Joanne's nuts if she thinks we'll rehearse with a stiff in the house."

"I beg your pardon?"

"A stiff. A body. *Sam*," Troy explained. "Sorry. I keep forgetting you English don't know the language all that well."

"Indeed," Saint Just said, gifting the man with a small inclination of his head, as if acknowledging the fellow's superior grasp of the language. "But if we can push on? I do think we should inquire once more as to everyone's whereabouts earlier today. Say, from breakfast on?"

Troy grinned. "So you think that's a good idea? Terrific! I knew it was a good idea. I got it from the script. First, we ask where they all were, then we tell them they all had motives—and then the killer makes some sort of mistake, and *bam*, we've got him. Let's do it."

"I can hardly wait," Saint Just said as Troy once more took up what he obviously believed to be center stage in the large room and clapped his hands, asking for everyone's attention.

"It's show time? Oh, goodie, I missed the first show," Maggie said from behind him.

"He's harmless enough, Maggie. I think we should help him out, volunteer our whereabouts for the day."

"You just want me to have to say you and I—you and me—that we were together in my bedroom. And you'd just love to volunteer that I had my portable CD player turned full blast, and the two of us were dancing while Sam hung around outside my window, and we didn't hear anything anyway because we were *otherwise occupied*. I'd rather be a suspect again."

As there was no real answer for Maggie's accusation other than the truth, which would damn him, or a lie, which would similarly damn him, Saint Just lightly pressed a finger to her lips to shush her as Troy began to speak.

"Time for alibis. Oh, yes, we're going to do this again, people," Troy was saying. "Again and again and again, until we get it right."

"Oh, you mean the way you always have to do it, Troy, if you need to say more than three words during a scene?" Evan asked, showing that, no, it wasn't that much of a stretch for the man to "method act" Lord Hervey, in or out of costume.

Nikki giggled, then turned another page in the magazine she'd been reading. "That's why he's always in bed with some bimbo on his soap—no dialogue, just pecs and abs. One of these days, Troy, they're going to want to see your ass, and it's good-bye career time. Hey! Hey, look at this."

Saint Just, who was standing behind the couch Nikki seemed to have established as her own, leaned forward slightly on the balls of his feet, looking at the magazine as she held it up for the company.

"That's you, isn't it?" she asked, pivoting sideways in her seat as she looked at Saint Just through the lenses of the small glasses she hadn't been wearing at any other time. "You're the *Pierre* guy. I didn't notice that before. Oh, that's it. I've got to get new contacts."

"She's resting her eyes, wearing glasses instead of contacts," Maggie told Saint Just quietly. "Colored contacts. I should have noticed. Her eyes aren't half as blue now, are they? Fake boobs, fake eye color. Do you think those are all her own teeth? I don't. She's probably bald, too."

"Thank you for that explanation, along with the unnecessary editorial comments. I had wondered," Saint Just said, then bowed to Nikki. "Guilty as charged, Miss Campion. For my sins, I am the public face of Fragrances by Pierre, yes."

Marylou, who had been wandering about the room carrying a tray she was loading up with dirty glasses and plates, stopped in front of Saint Just. "Dang, I couldn't hear that. I missed something, didn't I? What did I miss? Who are you? Are you somebody?"

Saint Just smiled at the young woman, who really should have been kept under her parents' wing a lot longer, perhaps decades longer. "My dear, we are *all* somebody."

Marylou wrinkled her nose. "Yeah, but not so as it

counts, you know? But I'm getting there. Sir Rudy has a title, you know."

Maggie laughed shortly as Marylou moved on, picking up another glass. "Lucky Marylou," she said. "I guess Sir Rudy gives her another entry in her *'Celebrities I Have Banged' Diary—Overseas Division*. And you like her, even feel a little sorry for her, so you're going to pretend I didn't say that, right?"

"Exactly," Saint Just said as Troy, who had been looking at the advertisement, called himself back to attention.

"This isn't getting us anywhere, so I'll start, okay?" Troy suggested, tucking the sword cane beneath his arm. "I got up around seven, dressed, came down here, and ate breakfast. I saw you, Evan, and you, Nikki—and Sam."

"Then Arnaud, you came in, right? I left everybody to go run the stairs a couple of times, then do my ab crunches. But I remember that Sam was really getting hot about the writer, how she was driving him nuts," Nikki added. "I remember that."

"Hey," Maggie cut in when everyone turned to look at her. "I don't kill people."

"You write about killing people," Troy said, except his tone made the words an accusation, one that faltered badly as he added, "It's almost the same thing."

"Right. You run up and down the stairs with that one a few times. Jerk," Maggie said in disgust, so that Saint Just knew he had to step in, yet again. No wonder he'd decided to *pop* into Maggie's world. Somebody had to protect the dear girl from herself.

"Maggie, if you'd tell us, please, about your last encounter with Sam Undercuffler?" he asked smoothly.

She was still glaring at Troy, her lower jaw thrust out, her green eyes sparkling. "The last time I saw him was this morning, out there, on the landing. *Alive.*" She turned to

Saint Just. "Then I was with you for a while, on the stairs, remember? Then I fell asleep in Sir Rudy's study. Then I heard some—"

"Yes?" Saint Just prompted when Maggie suddenly closed her mouth with the sort of quick finality that told him she didn't plan on opening it again any time soon. Perhaps never.

"Nothing. I didn't hear—that is, nothing happened. I heard the storm, that's all. Thunder. I fell asleep, I woke up, I grabbed some sandwiches in the kitchens, and I visited with Bernie for a long time. I went back to my room, you came in, Alex, we talked, I pulled back the drapery—well, we all know that part."

"And yet there remains a *part,* some sequence of events, we clearly don't know," Saint Just whispered as Troy turned to Evan Pottinger to query him about his whereabouts during the time in question.

"I was going to tell you," Maggie whispered back while Troy and Evan argued, which wasn't really a fair fight. "I woke up in the study and heard two people arguing, but I couldn't understand what they said, or even what sex they were. Just a couple of words, and I've forgotten most of those, damn it. Maybe the same argument Evan heard parts of too. Something about having something, looking for something. Friendship, maybe? Anyway, it's probably nothing."

"Saint Just?"

Both Troy and Saint Just turned around to look at Sterling. "Yes?" they said in unison.

Sterling's eyes went wide behind his gold-rimmed spectacles. "I . . . I mean this one," he said, pointing at Saint Just.

"Him?" Troy exclaimed, then threw back his head and laughed. "Har. Har. Har." A really *bad* attempt at an amused, sarcastic laugh. "Look at me, you knavish, dizzy-eyed varlot. What do you think this costume is all about? Does *he* look like Saint Just?"

"Well, um . . . *yes*. He does," Sterling said. "He's always looked like Saint Just. Haven't you, Saint Just?"

"My turn," Maggie said, stepping in front of her creation. "I modeled the fictional Saint Just after my distant cousin here, remember, folks? And Sterling Balder after Alex's friend, Sterling Balder. Alex Blakely became Alexandre Blake, then I tacked on the Viscount part. I didn't even change Sterling's name, and now Sterling calls Alex Saint Just as a sort of joke. See? Simple explanation."

Arnaud Peppin pushed himself out of the chair he'd been sitting in, his legs drawn up on the seat in rather a fetal position. "Good casting, sweetheart. Now, if your cousin could only act, I might be talked into giving this movie another shot. Troy, you're pathetic."

"Oh, yeah? And . . . and you're Arnie Peeps," Troy shot back.

"Why, you—"

And they were off, the two men standing a good fifteen paces apart, screaming at each other, Arnaud's high-pitched voice particularly grating on the ears.

"Alex? Aren't you going to stop this? Alex?"

Saint Just snapped himself back to attention. "Pardon me? I'm afraid I was once again considering myself in the role of . . . well, of myself. Still a tantalizing prospect, wouldn't you agree?"

"Only you could think that. The fictional-hero-turned-real Saint Just would play the fictional Saint Just. Talk about not being able to tell the players without a scorecard. Hey, where's everybody going? Alex? Everybody's leaving the room. Stop them."

But it was already too late. Arnaud's screaming obviously

had chased them away. As if Noah had just announced last call, off everyone went, two by two.

Tabby with Dennis/Clarence.

Bernie with the hot-water bottle Marylou had filled from the kettle on the gas stove in the kitchens.

Marylou herself with a widely grinning, all-but-preening Sir Rudy.

Sterling and Sterling . . . Sterling and Perry, Saint Just corrected mentally.

Joanne, dragging along a suddenly panicky-looking Evan Pottinger.

Byrd Stockwell with Nikki Campion, who was already opening the buttons on her blouse.

And, belatedly bringing up the rear, Arnaud Peppin with his beret (rather damp on one side) and both a glass and the decanter of Scotch.

Which left, oh joy of joys, Maggie, the Troy Toy, and himself.

"No, no," Saint Just said, taking Maggie's arm. "I vote we leave our master sleuth here by the fire. You?"

"Nobody really should be alone, Alex," Maggie said, looking at Troy, who had dropped into one of the chairs, his expression—well, blank. He may have meant it to be something else, but *blank* was about all he seemed to manage. "And we haven't even asked Joanne why she isn't wearing her stopwatch, remember?"

"In good time, in good time," Saint Just said, then gave in to his lamentable soft heart and said, "Troy? If you don't want to be alone, may I suggest you toddle off after Arnaud? I believe he's heading toward the study."

"Alone? No, I don't want to be left alone. But where are you two going?"

"Bathroom," Maggie said quickly, then winced. "I

mean, *I'm* going to the bathroom. Alex is going to stand guard outside."

"Oh, well, I don't want to do that," Troy said. "Guess I'll go kiss up to Arnaud. Never burn a bridge, right?"

"Absolutely," Saint Just agreed, then took Maggie's hand and headed for the landing, where he turned to the right and led her down to the ground floor of the large mansion.

# Chapter Twelve

"Why are we going down here?" Maggie asked, glad she'd exchanged the oil lantern for one of the larger flashlights, which she kept trained at her feet, not exactly a big fan of falling down the stairs. "What's down on this floor, anyway?"

"Other than the kitchens, various storage rooms? Only the entrance foyer and a small public receiving room for lesser humans, I believe. Solicitors and such. I'm of the opinion the plan for this building was to keep as much of it above ground as possible. The owners would have done better to dredge the stream and pond every year, although that's only my opinion. Careful, watch your step."

"I would if I could *see* the steps. Slow down."

He did. "Forgive me, my dear, but I am beginning to feel some slight urgency in my need to solve this case."

"And that's your first problem. This *isn't* your case. If anything, it's *our* case. I'm in this, too, remember?"

"Correction noted." Alex stopped at last, on about the third step from the bottom, turned about, and lifted his oil lantern, holding it close to the wall. "All right, here we go. Undercuffler had changed the final scene, if you'll recall, planning a duel between the Viscount and Lord Hervey on these very stairs."

"Well, whoop-de-do. So what?"

"So, I spent some minutes here earlier, considering the logistics of the thing, how the scene might be played out, and also amused myself admiring this rather unusual mural."

"Again, whoop-de-do. And another big *so what*?"

"Even knowing I, as you have just done, could possibly be redundant in saying this, all in good time, my dear. Now, precisely where did I see that?"

"I'll ignore the 'redundant' crack and just say see *what*? Alex, that mural is about forty feet high and just as wide. We've got that old guy in the chariot. We've got horses pulling the chariot. We've got angels and nymphs and various woodland creatures, who are actually supposed to be the original owner and all his descendants. We've got—hell, the only thing missing is Waldo."

"Who's Waldo?" Alex asked, taking her flashlight from her and training it higher on the mural.

"He was a little nerdy guy in a striped shirt and a cap, and some artist would draw him somewhere in crowded scenes, and then everybody would look at the drawings and try to figure out where—nobody important, never mind," Maggie said, holding onto the back of his belt as, slowly, they retraced their steps on the grand staircase. "This isn't going to work. There's not enough light. Whatever you're looking for, it will have to wait until morning. If the sun ever comes out again or the electricity comes back on, that is."

"No, no. You gave me only until the morning to solve our little murder, remember?"

"Sure. Let me believe I'm in charge of you. That would be different. Novel, even. *Novel*—get it? Oh, man, I'm losing it."

"No, no, you're doing just fine, all things considered.

And, I don't have to inspect the entire mural. What I believe I saw was in the bottom third, at the most. I really should have paid stricter attention, but then, who knew the thing would become important?"

"Well, while you're looking for something you don't exactly remember, something that could or couldn't be important, let's talk about the stopwatch some more, all right? Why didn't you hold it up in front of Joanne and tell her you found it? You know, the big *ah-ha, got you* moment. You live for those moments. Besides, I would have liked to have seen her reaction."

Alex turned about on the stair and motioned for Maggie to sit down, then joined her. "Maggie," he said in that maddening tone that told her he knew something—entire worlds of somethings—she didn't know. "If Joanne is involved in Undercuffler's untimely demise, and we cannot be sure that she is or isn't, we have to acknowledge that the woman could not have hoisted the body out of that attic window by herself. Agreed?"

Reluctantly, Maggie nodded, then shifted herself on the stair so that the bottom of her oversized sweatshirt covered her butt. "Agreed. She couldn't have done it alone. So?"

"So, my dear, if we confront her, she could react in one of several ways. She could exhibit delight that we have found her beloved stopwatch, which had somehow become misplaced. She could have very honestly lost the thing, and the murderer used it as a weapon of opportunity, without her knowledge. In other words, she could be innocent. An unlovely person, but innocent. Or, she could act nonchalant, take the thing, secretly delighted to have it back, and then dispose of it before the constabulary can be brought here."

"Wait. We're back to TV's version of crime scene investigating, right? You're sure jumping into the twenty-first century with a bang, aren't you? But I get it. The stopwatch is full of evidence. Epithelials—skin cells from Sam's neck, for one. From Joanne, too, and maybe even from someone else. DNA. God, you're right. We can't just give it back to her. But we could tell her we noticed she isn't wearing it. That could jump-start something. And you really should get that thing out of your pocket and into a plastic bag."

"I agree. But let's first consider Joanne Pertuccelli a while longer, if we might? Exactly what is her position, her relationship to this project? I'm afraid I don't really understand all the subtleties of the filmmaking industry."

"Neither do I," Maggie admitted. "Directors direct the actual filming. Where the actors should stand, how they should say their lines, what camera angles to use, I think. Anyway, in our case, that's Arnaud. Producers? I think they put up money, get investors to put up the money, then try to tell everyone what to do and how to do it, even if they make their real money selling soup or something, and they don't know squat about making movies. Sort of like a lot of book publishers these days. These conglomerates—"

"Yes, yes. However, alas, we have no time to climb upon one of your many hobbyhorses at the moment. But Joanne isn't a producer?"

Maggie was getting into it now; anything to help herself stay warm. "No, not exactly. At least, I don't think so. Actors, well, actors act. Marylou explained what she does. Screenwriters either write directly for the movies or adapt books—like mine—so they're more visual. Or so Sam told me. Mostly, I think they're like really bad editors who just want their *stamp* on everything they touch, even if the changes don't make the book better, but only different. My friend Virginia—you remember Virginia?"

Alex sighed. "Yes, I remember Virginia. She sent us another photograph of the baby last week, as I recall. Lovely child. But—"

"Virginia had one of those—one of those hands-on editors. Hands-on? Right. Hands, feet, teeth, you name it. God, he was a pain! Virginia finally told him to go write his own book. But, then again, everybody's writing their own book these days. Sam's was a screenplay, but you get my meaning, right?"

"Maggie, you're losing the focus of my question. While all of this has been extremely edifying, what does Joanne do?"

"Sorry. She works *for* the producer? The big money man? Maybe that makes her an assistant producer. I really don't know. She's over Arnaud, that much is for sure. And she hired Evan; he told us that. Maybe she oversees everything for the production company? Budget? Scheduling? Casting? Location? That sort of thing. Movies for television have smaller budgets, so they may be doing all of this on a shoestring, and Joanne's the one tying the bows."

"I see, thank you. All right, you sit here and relax, while I think about this," Alex said, getting to his feet once more, training Maggie's flashlight on the mural.

"Why not? I always relax by sitting on ice-cold marble steps. It's my favorite thing." Maggie tilted back her head and watched as Saint Just moved the beam of light slowly over the mural, almost inch by inch, working up the stairs to the top, then slowly making his way back down, the beam of light slightly higher on the wall.

After about ten minutes of this, Maggie was colder than ever and really, really bored. She stood up, wondering if her backside had frozen solid and might just crack and fall off, and asked, "You still don't remember what you're looking for?"

"Oh, I've always known what I'm looking for," Alex told her, stopping on the fourth step from the top. "I've been looking for this."

"What? Where? Let me see."

"Calmly, calmly. Look just up there slightly, to where I'm aiming the light. Do you see it? The adorable little cherub?"

"One of the dozens of adorable little cherubs, you mean. Oh . . . oh, okay. I see it. What's he holding?"

"That, my dear, is a diagram of this house."

"No. That can't be. You're pulling my leg."

"Another time, perhaps, if you ask nicely," Saint Just said, smiling down at her. "In any case, it would appear that the fellow who commissioned this mural was not only quite impressed with his family tree, but that he was also mightily taken with his architectual accomplishments and wished to share his brilliance with everyone. Over and above displaying his many ancestors and even the children he himself fathered, whose images are preserved for posterity in this mural."

"Yeah, well, he didn't have a digital camera, did he? Hold the flashlight steady. I can't really make out much of anything," Maggie said, squinting up at the unrolled scroll the cherub held in front of him. "I can see the outline of the building—both wings, huh?—but I can't make out the separate rooms. I've seen blueprints like this in some of my research books and can never really figure them out—them or the guide map to the Metropolitan Museum, for that matter. But this is only one floor of the mansion, right?"

Saint Just stood on tiptoe, examining the plan. "Well, that's disappointing, isn't it? You're right, Maggie. This plan is of the first floor. Here's the main saloon. The morning room. I see the study—I wonder."

"You wonder what?" Maggie asked, hanging onto him as he lowered the flashlight and the staircase was plunged into near-total darkness. "And warn me before you do that again, I nearly lost my balance."

"My apologies. Feel free to hold onto my belt again as we descend the staircase."

"Looking for?"

"Another cherub, of course, one holding the plan for the second floor. Sadly, while I believe cherubs balanced at either end of the mural to be highly likely, I doubt there is a third showing off the plans for the attics."

"Unless there's four? Four cherubs, four floor plans. One in each corner. Ground floor, first floor, second floor, attics. That's four."

"True enough," Alex agreed. "But let's concentrate on first finding another cherub, shall we? Although, thanks to the pitch of the staircase, this one will be considerably higher on the wall."

"Find it, and we can ask Sir Rudy where we can get a ladder," Maggie said, more excited than cold all of a sudden. "You're thinking the plan of the house will show another staircase somewhere? Maybe one that used to lead straight up to Uncle Willis's room before some descendant did some renovating? You English were always renovating. Is that what you're looking for? Or maybe a secret passageway? A priest's hole, maybe? I think I'm thinking the wrong century, but it's a possiblity?"

"Anything is possible, yes, and might serve to explain the lack of footprints in the dust. Ah, what have we here?"

"You found the second plan?"

"No, not yet. But look at this, Maggie," Alex said, taking hold of her hand so she could join him on the same stair. "Now, this is interesting."

"A drawing of the house and grounds. Boy, how'd they do that? Go up in a hot air balloon and sketch it that way? This is really pretty good."

"Ingenuity and talent did not begin with Americans, remember, or with the twentieth century. Why, consider the pyramids."

"You consider them. I'm looking at the grounds. Alex? There's the stream—see it? Goes almost all the way around the house. It's darn near a moat. And there's the drive we came down, the one that leads to the front door down there. See how it continues around to the back of the house, then splits to go to the stables? Probably the stables, anyway, although they're probably the garages now. Isn't that where the chauffeur said he was going—around to the back, to drop off our luggage? This is neat, I mean, this is really *neat*. Hold the light steady."

"Your wish is my command, as always. What do you see? Because I believe I also see it."

"Wait, I think I've got it. A marking that seems to indicate that there's a back road leading somewhere, right from the area of the kitchens? You think that's the area of the kitchens?"

"I do, yes."

Maggie, who'd been standing on her tiptoes, eased back down, moved her head from side to side, trying to release the cramp in her neck, the one she'd gotten peering up at the mural. "So what is it, Alex? Why is it there?"

"Tradesman's entrance would be my guess. It appears to hug the outer edge of the gardens before disappearing into that stand of trees. Why hadn't I thought of that earlier? Certainly drays and farm wagons weren't allowed to approach this grand pile on the front drive. I imagine it's still in existence and used by the household staff for their daily comings and goings. Do you suppose it's under water, too? After all, none of the staff was able to come here today."

Maggie rubbed the back of her neck. "Only one way to find out."

"True. Unless we ask Sir Rudy."

"Unless Sir Rudy forgot about it. He forgot about the roof leaking, remember? I don't think he pays much attention to anything except that he's now the owner. Oh, and Marylou, but let's not think about that. Come on, we've been looking at this mural forever and I'm bored with it. Let's go see. Maybe the two of us can walk out of here, go for help somewhere."

"Tramp on foot at least a mile to the village, in the dark of night, through the rain and wind, yes."

"Gee, you make it all sound so appealing." Maggie stopped on the landing and trained the flashlight back down on Alex. "What? What's the matter? You're afraid the local cops will upstage you before you figure out who killed Sam?"

Holding the oil lantern in front of him, he joined her on the first-floor landing. "That remark, madam, is beneath contempt."

"And right on target," Maggie said, grinning at him. "Come on, admit it. We weren't looking at that mural to find a way out of here. We were looking for a—*oooouuu*!—a secret *passage*. A *hidden staircase*. *Oooouuu!* You want to play the hero, Alex, and now maybe you can't."

"Bite me."

Maggie's eyes went wide. Then she giggled. "Bite me? That's all you can think of to say back at me? *Bite me*? That's my line, Alex." Then she slipped her arm through his. "Come on, think positive. Maybe the path is underwater."

"You can be the *most* annoying female," he said just as Nikki came down the stairs toward them, dressed once more in a skintight exercise outfit. She actually had a headband with a small miner's light stuck on the front of it, along with a flashlight in her right hand. Her face was sheened with perspiration; even her hair was wet. Leave it to the woman to be the only one who could work up a sweat in this mausoleum.

"Great, little Miss Perky," Maggie groused. "And I'm not just talking about the boobs."

"Hi, all," Nikki said, waving to them before jogging across the landing to the level of stairs Saint Just and Maggie had just climbed, and starting down them. "Gotta keep the leg muscles working. See ya on the way back!"

"She must have run up and down every staircase in this pile, twice, and there's bunches of them. I hate energetic people. Besides, I thought she was shacking up with the nephew," Maggie said, then looked at her watch. "Wow, we've actually been fooling around with that mural for over an hour, Alex. Still, I guess Byrd is a fast worker. Alex? Now what's your problem?"

"They all could have scattered everywhere, couldn't they?" he asked, frowning. "I hesitate to suggest we count noses yet again. After all, one or more of them is a murderer, not a potential victim, and none of them can actually escape."

"Unless the path at the back of the house is passable," Maggie reminded him, giving his arm a tug. "Come on. We can't just keep counting noses. Let's go do what we can do. There's a staircase leading down to the kitchens back past the study. I used it earlier."

"Yes, you're right," Saint Just agreed. "Undercuffler is the victim, and there's no reason to believe there might be another one. And yet, as we've not uncovered a motive, merely the manner of death? Yes. It is time to call in the local authorities. I shouldn't have delayed at all."

"Like any of us had a choice?"

Alex paused outside the closed door to the main saloon, then reached into his pocket and pulled out—a cell phone!

*"You've got a—"*

He clamped his hand over her mouth and pulled her to the far side of the hallway, away from the closed doors. "Quietly, my dear. I'm going to take my hand off your mouth now, and you're going to be quiet, correct?"

Maggie nodded, her eyes boring into him until he removed his hand, at which time, *whispering*, she said accusingly, "You've got a cell phone. How could you have a cell phone and not—oh, Alex. Alex, Alex, Alex. You just can't resist trying to play the hero. Solve the crime."

"I *am* the hero, remember?" he pointed out, smiling that infuriating smile of his. The one she'd imagined for her perfect hero. Intelligent. Arrogant. Knee-melting. *That* smile. "In any event, unless this service entrance is passable, we're still effectively cut off from civilization, remember?"

"Yeah? Well maybe the locals have a rowboat. Did you think of that?"

"Actually, no. You're very good at this, Maggie."

"I made you, remember?" she said, then swore under her breath as the doors to the main saloon opened and Troy walked out to join them.

"I thought I heard someone out here. We're back inside, most of us," Troy told them, then looked down at the open notebook he carried. "Let's see. Arnaud—we patched things up—Sir Rudy, Marylou, your two friends, Dennis. The Sterlings. Evan says he's staying in his room unless the place catches fire."

"I'm beginning to believe I really misjudged that man," Saint Just said, smiling.

"Uh-huh," Troy said, running his fingertip down the page. "Who else? Nikki's not here. Probably doing sit-ups somewhere, or her nails. She doesn't have any talent, you know, just the body. That goes and she's done, and she knows it. Paris Hilton without daddy's money behind her. She's thirty already, probably more than that, so she's almost gone now. I mean, really? Boffo Transmissions? Tabloid covers? Oh, here she comes."

Maggie turned to see Nikki bounding onto the landing. The actress waved again, jogging in place, as she asked, "Everybody back downstairs?"

"We think so, yes, except for Mr. Pottinger, who has barricaded himself in his bedchamber for the duration, I believe," Alex told her.

"Okay. Good. I'll go change. See ya!" she chirped, then took off toward the second floor.

"Bed aerobics, stair-climbing," Maggie said quietly. "I guess there's ways, and ways, to feel the burn, huh?"

"Troy?" Alex asked, clearly ignoring her remark. "I may have misinformed Miss Campion just now. You didn't mention the nephew or Miss Pertuccelli."

"Oh, right. Byrd's in there, and pretty pissed, if you ask me. He doesn't like that his uncle and Marylou are—you know. Hitting it off? I guess I wouldn't, either, if I was the old guy's only heir."

"And Miss Pertuccelli?"

"Hey, I can't keep tabs on everybody," Troy said, checking his list again. "Nope. I haven't checked her off. But I can check you two off now, right? It's good to be organized."

"Hold that thought, Troy," Maggie told him, then looked at Alex. "You wanted to see if there's any peanut butter in the kitchens, Alex, right?"

"Indeed, yes. I've developed quite a passion for peanut butter. But good work, Troy. Capital! We'll rejoin you shortly."

"Twit," Maggie said, shaking her head as Troy turned and marched back into the main saloon, still wearing his Regency Era costume.

"Ah, that's an interesting change. I believe, my dear, you have just put one of my words into your mouth. Although I totally agree, poor fellow. But he does try."

Maggie aimed the flashlight beam down the hallway as they made their way to the servant stairs leading down to the kitchens on the ground floor. "You're being awfully nice. I thought you couldn't stand the guy."

"As me, yes, that's true. Evan Pottinger would have done a much better job, much as it pains me to acknowledge that anyone save myself could do me justice. You've said that it's possible Joanne picked the actors for each role, or at least had a hand in the decisions, correct?"

"So why did she pick Troy Toy?" Maggie asked, sure that was Alex's question. "His Q rating, probably, or whatever it's called. And that, before you ask me, is some sort of gauge of how popular a person is with the viewing public. Then again, who can understand Hollywood? I mean, somebody thought Brad Pitt would be a real knockout in *Troy*."

Saint Just held open the door for her. "I beg your pardon?"

"*Troy*. The movie, not the Troy Toy. I just thought of that because the names are the same. But there's plenty of movies where the lead character is cast because the actor is a big star—not that our Troy is a big star, but he is a hit on the soaps, according to Sterling. I remember catching part of an old movie on cable one night. John Wayne—big cowboy movie star long ago—as Genghis Khan or something. The studio guys must have figured they could just stick him in any movie at all and have a hit. Hollywood is shameless."

"We all are, at one point or another," Alex said, entering the kitchens behind her. "Now, where would one keep plastic bags, do you think?"

"What? Oh, for the stopwatch? I don't know. Look around over there. I'll check the other room. Big kitchen."

"Kitchen, pantry, knife room, butler's and housekeeper's sitting room and bedchambers, etcetera. Estate kitchens were massive entities," Saint Just said. "Ah, here we go. Maggie?"

"Hang on a sec," she called to him, still poking around, shining the flashlight into dark rooms. "This is great, you know? I mean, there's books, there's the Internet, but this is actually *seeing* what I write about. I wish I had my camera. Hell, I wish we had lights."

"We do have rainwear, if that's any consolation," Alex said as she rejoined him, pointing to a wide, stone-paved hallway and a row of hooks holding several sweaters, coats, and four or five bright yellow slickers. There was a rack holding rubbers and boots below the hooks.

"Hey, this is a bonus," Maggie said, propping her flashlight on a low table as she grabbed one of the slickers.

"Look, aren't those Sir Rudy's waders over there? Come on, that's got to be the door to the outside back there. You want boots? I'm putting on boots."

"Rather unlovely," Alex remarked, holding up one of the slickers to examine it. "But serviceable."

"Wait a minute," Maggie said, snapping her slicker shut. "Before we go out into the monsoon, let's talk about the cell phone a little more, all right?"

"I'd rather not," Alex said, looking handsome in his own slicker—which really made her angry because she was pretty sure she looked like Rubber Duckie. "But, in my own defense, I believed at the time that concealing the fact that I still possessed a working cell phone was prudent."

"How so?"

"Think, Maggie. If we could have phoned for assistance, and received it, our entire party might have scattered to the four winds before the local constabulary discovered that Undercuffler's death was not, after all, a suicide."

"You would have told them."

"Ah, but would they have listened? And I'll admit to harboring a few lingering doubts of my own, until Joanne told us about the missing cell phones. Do you know what those missing cell phones mean, Maggie?"

"You're doing it again," she reminded him, bristling. "What do they mean? They mean we can't contact anybody until the water goes down. And, yeah, I agree, they mean Sam was murdered, even without the second rope mark on his neck, not to mention the lack of a suicide note. The guy was a writer, Alex. He would have left a note. A *long* note. You know, good-bye cruel and uncaring world—all that stuff?"

"You are the expert there, I'm sure," Alex conceded, smiling. "But what the missing cell phones meant to me, Maggie, is that Undercuffler's murder was impromptu, not planned. Gathering up the cell phones, indeed, opening the service doors down here to allow the water easier entry to the generators? Slapdash efforts to keep us isolated here for a while, for one reason or another. I'm attempting to assuage my conscience now for keeping my cell phone a secret, I know, but we are in agreement thus far?"

"You know we are. And I forgot about that one part. Sir Rudy did say someone left the doors open, didn't he? That wasn't an accident." Maggie clapped her hands together a single time in front of herself, then pointed both index fingers at Saint Just. "So that's it, Alex. It's the old story. Sam heard or saw something he wasn't supposed to hear or see while he was poking around, looking for filming sites, and they killed him. Somebody killed him. We'll say 'they,' because we already know Joanne couldn't have lifted Sam's body by herself and it was her stopwatch we found, right?"

"Joanne may still be innocent, remember? The stopwatch could have been misplaced, then appropriated."

"I'm not buying that one and neither are you, not really. She probably doesn't take that thing off even when she sleeps. We could ask Evan, I guess, since he slept with her. Anyway, they were interrupted in whatever it was they were doing. They weren't done yet, so they needed to stay here a little while longer, to finish whatever it was they'd started, which wouldn't happen if the cops showed up."

"Ah, but what had these nameless *they* started? Sir Rudy has some lovely artwork, I've noticed, but nothing anyone would consider priceless. And paintings would be missed, commented on. Still, a robbery of some sort is the most logical conclusion."

Alex pulled out his pocket watch, held it up beside the oil lantern. "Later and later. Shall we push on?"

"You're really willing to give this up, turn everything over to the local cops?"

"Lowering as that prospect is, yes. We've been at this

for hours, with no real, tangible results. If we were in Manhattan, I confess I would have contacted the good *left*-tenant by now."

"I miss Steve, too. I mean, the man carries a gun. I don't like guns, but there's a time and place for everything, you know?"

"Are you suggesting that I cannot protect you?"

Maggie sighed. "No, that's not what I said. I know you can protect me. I can protect myself, too. Don't put words in my mouth."

Alex's grin was positively wicked. "Poor dear girl. I believe I can sympathize with that particular plea."

"I'll have a smart comeback for that one, Alex—check with me in the morning, okay?" Maggie turned the large, old-fashioned key that was already inserted in an equally large, old-fashioned lock, and pushed open the door, immediately getting hit in the face by wind-whipped rain. The floodwater was easily seen, deep enough in spots to have its own whitecaps, which meant she was probably looking at the pond. Medwine Manor could have been picked up and dropped down in Venice, there was that much water everywhere. Unfortunately, there were no gondoliers poling past, singing "O Solé Mio" and asking if Maggie and Saint Just wanted a lift.

"Steady on," Alex said, taking her arm. "Perhaps you should stay here while I see if I can locate any visible paths above the water level. Someone must have been farsighted enough to have the paths elevated at the time of construction."

"Sounds like a plan, even while I think I should point out that *someone* didn't think to do that with the front drive," Maggie agreed, pulling the hood of the slicker closer over her face. "I'll keep the lantern, you take the flashlight."

Backing against the stone wall, out of the wind, Maggie

watched as Alex disappeared into the dark, walking with an ease and posture that hinted that he was having himself a lovely stroll on a sunny spring day. The man had panache . . .

"See anything?" she called out a minute later. "Alex? Can you hear me?"

"Still walking, Maggie, so that's encouraging," he called back to her. "The path is composed of rather slippery cobblestones and is nearly covered with water, as it borders the pond to the left, but I believe it could be passable for a single person on foot."

"What? I didn't catch all of that. Oh, hell," Maggie said, hoping the oil lantern wouldn't go out as she inched her way beyond the shelter of the stone walls.

Why would anyone build a house—a mansion, for crying out loud—at the bottom of a basin? And surrounded on three sides by a stream and a pond. That was just *asking* for it every time it drizzled.

"Alex? You still out there? Come on, talk to me, so I know you didn't step in a hole and drown or something."

"Go back, Maggie. There's rather deep water on either side of the path—the pond on the left, the flooding on the right. It's dangerous out here."

"For who? Whom?" she corrected, wincing. "For a *woman?*"

"Maggie," Alex called out, his voice coming to her through the sound of rumbling thunder. "Not *now!*"

"Right, bad timing," she said, figuratively slapping herself. Now was definitely not the time. She wished she'd never seen that drawing showing another exit to this swamp. She wished, if she'd had to see it, she hadn't pointed it out to Alex. Not that he hadn't seen the thing on his own.

She wished she was warm. She wished the rain would stop, and this night would be over, and the sun would come up, and . . . and that Alex could solve Sam's murder before then, because she knew he wanted to make it up to her for what he'd done to that miserable man back in Manhattan—who, yes, had probably deserved anything he got—but even heroes have to obey *some* rules.

"Alex? Come back! We'll wait until morning! Damn it, Alex—stop playing the hero!"

*I love you anyway.* That was the tag end for that sentence, and Maggie knew it. If she were writing this whole stupid story as one of her books, that would be the logical next line of dialogue. But she didn't say the words. She couldn't say those words.

Because she wasn't Rubber Duckie. She was Cowardly Chicken.

Her head down, Maggie plodded back along the slippery stone path toward the door, holding the oil lantern low, the better to guide her steps.

Then she got silly. Maybe she was tired, maybe she was even a little punch-drunk. Something. With a nervous giggle, she cast herself in the role of night watchman, one of the Charlies that once patrolled the streets of Regency England. "Ten o'clock and all's not *well-l-l-l-l*," she sang, swinging the lantern from side to side.

And that's how she saw it. That flash of bright yellow slicker on the ground just at the foundation and a good ten feet from the path as the light from the oil lantern skimmed over it.

She extended her arm, shining the light more fully in the direction of the splash of color as she carefully—and very reluctantly—picked her way closer. Then, for about the count of six, she just . . . just sort of stared.

Finally, Maggie found her voice. "Nine little Indians. Oh, shit. And I'm not going to faint. This time I am *not* going to faint. This time, I'm going to scream. *Alex*! *Alllll-exxxxx!*"

# Chapter Thirteen

Saint Just stood in front of the mirror in his assigned bedchamber, rubbing his wet hair with a thick white towel.

"Saint Just?"

"Yes, Sterling?" he answered, able to see his friend's reflection in the mirror as Sterling perched on the edge of the high tester bed rather like an apprehensive hovering angel.

"I . . . um . . . this is all beginning to be a little much, isn't it? I mean, first Mr. Undercuffler and now Miss Pertuccelli? Poor thing. That was a rather large knife stuck in her, wasn't it?"

"Where it remains—stuck in her, that is, as we wouldn't want to tamper with the evidence. And, yes, Sterling, a quite unfortunate demise. Very much unexpected—most obviously by me."

"It was good of Lord Hervey—that is, Mr. Pottinger—to assist you in carrying the body into the dining room. I would have performed that particular service with you, Saint Just, had you asked, although I will be eternally grateful that you did not."

"I somehow sensed that, yes," Saint Just said, arranging his hair as he employed the twin pair of small, silver-backed brushes engraved with his family crest. Or, at least, what Maggie had envisioned as his family crest. The brushes had been one of his small indulgences once his finances had taken such a sunny turn with the advent of Fragrances by Pierre into his life.

"Do you think Miss Pertuccelli is the last of them? Bodies, that is."

"We can only live in hope, as we're rapidly running scarce on laying-out tables," Saint Just said, slipping into a black cashmere sports jacket he had chosen to wear over black slacks and a black silk pullover sweater. "How do I look, Sterling? Properly funereal, I trust? I suppose I could hunt up something to serve as a black armband?"

"This is not a joking matter, Saint Just," Sterling said sternly, pushing himself off the bed. "Perry said we could all be dead by morning."

"Did he now? And where is your new friend, Sterling? I've discovered this recent obsession—that of counting noses."

Sterling frowned, then brightened. "Oh, yes, of course. He's with the others, I suppose, in the main saloon. I believe everyone was more than willing to obey your suggestion on that head. I never thought I could become so dreadfully disenchanted with England. Can we please go home, Saint Just?"

"As soon as may be, dear friend," Saint Just assured him as he located his quizzing glass and draped it over his head, sliding the glass into the breast pocket of his jacket. No matter what the ruckus, no matter how upsetting the situation, one must always strive to be well-groomed. "But it's good to know that at least we won't have to worry about everyone scattering willy-nilly all over the mansion. And, as Sir Rudy has put in a call to the local constabulary now that I've belatedly located my cell phone, we should be very shortly joined by those good gentlemen."

"Oh, I didn't tell you? So sorry. But as you were up

here, changing out of your wet clothing, you don't know, do you?"

Indicating with a small sweep of his arm that Sterling should precede him to the door, Saint Just said, "I know many things, Sterling. But you know something I do not know, yes?"

"Oh, yes. Sir Rudy was quite put out about it, as were we all, but it would seem that the local office of the police is rather small. Miniscule enough that everyone toddles off home at six, so that Sir Rudy could only leave a message on an answering machine. No one at the police station will come back on duty until the morning."

"Six, you say? Already too late, even if we had summoned them at once. And that, Sterling, would comfort me more if I wasn't aware that there doubtless are other calls Sir Rudy could make."

Sterling stepped to one side to allow Saint Just to precede him down the staircase to the first floor. "Oh, he did, he did. But there's still the bother of all that water, you understand. We've been told to sit tight until the morning and hope it stops raining. And it is well after midnight now, in any case. We're to stay together in the main saloon, just as you already said, although I don't think we're a very jolly party."

"Is Evan dressed and downstairs again?"

"Mr. Pottinger? Yes. And sitting with his back to the wall while dedicatedly drinking most anything he can find. He said something about Miss Pertuccelli not feeling any more dead than any other time he touched her, but nobody but Miss Campion laughed, and he really doesn't look at all in plump currant. Mr. Arnaud Peppin, who accompanied him to his room as a sort of guard, or swimming buddy, as Tabby termed the thing, is with him. Have we spoken earlier of the coincidence of all the *P*'s, Saint Just? Peppin. Pottinger. Pertuccelli. And Perry. Perry Posko. He's got two."

Saint Just paused at the foot of the stairs. "And you think this means something important, Sterling?"

"You mean as a clue? No," Sterling said, slightly abashed. "But it is interesting, isn't it? And somewhat confusing?"

"Life is often confusing, Sterling. That's what makes the thing so endlessly interesting, and what, most of all, prompted me to bring us here."

"And Maggie. You wanted to see Maggie. Be with Maggie."

Saint Just raised one expressive eyebrow. "I am as a pane of glass to you, aren't I, my dear friend? How extraordinarily humbling. Shall we join the others?"

"I wonder if Maggie's still shivering," Sterling said, pushing open the doors and stepping into the main saloon. "We piled her with blankets because she said she's so cold, but I think it may be more than that. Poor thing, she suffered more than one shock today."

"Discovering rather messily disposed-of bodies is probably never a jolly event, no matter how often one indulges in the exercise," Saint Just agreed, his gaze immediately going to Maggie, who sat curled on one of the couches, rather cocooned in blankets.

She looked so small, so very vulnerable. Frightened.

No, no, no. He couldn't have that.

"Well, there she is," Saint Just declared as he walked over to her, "our little heroine. Tell me, do you suppose this news will travel across the pond to be read by your dear mother in New Jersey? That should delight her no end—her trash-penning, hell-raking, still woefully spinster daughter embroiled in yet another scandalous adventure."

Maggie glared at him. "And don't think I haven't already thought about that one," she said, leaning forward to pick up the teacup on the table in front of her. "I'm thinking about a name change and move to Australia or somewhere. Care to put a shrimp on the barbie, Alex?"

"I think not, whatever that means. Once a person has resided in New York City, the center of the modern world, one could never be happy elsewhere. I know I shouldn't be. Shall we argue? I do adore arguing with you."

Maggie rolled her eyes. "Nice try, bucko, and thanks. But don't bother trying to divert me. I'm all right. I just want to know—" she looked around the room, lowered her voice, "—I want to know which one of these Looney Toons characters is a murderer, that's what I want to know. We're sitting here with a murderer until morning, Alex. Talk about being creeped-out."

"Yes. The Troy Toy seems particularly tense, doesn't he? The man's got a death grip on the sword cane."

"Do you blame him? Everybody's nervous. Arnaud's sucking his beret again. Sir Rudy and Marylou are in the kitchens getting more food and tea, but they'll be right back. Tabby and Dennis are stuck together over there like someone glued them to each other. And poor Bernie."

Maggie turned on the couch, looked toward the small settee in the corner, where her friend and editor was curled into a small ball beneath several blankets. "Oh, good, she's finally asleep. Which is a lot better than sneezing and blowing her nose all the time."

Saint Just looked across the room. "Ah, yes, poor thing, indeed. A small brandy in such circumstances wouldn't come amiss, would it?"

"I don't know. I almost poured her one myself. But she'll be all right. It's just a very bad cold, something she picked up on the flight over here. I think. Bernie thinks she's got bubonic plague. Anyway, we're all pretty much here and accounted for, now that you and Sterling are back. Although I could do without Nikki and Byrd billing and cooing over there."

"The robin? Oh, yes, there he is. A pretty yet entirely

useless ornament. And so very unlike Sir Rudy. Still, he is serving to keep Nikki occupied."

"Yeah, well, we could have just handed her a mirror. That would have kept her occupied, too, since nobody thought to bring a weight bench and some barbells. Now, which one of them is our murderer? Have you figured that out yet?"

"Unfortunately, no. We hung so much of our hope on the dearly departed Joanne, didn't we?"

"Doesn't mean she was innocent in Sam's murder, and we did think there could be two of them, so the other one might just have wanted to shut her up because she felt bad and was about to confess," Maggie pointed out.

"And keep her share of whatever profits are involved."

"Okay, that too. But I saw her face, remember? Her eyes were open in all that rain, and she looked so—so *surprised*. If we follow your idea that Sam was just poking around the house for shooting locations and tripped over Joanne and her partner while they were planning a robbery, then we *could* have a case of thieves falling out over who takes blame for Sam's murder. Because we both also agree that Sam's wasn't a planned murder. Or, if they didn't argue about Sam, then the age-old reason. You know, the standard double-cross?"

"A theory I've already mentioned, yes. However, knowing now that Miss Pertuccelli was not universally loved, to say the least, who would she have tapped as her partner in crime?"

"Good point," Maggie said, pushing out of the blankets as the conversation seemed to warm her, bring her back from her chill. "And there's still the question of what they hoped to steal. I know working in Hollywood isn't the greatest job security in the world. Maybe she was about to be fired and figured she'd make a big score first? Do you think Joanne saw Medwine Manor before they came here for the filming? She probably had to, in order to choose the place, right? Then she cased the joint, recruited a partner—*cast* someone who was going to be her partner?"

"That seems reasonable. And may I say, your love of the venacular is quite amusing. In my day, I believe Miss Pertuccelli, as the dimber-damber, would have gulled the gentry cove—Sir Rudy—as she locked her glimmers on the lay of the ken, then when she knew all was bob, called her carriers to dub the gig of the case before loping off." He grinned. "And Bob's your uncle."

"Cute. Real cute. Now what?"

"And here I was hoping you'd have a suggestion. Ah, but never mind. Here comes Sir Rudy now, carrying a lovely yet far-from-priceless silver tea service. "Shall we ask him what he has that might appeal to a thief?"

"Do we call him over and ask him quietly, or do you want to have a full Saint Just gathering-of-the-suspects scene? You're sure dressed for the part."

"I'll take that as a compliment, thank you. But I'm afraid the dramatic denouement will have to wait until we know more, so I'll make my inquiries as discreetly as possible. Excuse me."

"Not so fast, Sherlock." Maggie uncrossed her legs and made to stand up, nearly coming to grief as she momentarily became tangled in the blankets. "I want to come along."

"As if there was a doubt in my mind," Saint Just said, offering his hand as she stepped out of the blankets. "You'll be discreet?"

"You think I won't be? You think I'll just ask Sir Rudy if he's got anything worth stealing?"

"That is what we want to know."

"Okay. Just remember, you said it," she said, grinning at him as they came to a halt alongside Sir Rudy and the clinging Marylou, whose eyes had gone as huge as saucers a good hour ago and remained so now, leaving the impression she probably had not so much as blinked in the interim.

Marylou gawked at Saint Just. "You really *touched* her? You know, Joanne? How can you *do* that? Touch a body, I mean? I'm *so* scared. I told Rudy, he doesn't leave me for a *minute* until the cops get here. If I have to *pee*, he comes with me."

"Charming," Saint Just said with a slight bow. "Sir Rudy? This is awkward, at best, but Maggie and I would very much appreciate it if you would answer a few questions for us."

"Questions?" Marylou released her two-handed grip that had been clutching Sir Rudy at the elbow, and took two quick steps away from him, as if divorcing herself from her association with the man. "You think *Rudy* did it?"

"Not at all," Saint Just assured her. "Sir Rudy?"

The older man nodded his agreement, then said, "You want me to tell you who I think did it? Because I think it's that Troy fellow over there. Nobody's that dumb, right? And he's an actor. Actors can act dumb. Act dumb, act smart. Besides, he keeps accusing everyone else. That's a sure sign, don't you think?"

"Oh, brother . . ."

"Tch-tch, Maggie," Saint Just scolded, careful not to smile. "Everyone's opinion holds equal weight. Although I have as yet to ascertain a motive for either murder, Sir Rudy. Which, as it happens, brings me back to you. Maggie and I, amateur sleuths, to be sure, have been playing with possibilities, and it has occurred to us that, perhaps, there could have been a calculated effort to—"

"Oh, for God's sake. Some time tonight, Alex, okay?" Maggie interrupted, then poked a finger toward their host. "Do you have anything here worth stealing, Sir Rudy?"

"Worth? Do I? Well, of course I do. This whole place is littered with valuables. The furniture, for one. Dead old, all of it, and no more comfortable than a church pew, so it has to be valuable."

"Yes, and it is all quite lovely," Saint Just said before Maggie could interrupt again. "However, we were thinking of something rather more *portable*. The art, for example. Paintings, in particular. I have not had the pleasure of a complete tour, unfortunately, so I wondered if you may have a Rembrandt, for instance, in your possession? A da Vinci? A Botticelli? Two? Three? More? Or perhaps some fine Chinese pots? A collection of rare jade?"

Sir Rudy shook his head. "Afraid not. None of those things. The old girl sold that stuff off piecemeal years ago to keep this pile running. She'd made a good start on the silver, too, but then she died. Lucky for me. Why? You think somebody's here to rob me? I thought somebody was here to kill people. There are dead people, you know. I saw them."

"He sees dead people," Maggie said quietly, turning her face into Saint Just's sleeve. "Ready to punt back to me yet, sport?"

"Shhh," Saint Just warned quietly, although he, too, was rather amused. "Sir Rudy," he said, trying again. "Let me proffer another question, if I might? Did Miss Pertuccelli happen to *visit* Medwine Manor before arriving here to film the movie?"

Sir Rudy shook his head, dashing yet another possibility. "No. We met in London, as a matter of fact. Lucky for me, or so I thought at the time. Only up there for the day, you understand, to see my banker, and we met by chance, in a restaurant. Pricey place. I'll not go there again. Pay the earth and barely get two bites of food. Ate better when I was poor."

"So you met at a restaurant in London, entirely by chance?"

"I said that, didn't I?" Sir Rudy asked, frowning at Marylou, who was still regarding him much like a leper.

"She was wearing red, my favorite color. Package the Medwine Marauder in red, you know? She was sitting at the next table, as alone as I was, and we struck up a conversation. People do that, you know. Next thing I knew, she was telling me about her movie, and I was telling her how I've always wanted to have a movie filmed here. Not that I always wanted that. I only own this place less than a year. But once I thought of the idea, I was sure I'd always wanted to. All those lovely American actresses cavorting about the place in their skimpy clothes."

"All right. Thank you, Sir Rudy. Oh, and if I might have my cell phone? We'll probably all be leaving here in the morning, and I wouldn't wish to forget it in the rush."

Sir Rudy fished in his pocket and handed over the cell phone. "Here you go. Is there anything else you want to know?"

"Oh, right. Thanks, Sir Rudy," Maggie said brightly. "We'd like a ladder. Do you have one?"

"A ladder? What for? You two planning on climbing out a window? You'd just land in the water, like everyone else. You'd want a ladder to go up, not down. But I've got stairs. I've got more stairs than you'll ever need."

Saint Just was finding whole new worlds of meaning in the phrase "like pulling teeth."

"We would like the ladder, Sir Rudy, in order to get a closer look at the mural on the grand staircase, if you don't mind. You see, there's a diagram of the floor plan of this house and—"

"Sure, sure, I know that. Four of them, actually, one in each corner, not that you can see the ones up-top without binoculars. But you don't need a ladder for that. I've got drawings in my study, along with all those histories I told you about. Laid everything out on a table. Didn't I tell you about the histories? Being a writer, too, young lady, I would have thought you'd taken a look."

Saint Just smiled. If one waits long enough, most everything comes to one. "You said 'too,' Sir Rudy. Does that mean Sam Undercuffler *did* look at the histories you keep in your study? Perhaps saw the floor plans?"

"I don't know what all he looked at. He was in there for hours—that was before you people got here. Told you, nothing much to do around here in the rain," Sir Rudy said, shrugging. "But you don't need a ladder. I know that."

"Thank you, Sir Rudy, you've been an enormous help," Saint Just said, taking hold of Maggie's elbow and leading her toward the doorway, pausing only to pick up two of the larger flashlights and hand one to her.

"You're carrying your cane again," she said as they made their way to the study. "You looked sort of naked without it."

"And felt so, to be truthful about the thing," Saint Just told her smoothly. "It's much easier to carry a flashlight and cane than to lug one of those oil lanterns about everywhere. So? What do you think Undercuffler discovered in the study?"

"That's obvious, isn't it? No footprints in the dust, remember? Sam found a way into that attic room. Amateur sleuths? Come on, Alex, we're better than that. Which means, especially since we already know what we're looking for, we'll find what Sam found in half the time."

Unfortunately, Maggie's optimism didn't prove to be correct, as a good thirty minutes later, with one of the flashlights dimming, they had found nothing.

"Nothing," Maggie said, unknowingly echoing Saint Just's thoughts. "If there's a secret passage built into this pile, the old guy kept his secret. Which also means that Sam didn't find any secret passage. You have any more bright ideas, or should we just call it a night?"

"As long as we avoid the main saloon. We're still waiting for return calls from the good *left*-tenant and Mary

Louise. I'd rather no one else was aware that I placed calls to anyone."

Maggie propped her elbows on the ancient library table and dropped her chin in her hands. "Yeah, right. I know why you called Steve, but tell me again why you called Mary Louise."

Saint Just pulled yet another marble-backed book toward him, wondering why he would want to read about the third Earl and his notion that *Rotating Crops Is An Abomination Against Mother Nature.* "How odd. And here I am, pondering why I thought to call Wendell, when the first ten minutes of the conversation consisted mostly of the good *left*-tenant screaming in my ear. Anyone would think I *plan* to have all these little adventures."

"Anyone could, couldn't they?" Maggie sat back in her chair, sighed. "Okay, so Steve is checking the backgrounds of all our fellow guests. That takes time, so I doubt we'll get much of anything, although it was nice of you to call him, let him know how we're doing, even if you did wake him up. Now explain about Mare."

"You'll agree that Mary Louise is an inventive young lady?"

"I have completely forgotten that she's the one who made up fake identification papers for you and Sterling, your passports. That has gone totally out of my mind now that she's posing with you for those perfume ads. I even try to forget that she's younger than me, small and thin and beautiful, and that she's in on your Streetcorner Orators along with her cousin and his friend."

"Dear Snake. Dear Killer. Or, as we prefer to call them now, since they've left their budding lives of petty crime, our good friends Vernon and George. But all of that to one side, you will agree, Maggie, that Mary Louise is very intelligent, very creative. And rather accomplished."

"Yeah, yeah, yeah. NYU, all that good stuff. And a criminal mind. So?"

"So, Maggie, among her many talents, Mary Louise is also quite adept at surfing the Web. Indeed, she taught me everything I know. As we are without your laptop—"

"Don't blame me for that one. Everybody told me to leave it at home."

"True, including me. However, Mary Louise—"

"Is a computer whiz. She's going to Google everybody? And we don't have any power anyway, and I would have worn down the battery on the flight over, and nobody else has power left in their laptops, either, so let it go, all right?"

"Done now?"

Maggie nodded. "Sorry. I'm being snarky. It's late and, like Sir Rudy, I keep seeing dead people. Except I always get to see them first. So, Mare's going to search Google?"

"Yes. Among other searches. Actors are fairly public people, after all. She may discover something useful about one of our fellow guests. Wendell will only run the names, as he termed it, for criminal activity."

Maggie shrugged. "Okay. It's worth a shot, I suppose. Covers a few more bases. But nobody will probably know anything until tomorrow afternoon, anyway. Which leaves us where?"

"Very much back where we started, I'm afraid, as the house plans proved worthless. Unless you're interested in a small experiment?"

"If it keeps us from having to go back to that wake in the main saloon, I'm up for anything."

"Very good. But first, I'll straighten this mess we've made with the house plans while you run down the hall and fetch us another flashlight. Oh, and if you'd please gather up Sterling and Perry, and bring them back here, while you're at it. We'll each need one of them with us, as what I plan necessitates the two of us separating for a space."

"I get Sterling," Maggie said flatly.

"Oh, most assuredly, my dear, as I don't expect Perry to be anything but a dead loss. But Sterling will insist on this swimming buddy notion of Tabby's, and I don't want to upset him. Now hurry along, as we're running out of time."

"Meaning the cops will be here soon, and you want to hand them the killer on a silver platter. Okay, okay. So do I."

Saint Just piled up the marble-backed, handwritten histories and began folding the floor plans, all while running his mind over the voice-mail message from Socks he'd discovered on his cell phone.

> *Alex? You there? Pick up. Pick up, Alex. Damn. You're not there. Um, okay . . . I thought I should tell you. Maggie got this package? In the mail, not just left here or something like that other time, remember? With Sterling? I kept it for her, with her other mail, but it started to stink. I . . . um . . . I opened it just now, Alex. It's a rat. A dead one. Ripe, really ripe. No note or nothing that I could see, but I didn't look real hard, you know? Just dropped it all in a heavy-duty plastic garbage bag and put it in the basement. I'd call Lieutenant Wendell, but you'd skin me, right? So what do you want me to do? This isn't good, right? Call me!*

Saint Just had already returned that particular call while Maggie was busy reading one of the histories, telling Socks in a rather inventive spate of cryptic words, if he had to say so himself, to do nothing, as they'd be back in Manhattan in less than twenty-four hours.

Yet another reason, a very pressing reason, to solve these plaguey murders before morning . . .

# Chapter Fourteen

Maggie was halfway to the main saloon—not that long a walk, considering Medwine Manor was about as long as a New York City block—before it dawned on her. She was alone in a dark house. "Well, thanks, Alex. Nice to know you think I can take care of myself."

Then again, she had a mouth. She could scream. Unless someone came up from behind her and clamped his hand over her mouth while he dragged her into another room and—"Good. Keep thinking like a fiction writer," she told herself as she broke into a trot.

The doors to the main saloon opened just as she was reaching for the latches, and she stepped back, an involuntary squeal making it very obvious that she was approximately two heartbeats from total hysterics.

"Sterling! You scared me to death!"

"Oh, no, Maggie, I wouldn't do that," Sterling said, taking her hand and leading her into the main saloon. "I was just coming to see where you were. Sir Rudy wants to talk to you. You and Saint Just both."

"Not now, Sterling, all right? Saint Just has an idea, and he wants you and Perry to come with me. Bring lanterns with you, and another flashlight for me. A big one. And before you ask me, no, he didn't tell me his idea. You know Alex. He likes the drama. So let's just humor him, all right?"

"Oh, but Sir Rudy said you'd asked him a question, and he feels he didn't give you a complete answer."

For a moment, Maggie thought maybe Sir Rudy did have some priceless art or something here at Medwine Manor. But then again, how would even Sir Rudy forget priceless art? "I'm sure it'll keep. Go get Perry, okay? I just want to check on Bernie a minute."

"Tabby did just that a few minutes ago. Felt her head, offered her a cool drink, told her to blow her nose because she was snoring, and all of that. Bernie says she's feeling better now, although she doesn't look very much better. She's sleeping again. And, alas, snoring, although I'd never say so."

"That's because you're a gentleman to your toes, Sterling." Maggie peered into the darkness that hugged the farther areas of the immense room, outside the light from all the candles and the fireplace. "Okay. I'll leave her alone. Damn it, here comes the Troy Toy. What does he want?"

"He's been very busy, Maggie. We all have been. Discussing possible suspects."

"That sounds jolly, in a house with a pair of stiffs taking up space on the tables. Am I on the suspect list again? Because if I am, you may have to hold me back before I punch our pretty boy in the nose."

"No, no, no, you're not on the list. None of us is, as a matter of fact. Troy is now quite certain that Evan—Mr. Pottinger—is the culprit."

"Oh, really. Why?"

Sterling sort of lowered his head, although Maggie could still see the flush steal into his cheeks. "It . . . it would appear that Evan and Miss Pertuccelli were . . . um . . . that is to say, they've been . . ."

"Extremely friendly?" Maggie suggested, trying not to smile.

"Yes, exactly! Thank you, Maggie."

"You're welcome. What did Evan say?"

"He didn't say anything. He just threw his wineglass at Troy. Tabby got some club soda from the drinks table and dabbed at the carpet. We don't think it will stain."

"That's our Tabby. Having an extramarital revenge fling one minute, playing the Happy Homemaker the next. Okay, here he comes. Cover me."

"But . . . but with—?"

"Figure of speech, Sterling," Maggie said quickly. "It means I'm asking you to watch my back."

"I see. You could have said that. You know I have trouble with these modern sayings."

"Sorry, sweetheart." Maggie then smiled at Troy Barlow, who was still in costume and still holding his prop sword cane in a two-handed death grip. "Hi, there. Catch any dastardly murderers lately, my lord?"

Troy's handsome face reworked itself into what, Maggie guessed, was his stock *deeply serious* expression. "I've about given that up, since Evan threw his drink at me. Gleeking bat-fowling codpiece."

Maggie grimaced. "Do you have *any* idea what you're saying?"

Troy flourished the cane. "That's not important and it's a waste of my time memorizing all that baloney, too. Me solving the murders is important. Or it was. It's not like my agent is going to be able to use it now anyway. You know—star solves murder on set?"

"Life imitates art imitating life, you mean?"

"No. I don't think I mean that. I mean fantastic free publicity. But nobody's going to shoot this movie now. The writer's dead, Joanne's dead. It's like that old movie. Well, lots of old movies. I heard about them. Cursed sets. I think

*The Misfits* was one. Clark Gable, Marilyn Monroe. *The Exorcist* was another one, I think. And one where all the actors got cancer years later. Cursed sets. Nobody's going to touch this one again."

"That's beginning to work for me, to tell you the truth," Maggie said honestly. "As long as we all don't have to give the money back."

"Oh, no, no, we'll keep the money, although that's probably cursed, too," Troy told her. "So you don't want your books to be made into movies or a TV series?"

"Not unless I get a lot more say-so than I got this time, no. Look, Troy, it's been just grand talking to you, but Sterling and Perry and Alex and I are going to do a little more looking around, in case anyone asks. Has anyone else tried to leave the room?"

"Are you kidding? You'd have to be nuts to—well, you won't be alone, will you? Oh, and Sir Rudy was looking for your friend."

"Yeah, I heard that, thanks."

Sterling and Perry joined her, and she made it all the way back into the hallway before Sir Rudy, who had been half asleep on one of the couches, Marylou all but wrapped around him, caught up to her.

"I remembered," he said, grinning at her. "Although I don't think it's much help."

"You remembered something valuable? You've got so much that you could forget some priceless work of art?"

Sir Rudy gave a wave of his arms. "No, no, I know what I have, and I know what it's worth. I wanted this place, but I'm not stupid. Everything was appraised before I signed on the dotted line." He laughed. "Foolhardy, I know, considering the way we're all *floating* here, but I knew that going in, I did, I did. Knew the place was going to eat through money until I could whip it back into shape. But it's not often a small frog can get to be a big frog right in his own pond, eh, where all his old chums can watch?"

"You sure got the *pond* part right." Maggie liked this guy, she really did. But every moment spent with him was one less moment to figure out the murderer before the police got here and rained all over Alex's parade. "The something valuable, Sir Rudy?" she prompted.

"Yes, yes, I'm getting to that. You didn't read about it, in the histories? The book with the blue cover. It's the only one. Can't miss it."

Maggie shook her head. "No. No book with a blue cover. Only those marble-backed ones, all tan and brown. I think they're called marble-backs. No blue book."

"Oh, well, that's strange. I had everything all spread out on the library table for everyone. That's the one with Uncle Willis, you know. The blue one."

"The ghost Sterling and Perry were looking for," Maggie said, nodding. Time was a-wastin'.

Not that Sir Rudy seemed to notice that Maggie was shifting from foot to foot while she sort of backed down the hallway.

"They say that's why he never left."

"They? Who's they? Why do people always say *they*? Why don't *they* ever have a name?" Then Maggie shook her head. Now who was wasting time? "Go on. Please."

"I was going to," Sir Rudy said, looking confused. "We're talking about more than two hundred years ago, remember. Uncle Willis had huge gambling debts, so he pilfered all the family jewels and hid them. But then this place flooded, and he couldn't get away . . ."

"That sounds familiar," Maggie said, getting interested. Very interested.

"Yes, so he was questioned about the jewels, and his

uncle had him caned—they did that back in those days. Have your servants cane someone for you, you know?"

"Know that, too. Go on, go on," Maggie urged.

"There's not much more. Uncle Willis wouldn't give up his secret, so he was locked in that attic room so that he couldn't escape until he said where he'd hidden the family jewels—some rather lovely diamonds as well as much more. You can see most of it in the paintings of the ladies in the Long Gallery. The old lady never sold the paintings. She said they were the only way she could see the family jewels. There's one yellow diamond bigger than a goose egg, I swear."

"Is that good?" Sterling asked.

"It's good, Sterling," Maggie told him. "And about to get better, I think. What did Uncle Willis do, Sir Rudy? I take it he never escaped."

Sir Rudy rubbed at his chin, one of his chins. "Well, legend has it that the beatings were kept up, but Uncle Willis wasn't budging. Went on for months. Uncle Willis went mad as a hatter, and nobody found the jewels. We heard the old boy had made a map and hidden it somewhere, but nobody ever found it. Nobody's ever found anything, not in all these years. They finally gave up and just kept Uncle Willis in the attics."

Maggie could barely wait to tell Saint Just. "But the old lady—that is, the previous owner? The last of the line? She stuck it out here, even as the whole place started going downhill. She and the paintings of her ancestors, all wearing those jewels? Did she believe the jewels were here?"

"Everybody loves a legend. The young lads used to try to break in here and search," Sir Rudy said, then grinned. "I was one of them. We'd break a window in the kitchens and sneak in, then think we heard Uncle Willis walking around and run back out again. The old biddy was down to living in just a couple of rooms by then, and we probably drove her crazy. Chased me all the way to the end of the lane once, with a broom. But let me finish with Uncle Willis. He was mad as a hatter after a while, so they left him alone in the attics. He didn't even try to lope off. Must have been content. I read in the blue-backed book that he laughed a lot. Then one day they found him, hanging up there, in that room. More than a few slates slid off the fellow's roof before the end, I'd say."

"And anyone who read the diaries would know all of this? How extraordinarily interesting," Alex said from behind Maggie.

Maggie turned around quickly, and just as quickly tried to give Alex a sharp punch to the stomach, which he, naturally, adeptly sidestepped. "Don't *do* that. Don't sneak up on people like that."

"A thousand apologies, my dear," Alex said. "But think of all the time we've saved, now that you don't have to repeat the story to me. Sir Rudy? Do you believe any of it? Are *you*, perhaps, still looking for the stolen jewels?"

"Me? Oh, maybe at first. If I was in Scotland, I'd be keeping an eye out for that Loch Ness monster, too. But it's probably all a hum. I'll bet the jewels were found more'n a century ago and never reported. Taxes, you understand. The very devil here in England. In America, too, I suppose. No, the jewels were found, and then they disappeared, that's how I see the thing. But you did ask if I knew of anything worth stealing. You never found the blue book? Strange. Somebody must be reading it, don't you think?"

"Or has already read it," Maggie said quietly to Alex. "Let's go somewhere and talk."

Alex gifted Sir Rudy with a slight inclination of his head. "My profound thanks, dear sir, although I fear you are correct. The jewels are most likely long gone. Excuse us, if you please? We're off on a small excursion of our own. Fruitless, I'm already convinced, but it will keep us occupied until the constable arrives. Sterling? Perry? Do try to keep up."

"You just *love* taking charge, don't you?" Maggie gritted her teeth as she climbed the main staircase alongside Alex. "But do you think that's it? One of those people back there was bored, read the blue book, and decided to wait out the monsoon by looking for the jewels?"

"And found them?"

Maggie frowned. "Right. They would have found them. In just a couple of days, when everyone else has been looking for two centuries. That seems impossible. But why else would they—I'm still thinking it was Joanne and a partner—why else would they have to kill Sam, unless he stumbled on them right as they found the jewels?"

"Or the map leading to the jewels. Sir Rudy did speak of a map, remember, although that could all be conjecture, or wishful thinking, as everyone loves a treasure map with a large X marking the spot. And I agree, the idea of both the map and the jewels being hidden for several centuries, just to be discovered by chance by a pair of half-hearted treasure seekers anxious to ease their boredom? That does not, as you Americans say, compute."

Maggie had to half-skip to keep up with Alex's long strides as they turned into the wing holding their bedchambers. Which wasn't easy because Maggie, sadly, was one of those people who, if they can't see the floor in front of them, is of the opinion that maybe, just possibly, that floor may have disappeared and they were about to step off the end of the world.

"Slow down, will you?" Maggie grumbled, knowing full well that Alex knew of her fear of walking in the dark. "But yes, that's too many coincidences. The map or the jewels. That's one. That two of the crew would agree to work together when it's pretty clear none of them like each other. That they'd find in a day or so what nobody could find in a million years. That Sam would find *them* just as one of them was holding up the yellow diamond and saying, 'Eureka, we're rich!' "

"Unless Sam was one of the search party from the beginning?" Alex suggested, opening the door to Maggie's bedchamber.

"No," Maggie said, stopping dead. "Sam? But he's the innocent victim. I mean, we *cast* him as the innocent victim right from the get-go. I never thought about him as one of the bad guys."

"Yes, I do remember your feelings about the man. You were about to nominate the fellow for sainthood, I believe."

"Bite me. So I didn't like him. But you shouldn't speak ill of the dead, and all that bilge. I just assumed—"

"Shhh, we'll leave it at that and spare your blushes."

"Oh, yeah, right. You thought he was an innocent victim, too, right up until the Uncle Willis part. Admit it."

"If it will make you happy, I'll admit to anything," he said, then turned to address Perry. "You'll come with me, if you please, while Sterling and Maggie remain here. Safety in numbers."

"Where are you going?"

"Upstairs, to Uncle Willis's bedchamber-cum-prison, of course. I would like you to count to sixty and then begin to speak with Sterling here. Stand in front of the fireplace, if you would, and talk."

"About what?"

"My dear, must I do everything? Very well. May I suggest you begin with 'Into the valley of death rode the six hundred'?"

"Smartass," Maggie said, but she was beginning to understand. "You're thinking about those vents in Uncle Willis's room, aren't you? The ones that come off one of the fireplaces? You think they come off this fireplace? And that anything said in here can be heard upstairs?"

"That's part of it, yes, although that is not the be-all and end-all of my hopes. Perry? Shall we?"

So Maggie stayed in the room with Sterling, and counted, and fumed, and then walked to the fireplace and began reciting "Invictus," because it was one poem she'd had to commit to memory in school that she actually remembered. Well, the first verse, anyway.

She was about to recite the poem for the third time when Perry reentered the room. "I'm sorry to report we couldn't hear anything. Alex would like you to move to the next room on this side of the hall now, please, and do the same thing. Oh, and can I stay downstairs with you now? I don't want to go back up those narrow stairs in the dark."

Sterling cheerfully offered to trade places with Perry, but Maggie wasn't in such a jolly mood. It was dark up here, it was cold up here, and she was getting really tired of "Invictus."

"Wait, before you go. Whose room is next door, Sterling? Do you know?"

"Not mine or Saint Just's, as we're on the opposite side of the hallway. I think, perhaps, that it is the chamber occupied by Mr. Dennis Lloyd. Tabby's, um, friend."

Maggie grimaced. "You mean I was sleeping next door to the love nest? Because I saw Tabby's room and they weren't in there, and they've been . . . together almost since we got here. Okay, go back upstairs to Alex, and let's get this over with."

Another count of sixty, and nearly five choruses of "Row, Row, Row Your Boat" later—Perry Posko actually had a very nice tenor voice—Maggie heard something and shushed her duet partner as she stepped closer to the fireplace in Dennis's bedchamber.

"You hear that?" she asked Perry, who just bit his lips together and shook his head. "I hear it." She stepped even closer to the fireplace. "Alex? Alex! Is that you? *Talk* to me."

"I still don't hear anything," Perry said. "Must we sing again?"

"No, no more singing. I'm going up there."

She got as far as the door before Alex and Sterling appeared.

"Recitation, Maggie. I believe I suggested recitation," Alex scolded as he strolled into the room.

She followed him over to the fireplace. "You don't like my singing?"

"Do you?"

"No," she said, then grinned. "I know I can't sing. But you heard us? The vents to Uncle Willis's room come off this fireplace chimney? What does that prove? And why are you knocking on the wall?"

"I'm knocking, my dear, because I couldn't locate the latch from the other side. I'm hoping it will be easier from this side."

Maggie's mouth fell open even as her eyes went wide. "You found it? You found a secret passage?"

"A rather dank and dark little bit of ingenuity, yes, built almost directly beside the chimney, so that it would be disguised from the outside of the building."

"I want to hear everything," Maggie said, even as she moved to the wall beside him and started knocking on it.

"Very well," Alex said, inspecting a rather ornate sconce beside the mantel. "I discovered the vent as I followed the sound of your voices. It was located beneath a rather large wardrobe Sterling and I shifted. Ingenious invention, that vent. Inspection showed me that it is composed of a pipe that runs straight down the wall and into the side of the fire grate, not of the chimney itself, as that would be entirely too smokey. But it's not half as ingenious as the door cleverly fashioned into the wall and hidden by the wardrobe. In fact, if the wardrobe had not been there, and if I'd looked at the wall with no real interest, I wouldn't have seen the door at all."

"But you saw the door."

"We'll call it an opening, shall we? Not really a door. And I saw that opening mostly, I must admit, because, upon close examination, I also saw more drag marks in the dust where the wardrobe had been moved. Recently. After our discovery of Miss Pertuccelli's stopwatch, remember, we gave up searching the remainder of the room, which is my fault. From that point, it was rather elementary to find the door . . . the opening—"

"Call it a zebra, if you want, and it isn't your fault. We didn't know to look for a secret passage. How did it open?"

Alex was now carefully running his fingers down the side of the mantelpiece. "A small, hidden lever just at the point where—"

There was a small *click*.

"Yes, at just about that point on the wall. Strange that I couldn't locate it on the other side, but I'm sure I will when I look again," Alex said as a section of wall no higher or wider than three feet opened.

"You're right. It's not really a door. More of an opening. I should have realized. Your knees are all dusty."

"Easily remedied. There's a stone staircase leading from this floor to the attics, or from the attics to this chamber, depending on how you want to look at things. Would you like to be amused? I know I was, watching you and Perry. You were pretending to row your boats, I believe? Very inspiring."

"You *saw* us?" Maggie would have been embarrassed, but she was too curious. "How did you see us?"

"Take up that flashlight and take a peek for yourself. Although I warn you, if we wondered where the bats came from, we now know, as the roof is damaged and a passage is now open to the roof."

"There's bats in there?"

"I believe most have adjourned to the attic by now. Still wish to go exploring? Be careful not to trip over the vent pipe, as it hugs the floor just inside the opening."

Maggie took a deep breath, let it out slowly, then dropped to her knees and crawled into the passage, holding the largest flashlight in front of her. Once inside, she got to her feet. She trained the flashlight upward and saw the narrow, steep flight of stone steps and, higher still, a small, ragged square of what might just be the first faint light of dawn. Not that this mattered, because she sure wasn't going up there. She knew her limits. "Okay, what now?"

"Now look to your left and up, Maggie," Alex told her. "See the light?"

Maggie lowered her flashlight, at which point she saw two pinpoints of light shining into the passage. "What's that?"

"That, my dear, would be me, shining my flashlight onto the painting above the mantel. A lovely pastoral scene that quite effectively disguises the holes. Now, point your flashlight toward the floor. See the steps?"

Maggie did as he said and saw the three or four stone steps that led up to a narrow area stuck between the false wall of the room and the wall of the building. "Two peepholes," she called out, not really anxious to climb those steps to look through them. "I could use this in one of our books. But doesn't the chimney get in the way? Don't answer. I'm coming out. This place is giving me the creeps."

She took Alex's offered hand after crawling out of the passage and got to her feet. "Where are Sterling and Perry?"

"I sent them back downstairs. Sworn to secrecy, of course."

"Probably a good move. And I repeat," she said, looking at the pastoral scene above the mantelpiece, "doesn't the flue of the chimney get in the way? Why could I see into the room?"

"I didn't look too closely—all that distracting caterwauling, you understand—but I believe the chimney itself has to be slightly corrupted in order to compensate for the secret staircase. Curved, as a matter of fact, before rising straight up. A fire in this grate would be smoky and not very robust. I imagine a guest forced to stay here in the dead of winter quickly found a reason to bid his host a fond adieu and move on to another more hospitable residence."

"I doubt Tabby and Dennis noticed," Maggie said, brushing her hands on her slacks. "The passage goes only from here to the attics, not outside or anything? Why do you think the guy who built this wing built it?"

"I could only hazard a guess."

"Hazard it."

"Very well. The majority of the servant chambers are located in the other wing, with only the one room of any real size, in addition to a few smaller rooms, in the attics of this wing. If the master of the house wished to have a mistress among the serving staff, he could hardly house her with the other female servants. He could, however, give her a chamber in this wing, then visit her at night via the secret passage. Either he climbed up or she climbed down."

"Oh, she climbed down," Maggie interrupted. "He wasn't going to bend himself in half to go up to her."

"You're probably right. And nobody would be the wiser. Married couples rarely shared a chamber in those days, in any case, so no one would really know if the master of the house left his chamber for this one several evenings a week."

"No wonder, then, the passage wasn't marked on the

plans. Servant quarters didn't have fireplaces in lots of the old houses. They had to take coals from the kitchen in warming pans. But maybe the guy felt his mistress should have at least some heat as she sat in her attic waiting for him to summon her. What a prince. And now that we've had all this fun, what have we proved? Proven? Whatever."

"I would say that we have proved that Uncle Willis could, one, hear anything that was said in this room, and two, realized that he might just be able to escape via the secret passage—once he'd found it, that is."

"Sir Rudy said he'd almost escaped. But they must have caught him before he'd recovered the jewels from wherever he'd hid them, or they would have found them on him."

"True. And he would be watched more closely after that. I would imagine, once he'd realized the direness of his position, he went a little mad and eventually began contemplating doing away with himself."

"Then he hanged himself, and the location of the jewels died with him."

"My first thought, yes, until we discovered the passage. There is, after all, no record of the passage anywhere that we know of or Sir Rudy would have been overjoyed to show it to us. As a matter of fact, I think that Uncle Willis, broken and beaten in mind and spirit, as we are made to believe, actually had the last laugh."

Maggie looked at Alex from beneath her eyelashes. "Go on."

"Gladly. Shall we suppose that no one ever discovered how Sir Willis temporarily escaped his attic prison? Shall we suppose that his guard may have been increased, but the secret passageway was left unguarded? Shall we also suppose that, knowing he would never truly escape, or survive for very long if he did achieve freedom, Uncle Willis roamed the house at will after everyone was abed? Possibly raiding the kitchens for cherry tarts, possibly helping himself to his uncle's port and cigars? Living, as a matter of fact, quite well."

"And laying the groundwork for ghostly happenings once he was gone?"

"Yes, as a matter of fact, although that hadn't occurred to me. What did occur to me is that Uncle Willis *visited* his hidden jewels at some point and relocated them to an even safer place."

"The passageway. He sneaked out of his prison, grabbed the jewels from wherever he'd first hidden them, and hid them again in the passageway, where nobody would ever find them," Maggie said, ready to face possible bats, spiders, and anything else. "Let's go look."

"I have, alas," Alex said, closing the doorway to the passage. "There is, indeed, a hand-hewn niche cut into the wall. A rather large niche. But it's empty. The pattern of dust and, sadly, bat droppings tell me that until quite recently, there was something in that crude but carefully cutout niche. Something of a size approximately that of my hat box."

"And it's gone."

"Vanished."

"So somebody has it."

"A brilliant deduction."

"Well, hell."

"Yes, that, too."

# Chapter Fifteen

"If I please could have your kind attention, ladies and gentlemen?"

Saint Just leaned on the sword cane and waited until everyone in the main saloon was looking at him, and for Maggie to be done with glaring at him, before he spoke again.

"Thank you so much," he said, inclining his head slightly. "I am aware that we are all weary, cold, and quite naturally apprehensive, but I do believe I have news."

"*You* have news?" Maggie said out of the corner of her mouth. "What am I, chopped liver? Why didn't you tell me you were going to say something when we got back down here? What are you going to say?"

"Go wake Bernice, if you please, Maggie."

"No."

"Maggie . . . don't be contrary."

"I'll be more than contrary. What are you up to? I *hate* when you do this."

"My dear," Saint Just said as the occupants of the room variously pushed themselves out of their chairs or lounged more deeply into them, "I have absolutely no idea. But I will count most heavily on your assistance."

"You're going to wing it? Oh, Alex, I don't know . . ."

"What's going on?" Evan Pottinger asked, standing none too steadily, a glass in his hand. "Are the police here? Did you find another body? I don't want to be a spoil-sport, but I'm not touching another body that can't touch me back."

"No, no, no, Evan," Saint Just said, motioning for Maggie to go rouse Bernice as he himself stepped more fully into the room. "But thank you so much for providing me with my jumping-off point, as it were. For we have found something I believe will be of interest. If everyone would care to adjourn upstairs?"

Tabby, still wrapped in blankets beside Dennis Lloyd, said, "Oh, Alex, do we have to? I was just getting warm. And you're letting a draft in here with those doors open. I feel like I'm in a refrigerator."

"You want to feel cold," Evan said, pouring himself more wine, "try touching a dead body. That's *cold*."

"Do you *have* to keep talking about Joanne that way?" Nikki Campion asked, then buried her head against Byrd Stockwell's shoulder.

And that's all it took, unfortunately, before everyone in the room began speaking at once.

"Try a cold, wet, *hanging* body, Evan, if you want nightmares. We had to spin Sam around twice before we could get a good hold on him. Sam the Piñata. Cripes!" Arnaud Peppin declared in his high-pitched voice, which had increasingly become a whine as the hours passed.

"And how about me?" Troy asked, once more brandishing the sword cane he'd claimed as his own. "Huh? Huh? How about me? Is anybody ever going to pay attention to *me*?"

"*No*," at least four voices chimed at once, and the arguing began again.

"And once more, the inmates have taken over the asylum. It's easier when I write all the lines and then feed them to you one by one, isn't it?" Maggie asked, coming to stand beside him once more. "You want me to whistle them to order? I can do that, you know. You put your little fingers in each corner of your mouth and—"

"Anybody got a tissue? I've run out of tissues. And who do I kill for waking me up again, you or Alex?"

"Oh, Bernie, go sit down, honey," Maggie told her worse-for-wear friend. "I'll find you some tissues. Oh, and I woke you, but you want to kill Alex. I'll hold him for you."

"More coffee, anyone? There's plenty," Marylou chirped, circulating with a silver pot as Sir Rudy trailed behind her with containers of cream and sugar, and a besotted expression on his face.

Saint Just was momentarily nonplussed, although he'd never admit that to anyone, most especially Maggie. He'd come back to the main saloon without the glimmer of an idea as to what to do after announcing the existence of the secret passageway, and that clashed badly with his need to have this unpleasant adventure over and done so they could all get back to Manhattan . . . and the rat.

Wendell hadn't called. Mary Louise hadn't called. He was faced with two dead bodies and a room full of decidedly uncooperative murder suspects who didn't seem the least bit interested in hanging, breathless (Lord knew, none of them *ever* seemed breathless), on his every word.

The idea of taking everyone upstairs had popped into his head, thanks to Evan's inquiry, however, and Saint Just was liking the notion more and more.

If only he could find a way to stifle everyone long enough to listen to him.

"I say, Saint Just, they're an unwieldy group, aren't they?"

"Yes, Sterling, they are. The term 'herding cats' keeps running through my mind. Ah! Excuse me, Sterling," Saint

Just said, extracting his cell phone from his pocket. "Perhaps this will be good news from some quarter."

He stepped into the candlelit hallway and closed the doors behind him before opening the phone. "Blakely, here. Speak to me."

"Where's Maggie?" Steve Wendell demanded, his anxiety obvious even though the man was more than three thousand miles away. "You did what I said and didn't snoop around, right? You waited for me to get back to you? You're waiting for the local cops?"

"Is there any question in your mind, *Left*-tenant?"

"Damn straight there is. Look, I ran those names myself, all of them. And nothing, not that any of them are Boy Scouts. Peppin, the one you said is the director or something? He got picked up once for indecent exposure, and Evan Pottinger has a couple of DUIs—driving drunk. Troy Barlow was caught with a lid of marijuana a couple of years back; using, not selling. Par for the course out in La-La Land. I think they throw parties if their mug shots make it to the tabloids. But that's it. Except for one of your stiffs."

"I beg your pardon?" Saint Just asked, opening one of the doors just slightly, to hear that mayhem still pretty much reigned in the main saloon. "One of the *victims*?"

"Right. Undercuffler. He's got a short sheet. Some juvey stuff that's sealed, so I can't get it—something he did when he was underage, if you don't know what that means. That could mean anything, from shoplifting to hacking up his parents with a butcher knife."

" 'Juvey' being cop talk for 'juvenile,' I suppose. I'm certain I would have worked it out, but thank you," Saint Just said, pacing. "Yet there's more, isn't there?"

"Yeah, there's more. He has a B and E—breaking and entering. Nothing big. He rolled over on his partner and did eight months in the local lockup in Los Angeles, then probation. But he's been quiet for about six years, far as we know."

"Meaning?"

"Meaning either he cleaned up his act or he got better at it."

Saint Just thought about this long enough for Steve to begin calling his name, asking if he was still there.

"I'm sorry, Wendell. I was just thinking about your last statement. You have a record of Undercuffler's adult misdeeds, but does the rest of the world? In other words, if anyone wanted to keep such a criminal background concealed, is that possible?"

"If he kept his mouth shut, probably. But he has to admit to it when he applies for a job. Many don't do that, but if anyone finds out, the guy's ass is fired, so it's smarter to just list the arrest up front, on the employment application. Why?"

"Oh, nothing. I was only wondering if any of our small party here might be aware of Undercuffler's less-than-pristine past."

"And threatened him?"

"Possibly. Or invited him to join the party." Believing he'd revealed enough, Saint Just said, "A thousand thank-yous for all of your help, but if there's nothing else . . . ?"

"There's a *lot* else, damn it. I want to talk to Maggie. Now, Blakely."

"Of course, you do. Unfortunately, she is at the moment indisposed. I'll have her phone you as soon as possible, as I am expecting another call. Again, thank you. You've been a tremendous help."

"Another call? What, you called out for pizza and a canoe? Damn it, Blakely, don't hang—"

Saint Just closed the cell phone and slipped it in his pocket before returning to the main saloon.

"Sterling told me you got a call. Who was on the

phone?" Maggie asked him in an, unfortunately, accusing tone. "Was that Steve? I'll bet that was Steve, and I'll bet he wanted to talk to me and you wouldn't let him."

"We are rather in the middle of things, my dear. I told him you'd phone him back. Or would you choose to bill and coo rather than solve two murders? If so, may I say I'm crushed, truly crushed?"

"Don't push, Alex. Just don't push," Maggie told him, then turned and stuck the little fingers of both hands in her mouth and quite literally whistled the room to order. "Works every time. My dad taught me that when I was ten. He couldn't do it before that because I didn't have my second teeth yet. Gosh, a good childhood memory surfacing. I ought to write it down," she said as everyone immediately stopped what they were doing and came to attention.

Most especially Sterling, who raced up to her, grinning, to ask how she'd done that, and, "Will you teach me?"

"Sorry, Sterling, but Alex says everything goes to the back burner while he takes center stage to play the big macho hero."

"The back . . . ? Oh, Saint Just, you've solved the crime? I never believed for a moment that you wouldn't do it. Isn't that above everything wonderful!"

"He's solved what? He's solved the murders? Spanking jolly good for him." Sir Rudy, still holding the sugar and creamer aloft, grinned broadly. "Well, then, let's all have some coffee, eh?"

"Thank you, Sir Rudy, and may I say, spoken like an innocent man," Saint Just said, amused, and very aware that everyone in the room was listening to him now. "But I have only just deduced the *how* of it, and the *why*, but not the *who*, which is why I would ask that everyone adjourn upstairs to Mr. Lloyd's bedchamber."

"*My* room?" Dennis Lloyd leapt to his feet, sending Tabby quickly sideways on the couch, so that she had to right herself, which she did, straightening her scarf as she, too, got to her feet. "Are you saying I killed Undercuffler and that wretched woman?"

"Oh, Alex, that can't be true," Tabby said, using both hands now to fluff her hair—a woman who believed appearance counted for much, even in the midst of chaos. Saint Just had always admired her for that trait. "He was with me the whole . . . that is . . . that can't be true."

"I am not proposing that it is, Tabby," Saint Just said quickly, hoping to spare the woman's blushes. "Now, if you would all be so agreeable as to follow me? Sterling? Perry? Torches and lamps for everyone, if you please."

"Not for me."

Saint Just cocked one eyebrow as he looked at Troy Barlow. "I beg your pardon?"

"I said no. I'm not going. Why should we follow you anywhere? Nobody listened to me, so I'm not going to listen to you. Besides, it's cold out there."

"Oh, good grief," Maggie muttered, then pasted a very false smile on her face. "Troy? Come with us and I'll give you a cookie."

"Or stay here and appear guilty," Saint Just added, believing that while she was certainly amusing, Maggie wasn't being of much help.

Now everyone was looking at the Troy Toy.

"He's always blaming someone else," Evan pointed out. "Guilty people always do that. I watch *Columbo* reruns. Be helpful, direct attention away from themselves. Why'd you do it, Troy?"

"I didn't . . . I didn't do *anything*!" Troy said, turning in circles, looking pleadingly at everyone. "You've got to believe me. You've got to believe me! I'm innocent! *Innocent*, I tell you!"

"Now look what you've started," Saint Just whispered to Maggie. "Happy now?"

"He *is* overacting," Maggie said. "Then again, maybe the whole dumb-blond thing is an act. Did you think of that one?"

"Maggie, the man is either the greatest actor ever born or the greatest fool ever breeched. Having spoken with and observed the fellow at some length, I believe the latter rather than the former."

"Me, too, but it was a thought. They're all suspects, although I notice you've just ruled out Sir Rudy. I agree on that one. Okay, here are Sterling and Perry with the lights. Let's go, before Evan turns this gang into a lynch mob."

Once more calling everyone to order—really, it was so fatiguing—Saint Just and Maggie led the way across the large landing and up the main staircase to the second floor, Sterling having taken up the rear without being asked, to make certain there were no strays.

"Do you know what you're doing now?" Maggie asked Saint Just quietly as they made their way into the unrenovated wing and toward Dennis Lloyd's bedchamber.

"I do, up to a point. I would ask that you not look at me as I reveal the existence of the secret staircase, but rather concentrate your attention on our fellow guests."

"You expect one of them to make a break for it?"

"No, my dear, that would be too obvious. But I would be most appreciative of any sign of discomfort or apprehension in someone's expression or posture that you might detect."

"And if nobody blinks?"

"Ah, the well-known Maggie Kelly pessimism. Always so welcome at a moment like this."

Maggie grinned as she held up the large flashlight she was carrying. "Hey, anything I can do to help, Sherlock."

Saint Just ushered Maggie into the bedchamber and indicated that both he and she should take up their positions in front of the cold fireplace as everyone else moved into the thankfully large room—Tabby more quickly than the others so that she could pick up some lacy item of clothing from the rumpled bed and stuff it underneath her sweater.

But not without being noticed.

"What have you got there, Tabitha?" Bernie asked, winking in Maggie's and Saint Just's direction. "I wonder. Is it a good thing or a bad thing to be able to go braless at forty-two and nobody can tell the difference?"

"Forty. You're five years older, remember? And everybody can tell the difference with you," Tabby said quietly. "Especially when you lay on your back."

"Silicone can be your friend, Tabby, I promise," Bernie said, pulling a tissue from her slacks pocket as she gave a jerk of her head toward Nikki Campion. "Unless it's overdone, of course. Those things are just plain dangerous."

Maggie tugged Bernie by the elbow, pulling her beside her. "Could you can it for a minute, Bernie? We're sort of trying to solve a couple of murders here."

"I'm sorry, Mags. I feel like hell, and I'll apologize for teasing Tabby, I really will. But she said I snore. I do *not* snore. Besides, *I* get the men, not her. Not that I want old Dennis over there, but I'm talking the principle of the thing here."

Saint Just, for the most part, ignored this feminine exchange, as he was once more counting noses.

Their own small party of five, Maggie, Bernice, Tabby, Sterling, and himself, all present and accounted for.

Sam Undercuffler and Joanne Pertuccelli, definitely still where he'd last put them.

Leaving Arnaud Peppin, the director; Troy Barlow, the idiot; Nikki Campion, the—well, he was still undecided about her; Evan Pottinger, the not-so-courageous villain; Dennis Lloyd, the lover; Marylou Keppel, the ambitious gofer; Sir Rudy, their host; Sterling's double-*P* friend, Perry Posko; and, lastly, Sir Rudy's nephew, the robin.

"Mr. Stockwell?" Saint Just said, visually scanning the assembled parties and not seeing the man who should by all rights be standing next to Nikki. "Has anyone seen Byrd Stockwell?"

"Coming!"

"You were unavoidably detained between here and the main saloon, sir?"

Byrd Stockwell pushed past Arnaud Peppin to stand beside his uncle. "Took a moment for a trip to the loo, if you must know, since nothing was going on in here, unless I missed a catfight. Not that I think this whole thing is more than nonsense. What are we doing here?"

Before everyone else could echo that particular question—which, by the way all their mouths opened in unison like those of baby birds whose mama was approaching with a juicy worm, Saint Just believed very possible—he announced, "I have, through diligent search and considerable luck—"

"And *my* help," Maggie added.

"Yes, and with Miss Kelly's kind assistance, I have—that is, *we* have—discovered a heretofore hidden passageway in Medwine Manor."

Saint Just then waited patiently for the all-too-expected hubbub to calm down even as he and Maggie watched the faces of the others. He wondered if Maggie had seen what he'd seen, then felt sure she had. He did so because he knew Maggie to be both intelligent and observant . . . and because she had just now pinched him two inches above the elbow with some force. His Maggie, always so subtle.

"If you could all refrain from shouting out your questions," Saint Just went on, "I will explain."

"Everybody stubble it!" Sterling called out when nobody obeyed Saint Just, then he stepped back a pace, looking slightly startled at his own outburst. "Sorry, and all of that, but we really do need to listen. Saint Just is going to be brilliant. Aren't you, Saint Just?"

"Stop calling him Saint Just," Troy objected, brandishing the sword cane. "I'm—oh, hell, no I'm not. I don't want to be, either. I'll never get the accent right. I don't know why my agent said this stupid movie would be such a great career move."

"That makes about an even dozen of us," Evan Pottinger offered, still nursing the glass he'd brought with him from the main saloon, a glass he seemed personally attached to now.

"Me, too," Maggie said. "I mean, why you're in it, Troy, not why everyone else is. Did your agent call Joanne, Troy, or did she call you? I'm just curious."

"I can answer that one. His agent is Joanne's most recent ex," Evan said, hefting the decanter he'd brought with him and refilling his wineglass. "My bet is they swapped something under the table for Troy. A marital asset in exchange for a leading role. Probably the family pooch, right, Troy? You've got to be worth at least a schnauzer."

"You're drunk, and that's a lie," Troy said with more feeling than Saint Just had heard from the man to this point.

"People, people," Arnaud piped up, clapping his hands. "Fight later. Let's get this done."

Saint Just favored the director with a slight bow. "Thank you, Arnaud. As I was saying—"

"Before you were so rudely interrupted," Maggie said, grinning. "Sorry. Couldn't resist. It's just that that's right up there with 'I'm innocent, innocent, I tell you.' "

Saint Just reminded himself of how he adored this woman. "Yes, I know, my dear," he said quietly, "and may I say how prodigiously pleased I am that you're pleased. When we have a moment, however, you might want to consider a restorative lie-down. I believe you're becoming a tad giddy with quite natural fatigue."

"Bite me."

"And snarky as well, as you say."

"I'm getting cold up here, Alex. Start talking before we lose them again. They've all got the attention spans of fleas."

He nodded his agreement and turned once more to the semicircle of interested faces. "Now, as I was saying, ladies and gentlemen, we've discovered a secret passage in Medwine Manor. A passage, as it happens, that runs from this chamber to the attics. To the very room in the attics in which, as you may or may not know, Sam Undercuffler was attached to the scaffolding that surrounds this wing."

"Tell them about the dust. Don't forget the dust." Maggie was fair to dancing in place, whether from the chill or excitement, he didn't know.

Saint Just sighed, knowing, however, when he'd lost a battle. "Oh, why don't you just do that, my dear. I'm convinced you'll tell it all so much better than I."

"I'll pretend you didn't mean that as an insult," Maggie said, then rubbed her hands together in front of herself. "Okay, here's how it goes. When we went up to the attics—gosh, it seems like days ago—we noticed that there were no footprints in the dust in the area that leads from the stairs to the room in question. Uncle Willis's room, which is the same room used to hang Sam out the window. You with me so far?"

"They're *hanging* on your every word, if you'll excuse my descent into questionable sensitivity where the late Mr. Undercuffler is concerned," Saint Just assured her.

Maggie grinned at him, then continued her explanation. "Well, this got us thinking—I mean, it would have to get you thinking, right? How did Sam get to the room without disturbing the dust? How did the killer—or killers—get to the room? They didn't *fly* there. So we—Alex and I—we went looking for plans to the house, figuring there had to be some other way, some secret way of getting to the attics. Alex? You want to tell them about the mural? Because that one was your idea."

"I think we can safely dispense with that small side trip in our investigation," Saint Just said, mentally attempting to recall what Maggie would term the time line of the past now-nearly four-and-twenty hours.

"Right. Okay. We'll skip that part, since it didn't work anyway," Maggie agreed, the bit firmly between her teeth now, bless her. "So what we did was some simple investigating—simple, but pretty brilliant, really—and we found the secret passage."

"'Row, row, row your boat' is brilliant?"

"Try to forget that part, Alex, okay?"

Sir Rudy was all but drooling now. "Where? Where is it? It's in this room, you said, didn't you? I've been waiting forty years to get some of my own back on that old lady. Chase me with a broom, will she? Laugh at me at my pub, will they? Show me!"

"Over here, Sir Rudy," Saint Just said, stepping over to the wall beside the fireplace. "Just behind this wall is a set of very narrow, very steep stone stairs that lead up to the attic room once occupied by the man you all now know as the ghostly Uncle Willis. Maggie?"

"I'm thinking, I'm thinking. I want to get this right. I wish I could write it all out on file cards, then shuffle everything until I get it all in order."

"Let me help you there," Saint Just offered. "We begin very early yesterday morning, with Mr. Undercuffler dining with a few members of our party."

"Right," Troy said, as he had been a part of that small party. "That's when Sam told us about Maggie here, how she was being such a bitch about his screenplay."

"Gee, thanks for remembering that," Maggie said with a near-sneer. "I saw Sam after you all ate breakfast, when he showed up in my room, and we came downstairs together, but I didn't see him after that—until I saw him hanging outside my window at—when was that, Alex?"

"Much later," was all Saint Just said, as he was concentrating on something else entirely. "The electricity became disabled sometime during the night, correct?"

"Yes, but the generators kicked right in like clockwork," Sir Rudy pointed out. "Until they got flooded. I sure want to know what idiot left those doors unlatched."

"Our killer, I would say," Saint Just said, knowing he now had everyone's attention once again. "Tabby? I promise to forget everything you say once you answer my questions, and please forgive me, but where were you and Mr. Lloyd, from the time you left the main saloon until you were asked to join everyone there once more?"

"Alex," Tabby pleaded through clenched teeth. "Do we have to?"

"Ah, Tabby, honey, I think we do," Maggie said, stepping in front of Saint Just. "Because I think I can see where Alex is going with this. I . . . well, I went to your room around noon and you weren't there, but it looked like maybe you had been there?"

"I'll pay you back for this some day," Tabby said, stepping close to Maggie. "Yes, we were in my room all night. But then we went to Dennis's room around eleven or so in the morning because we'd run out of—well, just you never mind. He had some granola bars, too, because we were hungry. And we stayed there until someone told us to come downstairs, that the generators were out. There. Satisfied?"

"I don't know, I usually do all of this on paper before I write." Maggie looked at Saint Just. "Are we satisfied?"

"Yes, I think we are."

"Well, good for you," Byrd Stockwell said. "Now tell us."

Saint Just obliged. "Happily. I can verify that Sam Undercuffler was alive at nine o'clock yesterday morning. I understand that Miss Pertuccelli had requested that he investigate the premises, looking for possible locations to film outdoor scenes that, because of the flooding, would most probably be relocated inside the building."

"You only use dialogue in movies, not all my scene setting," Maggie offered. "Although there'd be some reworking needed to change the rooftop duel to one on the stairs. Then again, this was supposed to be made-for-TV, so you guys will probably just fake it all. Not that Sam and Joanne probably weren't faking it, giving Sam a reason to disappear for a while."

"You know, Hollywood does make some quality films, Maggie," Arnaud said, obviously smarting. "Although I will agree that sometimes we cut a few corners. I know you writers think you are more important, but, as Lloyd Kaufman said so well, 'It's up to us to produce better-quality movies.' "

Maggie shook her head. "Kaufman? I don't know who that is."

And yet again, Evan came to the rescue. "Lloyd Kaufman produced that classic American movie *Stuff Stephanie in the Incinerator*. No lie."

Everyone laughed, and for a moment, the tension eased.

"Where was I?" Maggie asked. "Oh, sorry, Alex. I was jumping ahead, wasn't I? Go on. I see where you're going. Bless you, Bernie."

"Thanks," Bernie said after her loud sneeze, then blew her nose. "This had better be worth pneumonia, Alex. Come on, show us the secret passage."

"First things first," Saint Just told her. "You will all

please remember that what I'm about to say is conjecture only and I've no real proof. However, I believe that Mr. Undercuffler, a known criminal—"

"Whoa! Back up, Sherlock," Maggie said. "A *known* criminal? I thought we were just guessing that he was part of it. Is that what Steve told you? Sam was an actual criminal?"

"Yes, indeed, although possibly reformed. But, following your example, I am getting ahead of myself, aren't I? We'll step back in time a moment and consider Miss Pertuccelli, shall we?"

"Why?" Nikki asked, blowing on another recently filed nail. "She's dead. They're both dead. Can we go downstairs now? What do we care about secret passages?"

"I want to see the secret passage first," Sir Rudy protested. "I paid for it."

Saint Just, always accommodating, proceeded to drop to one knee and run his hand down the side of the mantelpiece until he felt the slight indentation, then pushed.

As before, the opening appeared, this time to oooh's and aaah's and one heartfelt "And it's all mine!"

"I think it best that we don't further disturb anything inside the passageway until the constable has been," Saint Just told them, shutting the panel once more. "Fingerprints, that sort of thing. But I will tell you all my theory."

"Our theory," Maggie added. "I give *you* credit."

"Our theory," Saint Just concurred. "It is our theory that Miss Pertuccelli was aware of Mr. Undercuffler's dubious background and, either by plan or happenstance, enlisted him in her hunt for the missing jewels, the jewels allegedly hidden somewhere in Medwine Manor by the late and reportedly lingering Uncle Willis."

Maggie shrugged. "Okay, so I didn't know about his record until now, but I was right about her hiring Sam as a partner in crime."

"Possibly. Probably."

Sir Rudy clapped his hands. "The stolen jewelry, of course! That's where Uncle Willis hid it all. They found it? I'd always hoped, but they really found it? A fortune in jewels?" He dropped his hands to his sides. "Oh. That's not good. Because they're gone again, aren't they?"

Maggie nodded her agreement. "Right. But let's get back to Sam because he's our first victim and the murders are more important than the jewelry."

"Says you, missy," Sir Rudy grumbled, looking crestfallen.

Maggie pushed on. "Instead of sending Sam looking around for places to shoot the movie, Joanne was really sending Sam off to look for the jewels. Except she already had a pretty good idea where they were, and I don't think we understand that part yet. Do we, Alex?"

"A detail that will fall into place in time," Saint Just told her. "For the nonce, we'll concentrate on Sam, as you call him, and Joanne. Joanne sent Sam off, the hiding place for the jewels was discovered, and the jewels recovered, all via this room and the secret passage. At which point there may have been a general falling-out or a planned severing of an uneasy partnership."

"She killed him and left him in the attic room, maybe even dragged him up there," Maggie clarified for their very attentive audience. "Sam didn't hang himself or get himself hanged. We told you it was murder, but I don't think we told you how we knew. He was strangled with Joanne's stopwatch cord and not hung up until hours later. That can be proved by the marks on Sam's neck, but we won't go into the how of that right now, either. We found the stopwatch behind a bureau up in the attic room right above us. We're figuring he died maybe an hour after I last saw him."

"But then there was a problem, as is often the case with

impulsive acts," Saint Just said, taking up the story, pleased as he could be at how he and Maggie seemed to so neatly dovetail each other. "It would seem that Tabby and you, Mr. Lloyd, had decided to adjourn to this room, with the first murder committed and Sam's body still in the attic above you. And, quite possibly, the jewels were still there as well. You had to be removed from the room. Thus the open doors to flood the generators."

"Why not just climb the stairs to the attics, Saint Just?" Sterling asked.

"A good question, but I believe I have the answer. The dust. Once the murder was done, the murderer or murderers had time to think, to come up with a plan. Footprints in the considerable dust would leave a trail showing that more than one person had climbed those stairs and walked those attics, both coming and going—that one person being the supposedly suicidal Sam Undercuffler, who could not possibly have made *two* tracks of footprints if he was dead by his own hand."

"They could have just swept the attic and gotten rid of the whole dust problem," Maggie said.

"True, but we've had more time to consider alternative possibilities. The murderers did not. They were, as you would say, *winging* it. To continue, the lack of footprints in the dust also would delay anyone's curiosity in searching for the writer in this particular attic of this very large pile, at least long enough for the murderers to make good their escape."

"Besides," Maggie interrupted yet again, "Sam was *only* the writer. If Joanne didn't ask about him, nobody would probably even notice he was missing. Except they didn't count on us."

"Thank you, Maggie. And once a serious search party was mounted, there would be so many footprints that the former lack of them would never be noticed. And not to offend the ladies, but the cold would also have served to keep Undercuffler's body undiscovered."

"So they could just have left him in the attic room," Evan Pottinger said, obviously not as drunk as he might appear. "Why'd they go back and hang him out the window? Oh, right, maybe they had to go back for the jewelry anyway. And the suicide angle. You're figuring they didn't decide to fake the suicide until after he was already dead. I forgot. And we're saying murderers now. Plural. There's more than one?"

Maggie jumped in to answer. "Joanne's stopwatch cord may have been used as the murder weapon, but the woman most certainly did not lift Sam's dead weight up and out the window while tying him to the scaffolding. Not alone."

"She's right," Arnaud said, shaking his head. "It took the two of us just to cut him down again. Joanne couldn't have done it alone. But she killed him?"

"I'm afraid we can't ask her that," Saint Just said, stepping away from the fireplace. "But there you have it. Unbelievable as it may seem, it appears that Joanne Pertuccelli and Sam Undercuffler, and one as-yet-unnamed cohort in crime, heard about the missing jewels, discovered the hidden passage, found the jewels, and then had a falling out that ended in the murders of two of the three accomplices. It is only left to discover that third party, who is, sadly, one of us, unexpectedly trapped here with us at the moment. And the jewels, of course. When we discover the one, we will find the other."

"I don't understand," Troy said, frowning. "How did they know about the jewelry?"

Saint Just, who had previously been annoyed with Troy Barlow's thick skull, wished the man hadn't taken this moment to at last appear incisive.

"We don't know. We're working on that, just as I am still wondering why the miscreants didn't simply shut Sam's body in the secret passage and be done with it, allowing everyone to think he'd simply gone missing—at least until the heat of summer. Perhaps the faked hanging was a natural thought progression for someone in the very visual movie industry? Or perhaps the method of demise for Uncle Willis spurred their imaginations?"

"Stuff him behind that wall? And you said summer. *Eeeeuuuwww*, you mean he'd start to smell when it got hot." Marylou put her hand to her mouth, then buried her head against Sir Rudy's chest. "That's just too gross."

"Indeed," agreed Saint Just. "Now, if there are no further questions, and if no one is prepared to confess, I suggest you all adjourn once more to the main saloon and the warmth of that quite delightful fire while we await the arrival of the constable."

"That's it? That's all? Sam and Joanne were bad guys, and they're dead—and so what? And there's still a killer in the group? No way." Evan Pottinger lifted the lead crystal stopper from the decanter he held and threw it in the general direction of the bed. "I say let's frisk everybody, find the jewels. I get to pat down *Boffo* girl." Then he drank straight out of the decanter.

Saint Just was tempted to agree with at least the spirit of Evan's suggestion. It was time every guest's bedchamber was searched, as, judging by the size of the outline in the dusty stone niche, the amount of jewels was considerable, certainly more than could be concealed on anyone's person. "I think personal searches are unnecessary, Evan. However, as you all return to the main saloon, please, Maggie, Sterling, and I will conduct searches of each bedchamber until such time as the constable can ford the flood."

"I don't want you poking around in my room. You're no cop," Troy said, pouting. "I'm going with you."

A chorus of "me, too's" followed. Naturally.

"Very well. But we'll all go together, room to room."

"Like a group toidy," Bernice said, and Maggie giggled.

"Please don't explain that, ladies," Saint Just said. "Now off you go, two by two, as has already been suggested."

"She's gone." Byrd Stockwell turned in a full circle. "Nikki's gone! Son-of-a—"

"Nikki?" Maggie looked up at Saint Just, wide-eyed. "No. *She's* the third one?"

Saint Just was confused. Really, really confused. How could he have been watching the wrong suspect? "There was always the hope someone would, as you Americans say, make a break for it. But Miss Campion? Perhaps she, too, had need of the facilities?"

"Yeah? Well, let's go find out," Maggie said, already heading for the doorway to the hall, hard on Byrd Stockwell's heels.

"You go with the others, Robin," Saint Just said, taking hold of the man's arm and turning him about. "Sterling? Please see that our Robin Redbreast remains with the others."

"Really?" Sterling blinked several times, then stood up very straight. "Perry and I will see to it, Saint Just, have no fears on that head. Perry? You take his left, I'll take his right."

"Anything you say, Sterling."

"Don't you dare," Byrd said, backing away, only to bump into Bernice, of all people, who had picked up a very substantial-looking brass figurine and was now holding it with the same intensity with which Saint Just's favorite New York Met, Mike Piazza, gripped a baseball bat.

"Go on, try to run, I dare you," Bernie said. "I've been looking for someone to beat on all night. If I can't drink, I can get my jollies this way."

"Thatta girl," Maggie said, then took off for the other

wing, Saint Just beside her. "I know which is Nikki's room. I saw it yesterday morning."

"This doesn't make sense," Saint Just told her as they broke into a jog. "You saw the robin look at the wall when I announced we'd found the passage—*before* I revealed the location of the opening?"

"I did. And he's logical. Nikki isn't. One thing's for sure—the robbery itself was *planned*. Only the murders were unplanned."

They were past the main staircase now, and Maggie suddenly stopped, then turned back.

"I thought you said you knew the location of her bedchamber."

"I do, but she went this way," Maggie said, holding up her flashlight as she grabbed the railing and started down the stairs toward the candlelit first floor.

"How do you know that?"

"Because I can smell her perfume, and the smell died off when we got past the staircase," Maggie said, moving faster on the stairs than Saint Just ever would have supposed; obviously a woman on a mission. "She went this way."

"Very good, Maggie."

"Not really," she said as they reached the bottom of the staircase and then sniffed again before heading back toward the study and, beyond that, the servant staircase leading to the kitchens. "She *pours* on the perfume. A Chihuahua with a deviated septum could follow her scent. Come on, Alex, she's getting away!"

# Chapter Sixteen

Maggie ran until she realized she probably should slow down before she fell and broke something—most probably herself—and then hesitated as she and Alex got to the servant stairs.

"She went down. And you know why? Because she *knows* to go down. Do you know *why* she knows to go down?"

"Maggie, she's down. And very soon to be out and about, so we can probably leave this discussion for later, yes?"

"Good point. But I know how she knows how to get out, so file that—I knew first."

"My compliments," Alex said, indicating with a slight bow that she should precede him down the stairs to the kitchens.

Maggie felt the breeze before she saw the door open to the outside, and she was off again, hot on the heels of a woman who really, really got on her nerves . . . and it had nothing to do with Nikki's great looks or her even greater body. Really, it didn't. At least not much.

"We'll need Wellington boots and raincoats," Alex said, grabbing her arm as she was halfway out the door into the downpour and the growing gray light of dawn.

"We don't have time for those."

"We do if we have to go more than ten feet to find her, and I'm sure we do. We've been out there before, remember? At least the Wellingtons, Maggie. You'll fall without them."

"Sure, okay, you're right," she said, smiling at him. Then she waited until he'd sat himself down on the old wooden bench before she bolted. "She's *mine*, Alex!"

The cold rain hit Maggie with only a little less than the impact she'd expect from a bucket of ice water being thrown at her, and she blinked, sputtered . . . and pressed on, already knowing the location of the path Alex had investigated earlier.

She felt her feet slipping out from under her as she staggered along, rethinking her refusal of those time-consuming rubber boots to cover her leather-soled shoes. But she kept the flashlight beam headed straight ahead, not down, and kept moving along the narrow path that just barely rose above water, water, and more water.

"Maggie! Maggie, come back here!" Alex yelled—gosh, he'd actually *yelled*.

"I can't. She's got a head start," Maggie yelled back at him.

And then she saw a figure, darker than the dawn around it. Nikki Campion. Nikki Campion, who'd taken the time to pull on rubber boots and one of those ugly yellow coats.

The idiot woman also had two suitcases, one in each hand. Was she nuts? Who makes a getaway with Gucci?

"Halt!" Maggie cried out. "Halt or I shoot!"

Which really worked only in truly bad cop and war movies.

Nikki let go of the suitcases and broke into a trot, the miner's light strapped to her headband lighting her way.

"Damn," Maggie swore, rubbing her face with her free hand, trying to wipe off the rain that had already saturated her hair and was now running down into her eyes.

How was she going to keep up with the woman? Nikki ran flights of stairs for *fun*, for crying out loud. The last time Maggie could remember running was weeks and weeks ago, when she'd gone after that creep and tackled him, nearly getting herself killed in the process.

You'd think a woman would learn.

Then again, every once in a while, a woman catches a break. Even Margaret Kelly.

With a startled screech, Nikki Campion lost her footing on the slippery cobbles, or bricks, or whatever the old stones were, and, her arms waving wildly, over she went, into the pond.

Where the Boffo Transmissions girl, even with her built-in flotation devices, sank like a rock.

"I'll get her," Alex shouted, coming toward Maggie in his boots and slicker, carrying another slicker for her. "I knew she wouldn't get far. Here, put this on."

Maggie had her flashlight trained on the water. Wow, whitecaps. When this pond flooded, it didn't fool around. "I don't see her, Alex. We can't wait for you to get out of that stuff. And she's wearing it, too. She can't swim in that." She began stripping off her soggy sweatshirt.

"Maggie, no—"

Maybe if he'd said "please" she wouldn't have done it? No, she was going to do it no matter what Alex said. Jumping in after Nikki Campion was just the sort of thing Maggie always did. Jump first, think later.

As the water closed over her head, Maggie instantly gained a whole new understanding of the word "cold." She'd have to tell Evan.

She surfaced to sputter and to yell, "It's cold!" Treading water as she worked to toe off her loafers, she tried to get her bearings, but there was still no sign of Nikki. "She come up at all?" she yelled at Alex, who had trained both flashlights on the water.

"Only for a moment. To your left. Maggie, I—"

"Okay." Maggie took another deep breath and went back under, opening her eyes, as she hoped to see something in the dark water.

And she did see something. The glow from Nikki's miner's light, or runner's light, or whatever the heck it was.

Maggie's feet touched bottom—the pond was probably only about nine or ten feet deep in this spot—then pushed off the graveled bottom even as she reached out with one hand and grabbed for the yellow slicker by the back of the collar.

Except her fingers hadn't closed around a collar; they'd closed around a strap, a wide strap. She pulled, and the strap came with her—or rather, the large cloth bag attached to the strap came with her. But not Nikki.

Maggie let go of the bag and it sank to the bottom of the pond. She was a good swimmer, which came from living her formative years at the Jersey shore, but she had limits. Lung capacity was one of them. Good thing she didn't smoke anymore or Nikki would be a goner.

Maggie surfaced, took another deep breath, and went down again, this time with more of a plan. Locating the glow of the miner's light, she judged where Nikki's arms were and grabbed one on the second try, pulling hard on the end of the sleeve of the slicker.

Luckily, the slicker had been fashioned for a much larger person. Even luckier, Nikki actually *helped* her, if blind panic can be called help.

Her arms and legs thrashing, Nikki grabbed onto Maggie, attacking her rescuer. Typical. So Maggie, not really feeling all that sorry about it, brought up her knee and popped the actress one square under the chin.

*All in the name of rescue*, she told herself as she grabbed onto Nikki's hair and headed for the surface.

"I've got her!"

Maggie sank a little as she felt Nikki being pulled up and out of the pond, then resurfaced in time to see Nikki's legs being dragged out of the water. "Yo. A little help here?"

Alex left Nikki where she lay on her stomach, coughing and retching, and reached for Maggie's hand. "You are the most feather-witted, headstrong, unbelievably selfish woman I have ever had the misfortune to encounter, do you know that? You could have drowned."

"Yeah, I'm crazy about you, too," Maggie gasped out, holding onto his hand as she gripped the edge of the raised path. "I'm betting the jewelry's still down there. She had it in a bag around her neck like an anchor, the jerk. Keep the flashlight on the water. I'm going to go back down and get it."

"Maggie."

"Don't try to stop me, Alex. I've had it up to here with these people, and I'm going to get those damn jewels and get out of England."

"I agree. But perhaps you'd like to use this?" he suggested, retrieving Nikki's lighted headband and handing it down to her.

"Good thought," Maggie said, trying to smile, but her teeth were chattering, so she gave up that particular effort as a bad job.

One last dive did the trick, as the handle of the bag actually seemed to be waving to her as she searched for it, and she was back on the surface and then on the slippery, bumpy path a moment later, lying face-to-face with Nikki Campion as the gray light of dawn became a little brighter. "Come here often?" she asked the drenched Nikki.

It was morning, and the case was solved. Sort of solved. Most of it solved. She hoped Alex was happy. She was. Rapidly freezing to death, maybe nearing a slight case of fatigue-induced delirium, but happy.

"I believe you two have been introduced," Alex said, assisting Maggie to her feet. "Here," he added, draping a wet slicker over her shoulders. "This won't help much, but it's better than nothing. Can you navigate the path back to the house while I assist Miss Campion?"

"Don't . . . don't let her get away," Maggie told him, heading for the still-open back door to Medwine Manor. "I'm so cold!"

She wasn't quite halfway to the house before Sterling, looking really adorable in his own yellow slicker, came running toward her, gathered her close under his arm, and led her into the kitchens, where Perry was waiting with a large red-and-green-plaid wool blanket.

"I love you guys," Maggie told them, shaking all over. "Fireplace. Get me to a fireplace. I'm *so* cold."

And that's when the lights went on . . .

"I thought it was the generators, but they're probably ruined," Sir Rudy said, handing Maggie a cup of hot tea as she entered the main saloon. "Our local electrical council has certainly outdone themselves. I don't remember power being restored this quickly before." He held up the silver sugar bowl. "Sugar?"

"Yes, three, please. Or four, if that doesn't insult you," Maggie said, trying with all her might not to spill the tea because her hands were still shaking. She glanced at the mantel clock. It was after six. Gee, it was true: Time flies when you're having fun.

Tabby and Bernie had grabbed her almost the moment she'd climbed the stairs to the first floor, pushing her into the study, to sit and drip and shiver while Tabby raced upstairs for towels and dry clothing, and Bernie told her she was an idiot—and Maggie had agreed with her.

But now she was back in the main saloon, and the power was on, which meant the central heating had kicked in, and the fire was still blazing in the fireplace, and Maggie actually had a moment to wonder how she was supposed to get all her wet clothes into a suitcase, then explain them to an airline security guard.

Because she was leaving England today if she had to swim. Okay, maybe not if she had to swim.

"Where's Alex?"

"Here, my dear," he said, and she turned to see him standing to the far left of the large room, looking the epitome of the Gentleman At Home, as he had crossed one ankle over the other and was leaning, so nonchalantly, on the knob of his sword cane. "And, before you ask, here, too, are all our new friends, including Miss Campion and the robin. Although I don't believe either of them is pleased to be here."

"I was leaving," Nikki explained through chattering teeth. "A person can't leave a house before she's murdered? So I picked up someone else's bag by mistake. So what? A person can leave a place when a person wants to."

"This is ridiculous," Byrd Stockwell said, glaring at Evan Pottinger, who was standing over the seated Byrd, holding the fireplace poker. "She ran, which proves she's guilty. All I did was diddle the slut."

"So very charming. Always the gentleman, Robin, aren't you?"

"Really?" Byrd said with a sneer. (Maggie all of a sudden didn't think he looked half so handsome.) "At least I'm not trying to act like some stuffed-shirt English lord."

Alex put a hand to his chest and recited a line from Aeschylus. "'Oh me, I have been struck a mortal blow right inside.' Pardon me, Robin, as I toddle to my chair, a broken man."

And then he did just that, propping his sword cane against one arm of the chair as he sat facing Byrd Stockwell. "Now, if we could dispense with the histrionics and be on with this?"

Maggie walked over to stand beside Alex. "What have I missed? Have I missed anything?"

"A phone call from Mary Louise, as a matter of fact. A very interesting phone call from Mary Louise. But we'll allow that information to fall into our conversation as we get on with this, if that's all right with you."

"Do I have a choice?"

"Not really, no."

"Didn't think so," Maggie said, sipping her tea as she looked more closely at Nikki, who was shivering in a blanket on another chair dragged to this side of the room. And surprise, surprise, someone had tied one of her ankles to a leg of the chair. Good thinking. "Okay, go for it. I'm kind of tired anyway."

"I *hate* you," Nikki said, glaring at Maggie. "You tried to drown me. I'm going to sue you, you know. You won't have a pot to piss in when I'm done with you."

"Gee, I'm scared." Maggie looked at Alex. "You have the bag?"

"It's safe, yes," Alex told her, then got to his feet and turned to speak to everyone. "I am happy to announce, ladies and gentlemen, that we have both our miscreants safely in hand now, and there should be no further impositions on your time or constraints on your movements. In other words, you may go."

"Not until we know what the hell happened here," Bernie said, looking at Tabby. "You want to know, right?"

"Only if my name doesn't come up again," Tabby said, pouting.

"I think you've had your fifteen minutes with this one, Tabby," Maggie told her, grinning. "Come on, Alex, fill in the blanks here. I can fill in one of them—how Nikki here knew about the path. She knew because she spends all her time running around, up and down the halls, the stairs. She had to have looked out a window at some point and seen the path. Her getaway path. Once she'd found the jewels in Byrd's bedroom, all she needed was to figure out *when* to make her escape. I mean, it's not like acting was really going to work out for her anyway. But remember her running around with her hair all wet with sweat? That wasn't sweat; that was *rain*. And she was asking us where Byrd was because she wanted to give him the slip. She was just biding her time, her luggage and the jewels already stashed in the kitchen, and when we said we were going to search all the bedrooms, she knew it was time to make a break for it. It's all so logical now."

"Nikki?" Alex asked the woman. "Do you care to comment? Or would you rather I supply more details? For instance, the fact that your last name isn't really Campion. It's Campiano. And that your uncle is Salvatore Campiano, a gentleman with, as my informant told me, *connections*."

Maggie slapped a hand to her forehead. "Just when you think you know everything . . ."

"Shh, my dear. Miss Campion? We know now that Boffo Transmissions, a marvelously successful enterprise that had its birthplace in Brooklyn, is owned by your uncle, who was nice enough to pay for his favorite niece's nose job—I believe that's the term—then feature her in his nationwide television advertisments, thus making you a celebrity. Rather like Paris Hilton without the Internet photos, I believe my friend explained to me—known for being known. I really don't understand the concept. But I applaud you, my dear. Many wouldn't know what to do with a windfall of stolen jewelry. But your uncle would. Wouldn't he, Miss Campion?"

"Mary Louise knew all of that?" Maggie asked, impressed. "That's what she told you?"

"No, my dear. Our friends Vernon and George knew all of this, George's relatives once more proving veritable fonts of information."

"George is Killer, right? And Killer's Italian, right? How

could I forget that one? Does everybody in the five boroughs know everybody else? Why don't I know anybody?"

"Perhaps you should consider getting out more?" Alex suggested with a smile.

"I'm ignoring that. But you're saying you don't think Nikki here was in this thing from the get-go? Hers is what they call a crime of opportunity? What makes you so sure?"

"I'm not, actually. But this entire exercise, start to ignoble finish, has the air of slapdash and clumsy improvisation about it, don't you agree? Robin, put us out of our misery, please. Remember, confession is purportedly good for the soul."

Oh, goody, now they were getting to the really nifty part. "Yeah, *Robin*," Maggie urged, "you know the jig is up. Tell us everything."

Byrd Stockwell looked up at Evan, who had just noticed that his glass was once more empty and was wandering off, poker in hand, to correct that lapse.

"He said he'd hit me with that. You people are all crazy. Americans. Everything's *violence* for you."

"Yeah, yeah, shame on us," Maggie said, putting down her teacup, as she'd realized about three sips ago that Sir Rudy had laced the tea with brandy. Which was why she'd finished all of it, the warmth of the brandy doing wonders for her. "Now spill your guts. You and Joanne and Sam. Maybe Nikki here, too, maybe not. How did it start? How did you all get together? Come on, Robin. First one to roll over catches the break, but the offer goes on the table only once. Let's hear it, Robin—one, two, three, cop that plea."

"And you say I watch too much television," Alex said, shaking his head.

And then Byrd Stockwell surprised her. He crossed one long leg over the other, folded his hands in his lap, and became one hundred and fifty percent stiff-upperlip British. "Oh, very well. Only an idiot would not try to salvage something out of this ungodly mess. But I want to make this clear. I killed *nobody*."

"Don't try to blame me, Byrd Stockwell! You just shut up!" Nikki yelled, throwing back the blankets and jumping to her feet . . . only to fall forward, flat on her face, as she must have forgotten the rope around her ankle. It was beautiful to see, Maggie decided, grinning. Almost poetical.

"No, Nikki, *you* shut up," Bryd declared flatly. "Always walking around the room naked, hunting for your nail polish while prattling on in that annoyingly high-pitched voice of yours about how I should admire your biceps, of all things. That's how you found the jewelry, isn't it? *My* jewelry. I shouldn't have listened to Joanne."

"Listened to Joanne about what?" Maggie asked. "You talked to her about Nikki?"

Byrd rolled his eyes. "Joanne felt that we should behave as if we weren't already acquainted, although she didn't much care for the method I chose to allay suspicions on that head."

Maggie pointed at him. "*You're* the one I heard arguing in the study yesterday. You and Joanne."

Byrd shrugged. "Possibly. Probably. She was becoming a bit intense. Even unnerving."

"Being the object of Miss Pertuccelli's affections could very well be terrifying, I'd imagine," Alex suggested sympathetically.

"Funny, Alex," Maggie said, then looked at Byrd. "She loved you? She expected marriage?"

"You Americans. You need everything wrapped up in a fantasy, don't you? This was *business*, Miss Kelly."

Maggie believed she was getting closer now. "Except *American* Joanne didn't think so. She got jealous. She thought you were going to drop her for Nikki. So you killed her."

"Incorrect on all counts," Byrd said, pushing back his

blond hair, almost preening. "If you'd allow me to explain from the beginning?"

"Who's stopping you?" Maggie asked, then winced. "All right, point taken. At least it's only Alex and me talking this time. Go ahead."

And he did. He explained that he'd happened to meet Joanne in London. She was impressed ("naturally"), and he was intrigued by her tale of woe about an upcoming movie she'd been all but blackmailed into working on. Re-creating England on a California soundstage—ridiculous.

But the budget was limited, there was no choice, nothing she'd found in England could be had for a reasonable amount of money.

"She was all about money," Byrd said. "Probably why I was attracted, as I am also very concerned with money. I won't bore you with the details, but we came to conclude that I could help her and she could help me, and we both could get very rich. It seemed that she paid alimony to quite a few people."

"You set up that meeting between Joanne and Sir Rudy?"

Byrd brushed some invisible lint from his slacks. "Right down to the red dress, Miss Kelly. My jumped-up uncle so admires red. By the end of the evening, he believed it was his idea to offer Medwine Manor to the production company, gratis. He's a simple man, my uncle. Joanne, unfortunately, turned out to be much more complicated."

"So that's how the movie got switched from Hollywood to England at the last minute. Sorry, go on," Maggie said, even as she could hear Marylou saying, "There, there, sweetie, we had fun, remember? It's not all bad," to an obviously upset Sir Rudy.

And Byrd went on, Nikki being very quiet, to explain that he had somehow become persona non grata in his uncle's house, unfortunately just as he'd discovered an old set of plans for the house in the back of one of the silver cupboards. Someone, he told them, had actually used them to wrap up some godawful bits of blackened silver. Byrd took the plans, not knowing at that moment what they were, to wrap up "a few things."

"You *stole* my candlesticks," Sir Rudy said, speaking for the first time. "I barred you from my house, you ungrateful puppy. Told you I'd set the dogs on you if you showed your face here again—if I had dogs."

Byrd spread his hands, palms up, and looked at Maggie. "You can see my dilemma. I'd heard all the stories about the jewelry. About Uncle Willis. At some point, probably while bored, I unbent the plans, looked at them, and realized that there was a secret passage located directly inside Uncle Willis's attic prison. It led down to my usual room, as well. I'd been sleeping not ten feet away from that lovely jewelry! After all, where else would the man have hidden it, if not there? I had to get back in that room."

"Sir Rudy wasn't happy to see you the other day," Maggie said, taking up the story. "But you'd convinced Joanne to get the movie filmed here, because when you showed up, and the house was full of people, your uncle wouldn't make a scene, and you knew it. That's why you cut Joanne in on anything in the first place."

"A stupid mistake, I agree," Byrd said, nodding. "I think I enjoyed the intrigue of the thing. Besides, she told me she could, as you Americans say, get me into show business if I helped with her own cash flow. It was all very quid pro quo."

"You wanted to go to Hollywood and be a movie star? Another model-turned-actor? Oh, good grief, of course," Maggie said, shaking her head. "I should have figured that one out the minute you walked in the door."

Alex paced as Byrd kept talking, his hands clasped behind his back, his expression thoughtful.

"I won't be insulted by you, Miss Kelly," Byrd stated firmly. "And I won't be held responsible for any murders. It was Joanne's idea to bring that ridiculous brown hack into the mix without consulting me. And it was she who strangled him after knocking him unconscious as the fool leaned over the jewelry, telling us both how he would use his share to produce his own screenplay. I was completely shocked. But he had been very helpful in finding the latch for us."

Maggie looked at Alex. "Was there a bump on the back of Sam's head?"

"I didn't notice one," Alex said. "Perhaps I wasn't all that thorough, once I'd seen the pair of marks on his throat. Although I most sincerely doubt that, don't you?" He turned to Byrd. "You did help her hang him up, didn't you, Robin? You'll at least admit to that?"

"Stop calling me Robin."

"Forgive me, but I do so enjoy it. Back to the late Mr. Undercuffler. You were, according to you, and with no one else alive to gainsay you, shocked, dismayed at the murder of the man you hadn't wanted involved in the first place—splitting the profits three ways rather than two—and are completely innocent of anything other than robbery. However, you did assist Miss Pertuccelli in, shall we say, *disposing* of the body?"

At last, Byrd looked disconcerted. "I didn't know what else to do. We'd left him up in the attic, but that wasn't good enough, and Joanne was going crazy, totally off her head. I remembered Uncle Willis, and we decided to make it look like a suicide."

He looked at Dennis and Tabby. "But now *they* were in the room. I had to find a way to get them out so they wouldn't hear us up above their heads, dragging Undercuffler about. The man was, if you'll pardon me, a dead weight. Besides, Joanne had thrown her stopwatch somewhere, as if suddenly, somehow, it had turned into a snake she couldn't bear to touch, and we might have to move furniture to find the thing. We never did find it, but that really wasn't a problem for *me*, was it? I had the jewelry."

Maggie raised a hand. "So you didn't think about the dust? The only reason there were no footprints in the dust was because each time you guys went up to the attic room, you went up through the secret passage? Damn. I was so sure of that one."

"Even incorrect assumptions can lead to valid conclusions, Maggie. We would never have even considered the existence of a secret passage otherwise," Alex told her. "Now, if you will, Stockwell, on to the jewels. And Miss Pertuccelli's murder."

He spread his hands, shrugged. "I don't know. We'd planned to just hold onto them, wait for the water to go down, and I'd leave, take them with me. Nobody knew we'd stolen anything because nobody knew the jewelry even existed. But, as I've said, Joanne had to go and kill that idiot writer. That's when everything began to fall apart."

"Writers will do that for you—screw up everything," Maggie said, grinning.

"It doesn't matter. I did *not* kill that writer. I did *not* kill Joanne." He turned on Nikki. "*She* did! And she stole my jewelry!"

Everyone, Maggie included, turned to look at Nikki . . . and when they turned back, everyone was looking at Byrd Stockwell, who now held Alex's sword cane in his hand, unsheathed. And he looked like he might just know how to use it—who knew what English schoolboys learned in class?

"Hand over that bag. It's mine!"

"Of course, Robin," Alex said, bowing, "as you do appear to be holding the upper hand." He stepped back, slowly, then sort of *whirled* around, grabbing the Troy Toy's sword cane out of the actor's hands. A heartbeat later, it was unsheathed, and Alex was facing Stockwell once more, both of them in the *en garde* position.

"Alex, for crying out loud, that's a *prop*," Maggie said, really worried now. "You can't fight him with a prop sword. Give him the jewelry. He won't get far."

"I should, shouldn't I?" Alex said, not taking his eyes off Stockwell. "But this man murdered two people. We cannot allow him even an attempted escape."

"Oh, great, you're doing that *honorable* thing again, right? Well, cut it out!" Maggie looked behind her. "Where's the jewelry? Who's got the jewelry? Hand it over, okay?"

"Why?" Bernie asked, then blew her nose. "Alex and I already looked at it. It's fake."

Maggie worried that her eyes might just pop right out of her head. "It's—"

"Fake. Paste. Glass," Bernie elaborated. "I know my jewelry. Uncle Willis stole fake jewelry. Good fakes, so the pieces are worth something, but not all that much. Life's a bitch, ain't it?"

Maggie's head was spinning. Looking at Alex, who was looking at Stockwell—the two of them still squared-off—she tried to sort out this entire mess in her mind.

"You know," she said, "it could make sense. People back then often replaced their real jewelry with fakes when they needed money. Good fakes, too. But if Uncle Willis stole the jewelry and took it to a pawnbroker, then everybody would *know* the family was broke."

Now she was pacing, well clear of Alex and Byrd Stockwell, who were beginning to look a little silly posing like that. "They had to find that jewelry, and they couldn't let Uncle Willis out to tell anybody the family secret, either. If he figured it out once he actually inspected the pieces, and told anybody, they'd be ruined. Tradespeople would start calling in their accounts, they'd end up in debtor's prison, the whole nine yards. I mean, you think we all live on credit now? Those guys were ten times worse than us. And then, once he'd maybe figured out he was locked up for life and would be hunted down and killed if he escaped with what he knew—not just with the jewelry, but with what he *knew*—Uncle Willis went mad and got his revenge. God, I *love* this! I want to *write* this!"

"Appeals to your romantic, and often bloodthirsty, fiction-writing mind, yes, I'm sure," Alex said, still watching Byrd. "I believe, however, the late Mr. Undercuffler and the late Miss Pertuccelli might not share your joy."

"That's true," Maggie agreed, still running scenarios in her head. Yes, this could be a good story. She could drop Saint Just in the middle of it, have him solve the crimes. The idea was definitely better than the book she'd just finished. But Alex was still talking, so she really should pay attention.

"Stockwell, it's over. You murdered two people for paste and have been ungentlemanly enough to attempt to blame two females for your crimes. You weren't about to share with Mr. Undercuffler, and you killed him while Miss Pertuccelli watched in horror—even borrowing her stopwatch cord to do the deed. Miss Pertuccelli must have been terrified, realizing, as you did, that all the jewelry was much better than half. I imagine you discovered her trying to escape, flee for her life, and you stabbed her with one of the kitchen knives."

"So much for showbiz," Maggie said. "But Nikki here is all after the fact, right?"

"Miss Campion merely happened to discover the jewels and want them for her own, nothing more," Alex agreed. "Put down your weapon, Stockwell—which is, by the by, also fake. The real sword cane, *my* sword cane, is in my hand. Mr. Barlow has been very kindly keeping it safe for me."

"Really?" Maggie looked from one thin sword to the other. "Troy's been lugging the real one around? Honest to God, Alex?"

"You doubt me, my dear?"

Again, maybe it was the fatigue. Maybe it was the four teaspoons of sugar. Most probably, it was Sir Rudy's brandy. Maggie grinned at Byrd Stockwell. "Is it real or is it fake? Well, punk? Huh? Do you feel *lucky*?"

An audible sigh came from the couches as Dennis Lloyd said, "Americans. No wonder you don't appreciate Shakespeare."

Byrd yelled and went on the attack, only to be stopped in his tracks when Alex poked him hard in the solar plexus with the cane part of the sword cane. He grabbed onto his stomach and gasped for air. It was a simple matter for Sterling and Perry to, at Alex's suggestion, "Cage the robin, if you please, while we await the constable. Tie him up, Sterling."

Maggie watched as Alex retrieved both sword canes, reassembled them, then tried to hand one to Troy, who wouldn't touch it.

"Alex? Were you bluffing?"

"As in any game of chance, my dear," he said, smiling, "the winner is not obliged to show his cards once the other party has folded his. What do you think?"

"I think you switched them at some point. I don't know why you did, or if the Troy Toy just picked up the wrong one at some point and you decided that switch might come in handy and let it alone. But, yes, I think Byrd was holding the fake one. I think you even left it where Byrd might get hold of it because you were itching for a fight and it never occurs to you that you could lose a fight, even with a fake sword—except you're not that crazy, and you had the real one. I think I know you that well. So? Am I right? Alex, damn it, stop smiling at me like that. Am I right?"

# Epilogue

Sterling returned to his seat on the plane after yet another short constitutional, as Perry had told him that it was important to stretch one's legs while on long flights . . . and after Perry had made that statement clearer, Sterling had realized that he'd meant getting up and walking the aisles from time to time.

He reached into the pocket on the back of the seat in front of him and retrieved his journal, but didn't yet open it, as Bernie and Tabby were in the seats in front of him and they were speaking to each other.

"No, of course I won't see Dennis again. Isn't that what a fling is about—mad passion and then never seeing each other again? Besides, he told me his favorite movie line of all time is 'I'll alert the media.' "

Bernie laughed, then coughed.

"Okay, so that's almost funny. But you know what isn't, Bernie? Unless I tell him, David will never even know I had revenge sex. And even worse, if I do tell him, he might not care."

Sterling quickly opened his journal, believing he'd heard more than he probably should have, and pulled his pen from his shirt pocket. He really should finish his entry, as they'd be landing soon and he wanted to watch as New York appeared outside his window.

*How good it will be to be home again, dear Journal. And as I've already told you, we all travel together this time. Even Mr. Undercuffler and Miss Pertuccelli, although they are, most unfortunately, traveling below us, in the baggage compartment.*

*Saint Just told me as I spoke with him on this recent constitutional that, no, Mr. Byrd Stockwell has not yet made a clean robin redbreast of things, but Saint Just is confident that the man will not escape justice. He said there would be fingerprints and all sorts of what is called forensic evidence for the police to discover, although Saint Just is no longer interested, as there's really not all that much dash and romance—his words, dear Journal—in mucking about with such things.*

*Miss Campion remains in England, but on the much lesser charge of stealing fake jewelry, and Maggie assures me I'm not to worry about her overmuch, as the woman is bound to land on her feet.*

*Sadly, dear Journal, it would seem that the movie about Saint Just and myself will now be unavoidably delayed. Sir Rudy, who had seemed such a convivial gentleman, all but tossed everyone out on their ears the moment the rain stopped and the water receded.*

*Saint Just is convinced the man is a tad overset to learn that his lifelong dream has ended in a huge, horribly expensive house that sits in the middle of flood water several times a year, with no treasure to hunt for anymore and all his village chums openly laughing at him. I think he is pining for Marylou, who is also on this airplane, along with everyone else. She and Evan Pottinger seem to be hitting it off quite nicely, which is a surprise to me but not to Saint Just, who is rarely surprised by anything.*

*We saw very little of England during this short and quite eventful trip, sadly, but perhaps we will all return one day. In the summer, when it isn't raining.*

*But, dear Journal, all has not been murder and mayhem. Saint Just and Maggie have most definitely cried friends again, and once more my hopes run high in that quarter. After all, they are sitting side-by-side now, and Maggie had been resting her head against Saint Just's shoulder, which I consider an excellent sign. I even have begun to hope that they will soon Come To An Understanding.*

"What do you mean, *you* solved it?"

"Now, Maggie, you must admit that—"

"*Me*, Sherlock. *I* did it. Okay, so you helped. A little. You pulled that harebrained stunt with the sword canes, I'll give you that. But I'm the one who jumped in that stupid lake and—"

"I think you might wish to rephrase that, my dear. As in, 'I stupidly jumped into that lake.' "

"Oh, yeah? Bite me."

"Here? In first class? Is that acceptable?"

Sterling smiled, sighed, and wrote:

*Then again, dear Journal, perhaps it is not yet time for the fairy-tale ending I dream of. But at least things are back to normal . . .*